Praise for J. Dayne Lamb's
Teal Stewart Mysteries

****

UNQUESTIONED LOYALTY

"Teal Stewart is becoming a favorite."

The Snooper

"This series remains an enjoyable read."

The Boston Tab

"J. Dayne Lamb skillfully layers the suspense . . ."
Kate's Mystery Books Newsletter

"A satisfyingly intricate novel . . ."

Kirkus Reviews

****

A QUESTION OF PREFERENCE

"An absorbing page-turner."

Publishers Weekly

"Not to be missed! Twists and turns that keep you reading
past your bedtime!"

Mystery Lovers Ink

****

QUESTIONABLE BEHAVIOR

"*Questionable Behavior* sports one of the best opening scenes
of the last ten years!"

Jeremiah Healy, bestselling author of *Foursome*

BIG MIKE MYSTERIES
BY GARRISON ALLEN!

ROYAL CAT   (1-57566-045-8, $4.99)

More than mischief is afoot when the less-than-popular
retired teacher playing The Virgin Queen in the annual
Elizabethan Spring Faire is executed in the dark of night.
Her crown passes to Penelope Warren, bookstore owner
and amateur sleuth extraordinaire. Then the murderer
takes an encore, and it's up to Penelope and her awesome
Abyssinian cat, "Big Mike," to take their sleuthing behind the scenes . . . where death treads the boards and
a cunning killer refuses to be upstaged.

DESERT CAT   (0-8217-4503-4, $3.99)

Meddlesome, mean spirited Louise Fletcher was high on
everyone's least-liked list. An expert at backstabbing, she
is found with a knife between her shoulderblades and a
death grip on a bright new penny. Everyone in Empty
Creek, Arizona, has a motive. So, it's up to Penelope
Warren and her feline partner Big Mike to sniff out the
victim's secrets, paw through her past—and pounce on
a killer.

*Available wherever paperbacks are sold, or order direct from the
Publisher. Send cover price plus 50¢ per copy for mailing and handling to Penguin USA, P.O. Box 999, c/o Dept. 17109, Bergen-
field, NJ 07621. Residents of New York and Tennessee must
include sales tax. DO NOT SEND CASH.*

UNQUESTIONED LOYALTY

J. DAYNE LAMB

KENSINGTON BOOKS
KENSINGTON PUBLISHING CORP.

KENSINGTON BOOKS are published by

Kensington Publishing Corp.
850 Third Avenue
New York, NY 10022

First Kensington Hardcover Printing: October, 1995
First Kensington Paperback Printing: July, 1996

Printed in the United States of America

MONDAY

One

The woman with the bright hair rolled a tissue across the smear of red lipstick glistening on her lips. She crumpled the stained paper to a ball and let it drop on the sidewalk as she watched the revolving door spin. *Someone else working the weekend?* She felt like she'd been losing time and tried to think. *Could it be early Monday? Before the sunrise?* The disorganized buzzing in her head stopped long enough for her to blink and recognize the face as she raised her pale eyes. She extended her cup and grinned. Time to collect.

Teal Stewart stepped across a drift of magnolia petals curled with heat and brown at the edges and walked rapidly across Beacon Street. Long legs powered her forward as she cut every corner of the path meandering through the Public Garden. The frill of cherry blossoms arching over her head failed to delight this morning. She checked her watch for the fourth time, but the possibility that she would arrive late did not change. Her pace hurried to a trot.

Hope, habit, or loyalty pounded through her mind on a three-count beat in time with each footfall.

Hope?

Surely not. She as good as hated Hunt for expecting her to jump at his invitation to meet him for breakfast, no matter the tension that had been separating them for the past months. She hated herself for increasing the trot to a run.

Sweat soaked full around her waist by the time she crossed from Winter to Summer. Boston could change seasons that quickly, in the interval of a bisecting street. Winter to Summer, Milk to Water—the patchwork of cow paths turned into roadways made drivers crazy and left tourists queuing for the security of fake trolley buses. Teal slowed, sure in her direction and now close enough to see her destination.

The First New England Bank building punctured the skyline, pressing out and down to straddle a block of prime city ground in Hunt's controversial design. Teal's watch showed one minute to seven on a morning which promised a scorcher of a spring day. The cherry blossoms would drop by nightfall.

Teal leaned against a light pole and fished her office shoes from her briefcase. This was as good a place as she'd get this morning to make the exchange—comfort for torture, sense for vanity, Keds for spikes. Most days, she used the privacy of her office, but not today; she couldn't afford the time. Teal smiled at the irony since Hunt was the one to always arrive late, if he turned up at all. But something in his voice had assured her he planned to break their natural order. He would be there first, and impatient.

She had intended to refuse the invitation in the same cool voice with which she had refused all the others following their disastrous breakfast last summer. That meal had

4

been intended to celebrate her admission to the Clayborne Whittier partnership and his return to Boston from Chicago. She still blamed him for picking the fight.

So, why had she agreed to meet him today?

Habit? Teal groaned. Huntington Erin Houston, famous architect, once lover, now friend, had intertwined her life since she arrived new to Boston from graduate school too many years ago. They had lived together for a few years, and, when the wounds of breaking apart had faded, meals at the private Ivy Club on top of the FNEB building had replaced the eat-in kitchen of their old apartment. Breakfast remained the favorite until a different separation had further deteriorated their relationship.

The wedge of Teal's career ambition had made Hunt crazy.

Loyalty? Was it loyalty that set her in motion, hurrying across the street? Hunt hardly would agree. Their last conversation across the plates of Ivy eggs and cups of special-blend tea circled through her mind.

Hunt had raised black eyebrows in a blacker judgment. "You think Frank Sweeny is a jerk! You've always thought he was a jerk. Why offer to be his second partner on—"

"His one client big enough to get Clayborne Whittier in trouble? Figure it out Hunt," she'd snapped.

"Unyielding loyalty to the firm? Is that why they made you a partner—to cover up for Frank? Why should you correct their mistake?"

"Because now I am a *they*. And Frank has his uses."

"Like what?" Hunt had laid sturdy hands flat on the table as he leaned forward. "You partners could fire him."

"Firing partners is not in the Clayborne Whittier culture."

Teal remembered Hunt's snicker, his mouth tight with disapproval.

"What's happened to you?" he had asked later, as they stood. "The new-partner drugs getting to you?"

The old barb, turned against her now, hurt. Hunt had come up with the quip years before, when Teal had described the behavior of a once reasonable human being turned monstrous after admission to the partnership. "Must be a mandatory course of personality-altering drugs that comes with the big office," had been Hunt's observation. The running joke held less humor when Hunt had refused to let the subject of her complicity with Frank drop.

"So, the great firm can't admit they goofed, but you're talking to me, Teal. Be honest. Why should you help keep Frank from facing his mistakes?"

"Because he's my partner," she had explained, hearing the defensive edge on her voice.

"Oh, l-o-y-a-l-t-y to the great firm. They wouldn't thank you," Hunt had concluded.

Hunt had had a way of hitting the target. Clayborne Whittier wouldn't thank her and acknowledge their mistake.

"Damn," Teal muttered. She rammed her sneakers into her briefcase.

Hope. She could feel the signs, see hope in her outfit this morning. How long had she searched the closet to find the red linen dress Hunt loved? When was the last time she had used his favorite perfume? She was crazy, and late.

She sprinted for the revolving door, hand raised to push.

She wasn't paying attention to the ventilation grate. When her heel caught, she went down before she could be afraid. The pedestrians hurrying along the sidewalk kept their momentum, troubled only long enough to swing wide of her fall.

Temper and relief rose in a measure equal to Teal's vanity as her hands braced to absorb the shock, landed on something soft.

The homeless woman who cushioned the drop did not shake Teal's grasp from her shoulder. She did not ask for spare change, although her hand held a lipstick-stained Dunkin' Donuts cup as if extended for a donation. Two quarters rested in a curdle of cream in the bottom.

"I am sorry," Teal said. She saw the woman better as she straightened.

The woman's dress was arranged in a swirl around her curled legs. A little pillbox hat perched on tarnished hair smoothed into a french twist. Teal realized that under the patina of hard wear, the woman could be near her own age, over thirty, less than forty. Teal knew her as a part of the FNEB scenery many people chose to ignore. Usually a cigarette burned between the carefully painted lips from which she flung foul or gracious appeals for money, depending on inexplicable whim. The woman gazed at Teal with her lips turned down.

"Sorry." Teal held up her battered shoe. "Stupid of me."

The woman stared with wide eyes. Teal stared back, the smile contracting off her face. A less self-centered and preoccupied morning, and she would have recognized the truth at once. Kneeling at the woman's side did not change what Teal did not want to recognize.

Death had provided the woman with a permanent home.

"I didn't see a thing, Dan. Really," Teal repeated.

She clenched a fist behind her back, rolling newly polished nails into her palm before she shook her fingers free. First one hand, then the other, the tension spilling from her shoulder and down her arm. Detective Daniel Malley could not be hurried. Her right hand curled back into a fist.

Why had she called him from the FNEB lobby? Someone else would have noticed soon enough. Someone else would have summoned the Boston police. Someone else would have been answering Dan Malley's questions.

Or she could have taken just a minute to stop upstairs in her office to ask Kathy to make the report.

No. Kathy might love her job, but Teal's secretary was not available for this duty. Not now that Kathy had become Mrs. Daniel Malley.

"The thing is, her hat," Teal had said to Malley on the phone to explain her calling homicide. "It's all soaked with blood in back."

Detective Malley confirmed her worst guess as the hour set to meet Hunt at Ivy receded.

"Her head is b-b-bashed in," he said.

Teal squeezed her eyes shut. "I didn't see anything. Really, nothing. She's been around town, I don't know, on and off for years, I think. Sometimes she's at International Place, sometimes 75 State, sometimes here, in front of the FNEB. The guards asked her to leave and tried to make her uncomfortable, but she understands her civil liberties. Understood," Teal amended.

She shifted her weight from one foot to the other and wanted to get going, leave this sudden death to Malley.

"Must be she died sometime late in the night or early this morning—"

"So what did you expect me to see?" Teal cut in, irritated.

Dan shrugged. "Something that didn't strike you as right."

His tan eyes squinted against the glare off the FNEB facade as he scrutinized the woman.

"She's not going to be anyone's priority," he said, spreading his palms open like a benediction.

Teal heard defeat in his voice.

"No. I'm sorry, Dan. It's just . . ." *Just what,* Teal wondered. "She had nothing to do with me. You'll do better with the guard."

Dan eased his head up and down. *The youngest, smartest detective on Boston's force,* Teal thought. *Conscientious to a fault. He would make the homeless woman his problem.*

But she wasn't Teal's, not this time, not like when Dan and Teal had worked together before.

"If I think of anything, I'll call," Teal said, restless to be on the elevator, to see Hunt. *It was hope, damn it.*

Teal spun through the door into the FNEB lobby. *He might have waited,* she thought.

"Teal!" Roger Singer grabbed her arm as she stepped inside. "You aren't going to believe this—Frank is going off to Funsters. Right now."

Roger's voice betrayed sly pleasure.

"He showed me a letter, honestly, with *Funsters: An Action Oriented Meeting Place* at the top. He doesn't know, and I wasn't about to tell him."

"Letter?" Teal said, stupidly. She could not believe Boston's oldest and most notorious gay bar had a motto.

"It's got to be a joke off some PC!" Glee shook Roger's shoulders.

Teal couldn't decide if Roger was reverting to his former, more whimsical self or was simply hysterical. The transition to partner had failed to bring out Roger's best, or hers, according to Hunt. The thought made Teal uneasy.

"Did you send it?" she asked.

"Are you nuts?" Roger's grin dropped. "Someone pulled our prank."

She and Roger hadn't been the only Clayborne Whittier managers to consider Frank Sweeny an ass. Frank had crafted a career out of the behavior of a sycophant. A zealous, thoughtless loyalty to the great firm had been his admission ticket. He chased after any prospective client, no matter how misdirected his effort. Most of those he brought in were inappropriate to the practice of an international accounting firm. Roger and Teal each had worked on more than one of Frank's dogs as staff. Teal had enjoyed coming up with the unkind hoax.

"Funsters," she had suggested to Roger. "We'll send him a phony letter asking him to propose on the Funster's audit."

"Funsters is audited?" Roger had asked.

Teal couldn't believe Roger could be so dense. "Of course not, but what will Frank think?"

"Practice development!" Roger yelped.

"Can you imagine Frank walking through Funsters' door?"

They had taken a second to savor the image, the malice

in the humor, before both had shaken their heads. And that had ended Funsters three years ago.

Roger was back to grasping her arm.

"I'm not kidding. Frank waved the letter as he climbed into his car. I can't wait to ask him how the proposal is going—"

"Roger, this isn't really funny," Teal said.

Actually, it was, sort of, and they both knew it.

"If you didn't send it and I didn't send it . . ."

"Who did? Right?" Roger suggested. His concentration brightened. "Probably your Amy."

Teal's chuckle of dismissal caught in her throat. Amy Firestone, her best senior manager, Clayborne Whittier's best senior manager. Teal hoped Roger guessed wrong.

"You told her the story," Roger persisted. "You admitted you told her."

Teal grimaced.

"I never told anyone," Roger finished.

Of course you haven't, Teal thought, *just like you didn't come up with the idea in the first place.* Roger was another example of what the partners thought they wanted—someone willing to cede his imagination and autonomy. That's what she used to think in her least kind moments in the year between his promotion and her own.

"Frank'll be back soon. He's only going to Cambridge Street," Roger said as if Teal did not know.

She got the message. Frank had been sent on a tasteless practical joke to her part of town. Funsters was located on the commercial street which separated the West End from her neighborhood, Beacon Hill. This could look bad, except no one would imagine one partner could want to humiliate another, leaving Amy as the best suspect. *Damn*, Teal thought.

She made a show of checking her watch.

"Roger, I've got to run. Going up?"

"No." Roger squirmed. "Across the street—"

"To sign your jumbo mortgage?" Teal asked, glad to be off the subject of Funsters.

Roger evaded her direct gaze. Teal knew Barbara Singer, not her husband, had decided she wanted the move into a big, big house. Barbara could outspend Imelda Marcos. No wonder Roger looked trapped.

"You think it's safe?" Teal asked.

Roger pinched a wrinkle into his lapel. "I hear two years in the same office means you're safe from a transfer."

"Hmmm." Teal wasn't as sure.

"Well, I have to go," Roger said.

The elevator sped express to forty. Ten slow stops brought Teal to the Ivy Club at the top on forty-nine.

Walter spotted her scanning the dining room.

"Mr. Houston has left, Ms. Stewart." The maitre d' compressed his lips as if to say, what could she expect from Hunt.

Teal flushed with the prickly heat of dashed hope.

"Perhaps he stopped by your office," Walter suggested.

"Of course." Teal kept her smile until she left the club.

Kathy raised a blank face when Teal mentioned the architect.

"I haven't seen Hunt in ages, Teal." Kathy said. "Can I talk to you about something?"

"My office?" Teal offered. She swallowed her disappointment.

"I don't know if I should tell you this, but since you are friends . . ." Kathy shut the door behind them but did not sit.

Teal stiffened. If it was going to be about that stupid Funsters joke and Amy—

"Laura saw the list," Kathy finished.

Teal stopped thinking about Amy. Laura Smart worked for Clayborne Whittier's partner in charge, Don Clarke. Laura was his secretary, among other rumored things.

Teal had heard the talk, had planned to tell Hunt this morning. Frank Sweeny could get fired, after all. Clayborne Whittier's management committee was adopting a long-term strategy to transition out under-performing partners. The decision ended a ninety-year history of protecting partners from termination. All the talk in the firm in the last month centered on speculation about the names on the list. Nothing had leaked from a good source until this.

"Who?" Teal asked, alert with curiosity.

"I don't understand, Teal." Kathy's heart-shaped face suffered with confusion. "Roger."

"Roger Singer?" Teal's voice rose. *Mr. Competent? Mr. Safety? About to be canned? And not Frank? Roger had worried about a transfer like any partner, but termination?*

"That's who Laura said. And she flashed the memo at me." Kathy lifted her shoulders and let them drop.

Teal stepped for the door. "I'd better stop him."

"Stop him?" Kathy's emerald eyes blinked in confusion.

"He's about to sign a huge mortgage. If I warn him—"

"That's the other thing I don't understand. Laura acts like he already knows."

"He knows?" Teal repeated. "You could have fooled me when I saw him a minute ago."

Kathy squirmed.

"There's more?" Teal stiffened.

Ever since Kathy and Laura Smart had become friends, Kathy knew details about the partnership hidden from Teal. The shift had its discomfiting moments.

"The reason." Kathy bit her teeth together.

"I'm not sure I should hear this," Teal said, and she wasn't.

"But it's because of Emma Browne." Kathy's mouth contorted to a frown.

Then Teal understood. Kathy was warning her if she wasn't careful, she would be next.

TWO

Emma Browne compressed her thin lips into a thinner line. She didn't care what she saw when she looked into the mirror, but it sure had mattered to them—fortunately, as her lawyer started to explain again for perhaps the twentieth time.

"Americans don't like the idea that a corporation, or putative partnership in your case, Emma, can judge an individual's suitability for promotion on the arbitrary, subjective standard of appearance. Roger Singer made a mistake, and his words will prove to the court that Clayborne Whittier should pay."

Her lawyer's expression was smug. He'd better be right. He cost enough.

Tension squeezed her tongue to the top of her mouth. She swallowed, and her voice came out high and grating. "But can we make the bastards admit me to the partnership?"

A flick of displeasure, and his eyes slid past her face. No reassuring laugh followed in the moment of silence, no re-

15

peat of her name in his smooth voice, but he pushed back in his chair, to signal that he remained relaxed, in control.

"The monetary damages—"

"Forget monetary!" Adrenaline popped in her veins and the twitch started above her right eye. "No amount of money is enough, do you understand?"

She deserved to be a Clayborne Whittier partner, deserved admission on merit. Total billings from clients she had wooed to the firm exceeded $20 million last year, and they said she "lacked the requisite attributes required of a partner." She had more in mind than money for them to pay.

Poor Roger had meant to be nice last summer, the day he had called to console her on the disappointing news. His admission had come the prior year. He could afford kindness.

She could recite every word of their exchange.

"Maybe another lap will do it," he had said, as if it was just a matter of running the track, another year's waiting.

"Can you tell me the vote?" she had asked. "Yours, for example?"

"Uh. . . . The rules—"

"You're too fucking embarrassed!"

"Emma, please."

Roger had used that unctuous victor's voice, and she had wanted to puke. But she'd had patience. She'd outlasted his silence.

"Maybe you should give some thought to softening up a bit, Em. Wear a touch of makeup, you know, do what women do—"

"No, what do women do?" she had asked, her voice as soft as a cat's.

"Well, not swear so much. Don't be so hard on the troops, you know."

She pinched her mouth between thumb and index finger at the memory. "Don't be so hard on the troops" from the man who thought nothing of making staff work through lunch, skip vacations and forego a planned parental leave the first weeks after a child's birth!

"I shouldn't say this to you," Roger had said and sighed like she should appreciate his courage.

She hadn't even breathed support.

"I guess I can trust you and I want to help . . ." He had trailed to a stop.

You little turd, she had wanted to say. *You fucking coward.* But she hadn't been that stupid.

"We started together, Rog, remember? I saved your ass in the intro training course. Of course you can trust me." Emma hadn't bothered to smile. He hadn't been able to see her on the other end of the line.

"Okay, okay," Roger had said. "The . . . uh . . . consensus of the partners is you need to act on what I'm suggesting— you know, be more feminine and such—to have a chance next year."

"No, I don't know," Emma had spit into the mouthpiece before she had caught hold of herself.

Emma had relived the moment hundreds of times a week since that day. She could still bring back the sensation of the blood swirling in her ears, the length of the Massachusetts to California connection making Roger's voice wobble.

"I specifically should act more like a woman?" she had repeated.

"Well, yes," Roger said.

"Wear makeup?"

"Maybe a little."

Roger must be squirming, she had thought as he had amended the suggestion to "not a lot."

"How about my clothes?" Emma had asked. He hadn't been able to see her pulling the paper clip straight and jabbing it into the blotter. She had sliced his initials into the thick paper, then crossed them to a bump of fuzzy dust.

She had imagined him in his big, black swivel chair, the executive model, twisting around, unable to come to rest.

"There are nice, feminine business looks you might consider," he finally had said.

"Like Teal Stewart's?" she had asked. Teal had made the partnership but not Emma.

"Uh . . . no," he sputtered. "Teal is . . . you know—"

"She should wear suits? Like I do?"

"I guess. Maybe." Roger had not elaborated and Emma had not needed to press.

She had grinned as he'd dropped like a pigeon into her trap.

"That's what the partners said? Specifically? That I should be more feminine in how I act and dress? You guys said this out loud and no one told me?" She shaped her voice into something between concern and contrition.

"I'm telling you now," Roger had offered.

"And it's wonderful of you," she had purred. "Did your fellow partners ask you to be the messenger?"

"No, and I shouldn't be sharing a word of what goes on at partner meetings."

"Well, thank you for breaking the rule for me," she had said before hanging up to dial her lawyer.

Her lawyer had agreed she had a good discrimination case based on recent precedent at another of the Big Six international accounting firms. That battle over the legality of certain partnership-admission practices had gone all the way to the U.S. Supreme Court. The female plaintiff had ultimately won and become a partner. Emma liked to think she'd have Clayborne Whittier eating the same crow. Her suit would be a piece of cake, her lawyer had assured her.

Today, in her hotel suite in Boston, it still made Emma furious to imagine the Clayborne Whittier partners sitting around their fancy conference tables in offices across the country discussing her clothes, rather than the millions in billings she had brought to the firm. Not her technical skill. Not her qualifications or her MBA from the University of Chicago. Most of them were lucky to have managed a BS in accounting.

No, they had worried about her makeup. And found themselves in a lawsuit. A year of their attempts to make her settle for money had only made her angrier.

Her lawyer's unctuous voice broke into her thoughts. "You haven't been near the Clayborne Whittier office since you arrived, have you?"

Emma decided not to upset him with the truth, the details of her little bit of personal snooping or her appointment that night. "Just to walk by once on Friday—"

"Well, listen to me. You stay away from that place."

"Yes," she agreed. She listened; it was just that she didn't intend to comply.

Tomorrow her lawyer would depose Don Clarke. Don deserved to be first, in Emma's opinion. The rules at Clayborne Whittier meant someone would pay. She didn't have much expectation that it would be a partner in charge. She'd heard the rumor about Roger. Transitioning out. Emma snorted. Don blaming the messenger, no doubt.

Emma managed a narrow grin. She wanted much, much more.

The marble block arced through the air. Each time Roger tossed and caught the carved memento hand to hand, one shoulder or the other would dip with the weight of the stone. Now and then he used a fancy swing to send it around behind his back.

Teal caught his sudden lob with hands raised in self-defense. The weight made her arm drop. She rotated the black slab so that its chiseled side faced up.

"MICROANSWER CORPORATION INITIAL PUBLIC OFFERING," she read to Roger.

She did not go on with the engraved list of underwriters or the offering date. MicroAnswer had gone public in the most successful stock issue of last year. Clayborne Whittier had participated as the company's auditors.

"Not a bad day's work," she said.

"I was only the partner on the Massachusetts subsidiary—"

"But important enough to receive this baby." Teal knew the high status of offering trophies. "And isn't it cute to be shaped like a real tombstone."

She imagined that Ted Grey, the California partner who headed Clayborne Whittier's MicroAnswer team, would have received a marble slab and more, maybe a framed announcement from *The Wall Street Journal*. The announcements in the *WSJ* were referred to as tombstones because the blocks of print resembled grave markers. Someone had been cute with the paperweight design.

Teal could brag only of two plastic cubes with shrunken prospectuses inside. Corporate lawyers, certified public accountants, and underwriters added these souvenirs to their office decor like scalps. A ping of jealousy reminded her that she had nothing so fancy as Roger's marble.

"Have you seen Emma Browne yet?" Teal placed the expensive trinket back on Roger's desk.

Roger shifted his attention to the trophy. "Un . . . no."

"What's she like?" Teal asked, eager to hear, but Roger kept his eyes down. "As bad as they said out in California? The senior manager from hell?"

Roger shrugged.

"Honestly, Roger, she's your friend. She started with you here in Boston for a year before she transferred."

"Right. But we aren't supposed to—"

"The lawsuit," Teal said. "You can't say anything."

She could have kicked herself. What was she doing talking about Emma Browne to Roger after hearing the talk about Roger being fired? He had to be feeling miserable.

"She has balls." Roger chuckled, though his expression looked like he'd rather not. "Taking on Clayborne Whittier. Who's on the list for tomorrow? Don, me, then you as the deposition lineup?"

Teal realized she was staring.

"What are you going to say about the great firm?" Roger asked. "That we're a real equal-opportunity employer?"

Teal didn't want to think about what she would say tomorrow. She didn't like Roger's quip. How could he be joking with her? Hadn't he heard the rumor?

"Aren't you worried?" Teal asked.

"Because I gave her the ammunition? Do you think I should be? More worried than you?" Roger sniggered. "You're our great defense. Women make it to partner."

"Just not Emma," Teal said, uncomfortable with her own confusion with Browne v. Clayborne Whittier.

If knowledge was power, where had it got her? Uneasy for Roger's ignorance and unwilling to say more. She recognized why Roger thought she should worry, and she was worried. What should she say as the only woman in Boston to be deposed?

"Is Barbara excited about the new house?" she asked as she picked the black stone off Roger's desk and set it down as fast.

Roger hunched his shoulders to his ears and let them drop. "I guess."

"And you?"

He shrugged again.

"It's a big move," Teal said. "I expect big enthusiasm."

"It's her choice."

It's her choice.

It's your life, Teal wanted to scream. *It's your life that you are living, not your wife's. It's your life that Emma is out to ruin.* Teal stuck with the office rules and stayed mute. Getting personal at work was not done.

"I haven't seen Barbara in a long time. Kids keeping her busy?" Teal took a step back from his desk.

"I haven't seen Hunt in twelve months," Roger said.

Teal stopped walking.

"I see the picture," she said. *You have your relationship issues, I have mine. Period.*

"I was supposed to have breakfast with Hunt today but . . ."

But what, Teal wondered. *I stared into a poor, dead woman's eyes? I ran into you?* There were so many excuses for missing Hunt, and not one to make her feel better. She eased closer to the door.

"Aren't you a little worried about tomorrow?" she asked.

"Me? Worried?" Roger wriggled in his leather chair.

"The big mortgage and all . . ." Teal bobbed her head. A few chestnut hairs escaped her chignon and tickled her left ear.

The swivel mechanism in Roger's chair ground as he rotated front to side and back around.

"The mortgage?" he asked.

"Yes, remember? This morning?" Teal said, irritated he was making her remind him. It was his mortgage.

"Oh, right. Should I be worried?" he asked. His eyes narrowed. "You heard."

"Yes. Laura Smartee," Teal confessed, using Laura's nickname among the partners.

Laura Smartee drops her pants and all the partners have to dance. . . . The lyrics didn't get nicer.

Laura Smart's method for moving ahead could be described as the antithesis of Emma Browne's, yet here they both were, Emma in the middle of the lawsuit and Laura buzzing at the edge. And Roger primed to take the fall.

"That," Roger said. He was back to tossing the tombstone hand to hand in his game of catch.

Teal nodded. "But I can't believe it's true."

23

"Believe what you want."

"Is it because of the lawsuit? Emma Browne screws the partnership and they—"

"It's not *they*, Teal, it's you and me and the rest of the partners. Frank Sweeny—"

"Ted Grey, Don Clarke." Teal stopped herself. This was the argument with Hunt, except she and Roger were on the same side.

"Yeah, *they* aren't too happy," Roger said.

"I'm sorry, Roger."

"Don't apologize."

"Laura does like to invent nasty rumors," Teal said. It wasn't much.

"I'm on top of things."

Roger set down his toy and bent to pull a file from the smaller of the two workpaper trunks on the floor by his desk. His reputation as Mr. Detail, Mr. Protects-The-Firm-From-Lawsuits, was earned. Teal knew he would review every line on every schedule in the two trunks. They had to be from the audit of MicroAnswer since she knew most of the fieldwork had ended. She was pleased to see Roger had something to keep his mind occupied as she left.

"Teal?"

Teal spun around.

"Laura?" The pitch of her voice said, what are you doing here outside Roger's office?

Laura, like Teal, wore red. Her angora sweater crossed over her breasts in a low v-neck. The lycra skirt hugged a well-shaped rear. Red sequins sparkled from three-inch heels. Cropped blond hair showed black at the roots above a face able to take Teal's breath away even under the heavy makeup. What it must do to the men Laura gunned for, Teal could guess.

Gum popped in Laura's plum-outlined mouth. Laura Smart cultivated a unique look, and it worked, Teal admitted, strange as it was. Laura had moved from word processing to executive secretary on the strength of her many talents.

Laura had the expression of a cat after the last lick of a dish of cream.

"I was so worried I wouldn't find you." The plum lips pursed into a conspiratorial smile. "It's about your lunch with Mrs. Clarke?"

The confidential secretary and girlfriend of the boss with a message from the Mrs. Teal shifted uncomfortably. An aging certified public accountant and a young punkette, Don Clarke and Laura Smart made one unlikely pair; but they did make a pair, something Teal never let herself forget.

"Mrs. Clarke would like to move it up a half an hour. I checked with Kathy before I told Mrs. Clarke you agreed. Did I do right?"

Lunch with Julia Clarke. Teal tapped her forehead. She hadn't remembered.

"Thanks. You did fine, Laura."

They walked the corridor side by side.

"Kathy says you're the greatest boss?" Laura said.

The rising inflection caused Teal to narrow her eyes to navy slits. "On my better days. But surely no one compares with Don."

Laura, blond spikes and all, managed a coy look. "I guess not."

25

She stopped in a position that made it awkward for Teal to move past.

"Is there something else?" Teal asked.

Laura cracked her gum. "N-o-o . . ."

"The two most interesting women in the office, and the two I'm looking for, better luck." Ted Grey came up behind Teal. "We on for after lunch?"

"Still fine with me," Teal agreed.

"And you . . . " he said circling to Laura.

Ted had been in Boston for the last few weeks to visit the MicroAnswer facility. For the moment, Laura had two bosses.

Teal cut in. "See you later."

Teal walked away, thinking about her lunch date. When Julia Clarke had proposed Teal join the board of the Children's Charity Foundation, the offer had relieved Teal of the need to find an appropriate "partner's philanthropy" on her own. Julia had made the process easy, although their new relationship had begun to press the unspoken boundary between Teal's position as a partner and Julia's as spouse of the partner in charge.

Teal hoped this lunch would stick to the business of charity. She glanced back down the hall to where Laura talked with Ted. There were some things she did not want to know about the wife of Don Clarke. Julia's impression of Don's secretary, for one.

THREE

Julia Clarke snapped her compact closed and stared around the dining room. The Parker House continued to set an impressive table, even if the hotel's name now started with Omni and the New Hampshire family owners had sold out to a Japanese conglomerate. Everything had become a chain in her lifetime, a chain or a franchise. Not Clayborne Whittier, of course. Don loved to remind her that the great firm remained a partnership of one man, one vote.

She clicked the compact open again and regarded the reflection from the small circle holding her face. Mottled skin under her eyes, etched crescents beside her mouth to the left and right. She tapped at a shiny spot on her nose with the puff, then brushed it across her cheeks. The powder added a layer of ghostly white. She had hated the color, or lack thereof, but her Chanel consultant assured her the look was right, precisely in vogue for spring and summer. Who was she to argue with Chanel?

This morning seemed so close and so far away, like her face as she manipulated the compact to move the mirror in and out. Staring at the circle did not explain how the end of her life could start like any other day. Banal and ordinary and slow, Don in the shower when the telephone rang.

"I'll get it, honey," she had called to him from outside the bathroom door.

Had she loved him at that moment?

He was the companion of twenty-some years, father of her children, a good provider. No, a great provider, with his ambitions at Clayborne Whittier rewarded seven years ago with the latest assignment, partner in charge of the Boston office. And he expected to make it on to the management committee and New York next year. She had expected to be right beside him.

Even after she'd hung up the phone, she'd had moments of wanting that life. Moments? Hours. Hours and hours when she'd cried herself sick after his last good-bye wave from the drive. Sitting now in the dining room of the Parker House, she would do anything to bring back the security six words had shattered.

"Mrs. Clarke?" the voice had scratched over the line grating and high.

"Yes, this is she speaking," she had replied in the modulated tones of her private girls' school education, as if the caller had not known who spoke.

"Is Don available?"

The other party had not offered a name and Julia had not asked.

Julia had shaken her head. "Not at the moment. May I take a message."

The chuckle made her smile tighten.

"I guess you'll have to. Ask him to make up his mind.

Does he really want his little affair with Laura Smart to come out in court—"

Julia had gasped.

The caller had groaned. "Don't be so trite as to not know. I am sorry if I'm the one to tell you. You can remind him he doesn't have much ti—"

Julia had not banged down the telephone; she had placed her finger on the button and pushed ever so gently.

"Who was that?" Don had asked as he walked out of the bathroom.

She'd swung around to stare at the flaccid middle wrapped in the big, white bath sheet, his favorite, Porthault. *His little affair with Laura Smart.*

She'd gagged on rage. The alarm on his face had made her work the gag into a cough.

"Who?" Don had repeated when she'd stopped hacking.

"Never said," she had replied with complete honesty.

He must have assumed she'd meant wrong number, and she hadn't disagreed. She'd handed him his bag at the door, kissed his cheek, and waited for him to pull into the street before she'd screamed her anguish and collapsed to the foyer floor, their black Labrador nuzzling her cold hand with a soft nose.

She had not wobbled when she'd stood on cramping legs a half hour later. Her voice had held steady all through the conversation with Laura Smart, even while the tears had run into the holes in the receiver, making her wonder if she could electrocute herself.

Laura had agreed to find Teal Stewart and move up the lunch meeting, her manner ingratiating and sweet. Julia had even shared a joke with her husband's private and confidential playmate before they'd hung up. She had understood what could be lost if she messed up.

Reflections in the round mirror brought her back to the present moment. She stared into the silver disk and watched the activity over her shoulder. The captain headed for the table, Teal Stewart in his wake.

Julia Clarke pressed her palms against the black enameled case until the clasp caught and clicked, then she lifted her perfectly groomed face to Teal with a smile.

"So Laura caught you," Julia Clarke said. "I hope I haven't made a terrible mess of your schedule."

"Not at all," Teal murmured. One did not refuse the wife of the partner in charge. "Problems with the car raffle?"

Teal would never understand how she had allowed herself to become co-chair of CCF's annual car raffle. No, she understood—Julia Clarke comprised the other half. Teal had piped up the moment Julia had asked for a volunteer, grateful then that she and Hunt weren't speaking. How he would have disdained her apple polishing.

Julia patted Teal's hand, a sign that she misconstrued Teal's sigh. Both Clarkes patted, Teal realized—Don with hearty thumps to her back and shoulders, Julia with a motherly stroke. Of course, Julia was not that old, not close.

"The raffle is doing tremendously well. Five hundred twelve tickets sold, at least fifty ahead of last year at this point! Tonight we can give a positively glowing report," Julia said.

Teal smiled. Julia liked to speak on behalf of the raffle committee at CCF board meetings. Teal preferred to do no more than nod by Julia's side. The meeting this evening promised to be easy.

"I needed a huddle with you on a different matter. I hope you don't mind?"

Teal tried not to show her discomfort. Lunch was shaping up to be everything she had feared. "If I can help, please . . ."

The balance she left unspoken. *Please what,* Teal wondered. *Please don't involve me?* Julia didn't give her the choice.

"I'm worried about Don, the terrible hours he spends at work."

Julia's lips drew into a frown. A mark of lipstick stained one tooth like a fleck of blood.

"I need your insight, from a partner and a woman, not advice from a bunch of other left-out wives. Will you help?" Julia asked.

Teal hoped the shock didn't widen her eyes. They felt as big and obvious as shooting marbles.

"I'm not sure I know anything you haven't put up with for years, Julia," she hedged. "Clayborne Whittier makes everyone work too hard, even Boston's partner in charge."

Teal meant what she said. Late hours couldn't be new to a firm spouse. She tried not to inspect the older woman's face for a sign. *Did Julia know about Laura?*

Julia looked impeccable in her Karl Lagerfeld suit. Her expensively colored honey hair rose from a pretty, oval face before it curved into a tailored pageboy. Shell-pink enamel softened blunt and manicured nails.

Teal could not decide if the glitter in Julia's eyes signaled a morning spent crying. Embarrassment dimmed Teal's smile. Even if people at Clayborne Whittier knew the truth, and not everyone did, no one would have told Julia Clarke.

"He isn't acting himself, Teal. At the office past midnight, coming home drained and tired. If I didn't know better, I'd be worried he was having an affair." Julia arched plucked brows.

Julia was not the first wife to be the last to know.

Teal knew herself to be under the microscope. This particular executive wife counted as a friend, and Teal wasn't one of the boys. She arranged her face to express neutral support.

"There is the lawsuit. It's got all of us partners on edge."

"Emma Browne! That dreadful woman with the rasping voice. She seems to have everything under control." A fleeting brightness of rage rippled Julia's face.

Teal didn't know what she thought of Emma Browne. She knew she could not dispute the basic claim in Emma's lawsuit. Clayborne Whittier was no more hospitable to women than many other firms. Less, actually, if the statistics published in last year's *New York Times* remained true. Emma Browne likely had been blocked by the same institutional process which also kept Julia from discerning the truth.

"I've never met her," Teal said. "She left Boston right before I started."

"But you will meet her?" Julia asked.

"Yes," Teal agreed. "I think she plans to be there tomorrow when I'm deposed—"

"Deposed? You? But why on earth?" Julia asked.

Teal had wondered about that herself until she'd realized that Emma's lawyer might plan to argue that the few women who made it to the partnership had experienced similar prejudices and pressures to conform to the firm dictates, the difference between the ones who made it and Emma being that the ones who made it had caved in, subordinated their diversity to a stereotype of acceptable female behavior. Hunt would be amused.

"Her lawyer must think it will help her case." *And perhaps it will,* Teal added silently. She didn't know how she would answer the questions put to her. "Don's on the schedule, too."

Julia blinked. "I didn't realize. Foolish me. Do you go before or after?"

"I'm less important, so they want to get through with him first," Teal said. "All the partners are going to spend the morning with the firm's lawyer to discuss the case, then Don and Roger and I get to be deposed."

"You'll do fine." Julia smiled.

Julia always smiled. She would smile if mortally wounded. That was one part of what made the lunch odd. Teal sensed something terribly wrong, but Julia smiled. The older woman tapped Teal to attention with a finger on her arm.

"Don't you think Laura Smart is a dear? She offered to help with the raffle. I think she is much more clever than any of us suspect beneath those attention-grabbing clothes. Don tells me she makes a practice of leaving them in the office overnight. She wears even more outrageous things to go out in the evening! Have you ever heard of anything like that?"

Julia's eyebrows shot up again and the corners of her mouth curled high. Teal didn't know what to do. Look Julia in the eye? Not at this moment. Teal had heard the same story from Roger, and Kathy had confirmed Laura's actions.

"Does your secretary change her clothes at the office?" Julia asked, one eyebrow still in an arc.

"No." Teal smiled herself, imagining demure Kathy dressed as either the work or playtime Laura Smart.

"Why on earth would Laura do such a thing?" Julia persisted.

"Kathy says it's because Laura likes to stir up gossip." Teal repeated Kathy's explanation verbatim. She could have kicked herself.

"And does she?" Julia asked.

Teal grimaced. "We're talking about her, aren't we."

"You're right." Julia lifted her menu. "Should we continue to talk about her over food, or am I beginning to sound too much like a jealous wife? She's awfully attractive, but then so are you."

The muscles froze around Teal's mouth. It wasn't right, Kathy keeping Teal informed and other secretaries telling other partners while Julia Clarke, the most interested party, remained in the dark. The convention of a Clayborne Whittier affair had many rules, don't squeal to a spouse being the first.

Teal opened her mouth.

"Ready to hear our specials, ladies?" the server asked from behind Teal's back.

"Yes," she agreed too fast and hoped her relief did not show.

Julia felt she didn't need to mention Laura over the first, or any, course. Teal's eyes and voice and face had revealed

enough of the truth. Julia understood she must be very care-
ful. Don's dalliance threatened to ruin her life as she knew it.
Maybe Emma Browne had meant to warn her this morning.
Maybe Emma considered the gesture appropriate, nice. No,
Emma Browne had seen the affair as useful.

Julia chuckled.

"I wish I thought something was funny today," Teal
said.

Julia made herself pay attention.

"Unfortunately, I have to get to a meeting with Ted
Grey," Teal said.

"Must you?" Julia asked.

"If Ted and I don't come to some agreement, I think my
best senior manager may quit."

"*Best* senior manager?" Julia raised an eyebrow. "That's
going some."

"She is," Teal said. "Amy Firestone."

"Oh yes, Clayborne Whittier's dissident. Am I right?"
Julia grinned.

"According to your husband," Teal said. "But she's usually good for us. Amy is smart and able, if impolitic. Anyway, Ted insists he needs Amy with him out at
MicroAnswer's Massachusetts operation, but she's scheduled
to do my BiMedics quarterly review next week. He'll win, of
course."

"Why?" Julia said to be polite.

"Because he is the big-shot technology industry guru
from California, and in a contest with his needs I go second.
I shouldn't complain. Roger Singer has had to put up with
Ted every day since he arrived."

"Have you met Ted?" Julia asked.

"Yes."

"He's always seemed nice," Julia said. "Clayborne Whittier asks a lot from you folks. I think he's been transferred four times, never had space for a personal life or to enjoy a marriage. Oh, I am sorry . . ."

Julia felt the soft heat of her indiscretion, raising the subject of marriage with this single-minded career woman. Worse, she'd been a hypocrite, using the word "enjoy."

"It's okay. I might marry if I found the right man." Teal grinned.

Julia wondered where her sacrifices for Clayborne Whittier had gotten her in life. It wasn't a question she'd asked herself before Laura, when everything had seemed fine.

"Perhaps you and Ted?"

Teal laughed. "I don't think so. Oops, but I am about to make our V.I.P. visitor angry. I'd better run. See you at the board meeting tonight."

Julia inclined her head. "Don thinks Ted will be asked to take over in Boston when he gets sent to New York."

"So I should be nice. Thanks for the warning," Teal said.

"You'd do the same for me." Julia watched a shadow dim Teal's face.

She snapped her compact open after Teal had departed. Her hands trembled and smeared her lipstick. The face in the mirror still smiled. She scrubbed the napkin across her mouth until the white damask was stained crimson.

She had been so complacent, never challenging Don's decisions for their lives. And look where she found herself.

There has to be a solution, she thought. Panic fluttered in her heart. She refused to lose the achievements of a lifetime, not to Emma Browne, not to Laura Smart.

Julia reconsidered the situation. She was not going to take her own advice. She had no intention of being nice.

TUESDAY

Four

Teal raced through the Public Garden, oblivious to the stands of yellow tulips beside the walk. Vivid blooms swayed in the breeze, but for the second morning in a row, she stared at asphalt.

Why hadn't Hunt at least returned her call? She had apologized twice to his office phone mail and once to his disembodied voice at home, punishment enough. He couldn't hold that poor woman's death to her fault, so what was his problem?

The same as hers, she decided, her palm tightening around the handle of her briefcase. The leather envelope bulged with her silly heels, banging her leg with each stride. She considered tossing the case into the lagoon along with her relationship confusion. The tug of hope, habit, or loyalty—could the options be parsed so clearly?

Teal had to grin at herself as she crossed Charles Street into the Boston Common. The path moved up the incline of Beacon Hill to the crest, where the golden dome of the State House marked the top. She turned right.

Her grin faded. Where had Julia disappeared to last

night? The wife of Clayborne Whittier's partner in charge had never arrived at the CCF meeting, and when Teal had telephoned Julia at home right before, neither Clarke had answered. Teal had been left to punt on the raffle report.

She still wondered at Julia's purpose behind yesterday's lunch. Julia had wanted something. Confirmation of her husband's affair with Laura Smart? Teal worried that her reaction had offered proof, and no wonder, then, that Julia had skipped the obligations of philanthropy. She doubted Julia could enjoy many charitable impulses right now, and surely none toward the too clever Ms. Smart.

The park thickened with the crowd surging up from Park Street station on the subway. Cars honked and gunned down Tremont. Teal pressed back onto the sidewalk as a wedge of giggling young women crushed forward. They sprinted across the road between an onrush of cars. Teal followed with caution and waited for the walk signal.

Pushcart vendors were setting out T-shirts and food at the pedestrian intersection at the center of Downtown Crossing. Two mounted police in front of Filenes Department Store alternated slugs of coffee with shop talk from their saddles. Office workers hurried into the 101 Federal Street arcade to grab a Coffee Connection refill in their no-spill commuter mugs.

What she didn't want to think about was what she should say this morning. Teal knew the talk. Emma Browne was on a vendetta to ruin Clayborne Whittier. Roger faced being fired. Don and Julia might end up in Peoria instead of New York. Teal worried for herself. What would Clayborne Whittier's management committee think of her if she said what she felt? She'd get worse than Peoria.

The trouble was, she had more than hearsay evidence of gender bias at Clayborne Whittier. Her anecdotes might sound like nothing one by one, but the sum told a different story: the comments in each of her annual performance reviews that challenged her commitment to the firm, as if women could play at a career while men knew they must be serious; the accommodation to the client who had requested Clayborne Whittier send an audit team with which they could work late into the evening without causing talk (she and the other female staff had been rescheduled off the job); the partner who had encouraged her to find a position "suitable to a woman" right up to the year she'd made partner.

There had been remarks about her rather too stylish dress and autonomous attitude. But in the end, she possessed what Emma had not, with some willingness to compromise and the support of Don Clarke. Teal had been admitted to the partnership the year of Emma's failure. Teal and her fellow partners had adjusted. Not Emma.

Teal knew that Don's opposition to the former senior manager exceeded ordinary animosity. Teal found his intransigence about Emma hard to understand. Don Clarke had limitations, but she had never seen him carry out a personal vendetta, until Emma Browne.

And to which, Teal worried again—Clayborne Whittier, Don Clarke, or gender—did she owe her loyalty?

That was the question she must answer on the other side of Federal Street and up forty-eight floors. She took a deep breath and headed into the FNEB lobby. The elevator dropped her off at Clayborne Whittier. She intended to steal a minute of privacy before the meeting of the partner group forced her to confront her version of the truth.

Teal hesitated in the middle of the women's room for the third time and brushed back a haze of stray hairs. For the third time, she did not notice the pass of her hand tug the heavy gold orb looser from her ear. The sigh which burst from her mouth masked the earring's clatter when it dropped.

The orb skidded past three unoccupied stalls to slide under the far, closed door.

"Damn," Teal mouthed at her reflection in the mirror, but for a different reason. She wasn't seeing a thing.

The earring, trapped between a red sequinned toe and stiletto heel, set askew by the angle of the foot inside, spun to a stop.

Teal wet her palms and pumped out a mound of the useless foam the firm bought for soap. It didn't matter, her hands were clean. She rubbed them dry with a towel and looked back into the mirror.

Now here's a picture, she thought. Decisive, ambitious E. Teal Stewart in a situation where she felt lost. Nine years of work to realize her goal, admission to the Clayborne Whittier partnership, and the next hours on the other side of the bathroom wall could as good as make or break her career. Or she could lie.

"Damn!"

The conflict inside her vibrated off the polished stone walls. She heard Don Clarke's words in her mouth, heard his intonation as she spoke aloud.

"Not lie! Good God, Teal, do you think we'd ask you to lie?" Teal mimicked from some reservoir of auditory memory. Once, she had done Don so well she had her entire staff howling. Today, she glanced across a sink to find herself as audience. She did not laugh.

Don had summoned her to his office yesterday, as the sun paralleled his window with a blinding glare before it lowered to the horizon behind the Charles River. Teal remembered thinking the river looked a far more distant ribbon than from her Brimmer Street kitchen. Don's message, weighted with sports and team talk, contained his warning. *Don't embarrass the great firm. Don't find yourself on the other side of a them and us divide. Remember, you made it.*

"This is an hysterical, bitter woman, Teal. Be careful you don't get caught in her vengeance," he had said.

"I'm not sure a gender-bias suit against Clayborne Whittier is entirely without merit," Teal demurred.

Don Clarke had stared hard at her then. "Word of advice from an old mentor? Loyalty counts."

Teal grabbed the edge of porcelain and tilted toward the mirror.

"Right. And did you tell that to your wife last night?" Her breath fogged the glass as her low voice bounced around the room.

The woman with the red shoes didn't move a muscle.

Teal was done talking out loud, done thinking about the irony in Don's speech. Presumably, Julia would make him pay the piper in good time. Anyway, that was not Teal's business.

Teal fingered her watch. Eight A.M., the appointed hour. She smoothed the thin wool crepe of her sleek navy dress and checked her image seriously this time. She never had attempted to disguise her gender behind mouse-colored suits and silk bows at the throat of a man-tailored blouse, and she

45

hadn't been about to today. The chignon held her hair tight to the nape of her neck. Royal mascara emphasized the blue in her gray-shadowed eyes. The edge of her lipstick remained sharp. Everything looked in place, except—she touched a finger to her ear.

Her eyes scanned down. No earring glinted from the tile. She inspected the counter and sink. Nothing. She turned to the wall of stalls. Three open doors showed nothing but floor. The fourth was closed. Teal took a step to lay her palm on the cold metal. The hinge did not swing open.

Locked. A flush turned Teal's neck the color of Beacon Hill brick. She had been so sure she was alone. What had she said about Don and his wife? About Don't affair with Laura Smart? What out loud? Seconds ticked off before Teal could bring herself to clear her throat.

"Excuse me, do you see an earring on the floor? It's gold." Teal waited a beat and tapped her knuckles to the door. "Hello?" she faltered.

Why did this have to happen this morning.

"Hello?" She made her voice stronger.

No response. Teal sighed and folded her legs into a tentative squat. She glanced through the foot of open space under the door. Two feet splayed apart gave proof of an occupant.

"I can see it," Teal said, encouragement flooding her voice.

She waited.

"Just by your right shoe," she prompted.

The hollow echo made the room sound empty, but the feet confirmed she was not alone. She could see her earring nestled next to the red shoe. Teal's heart jumped and skittered in her chest as she straightened. She recognized the fancy pump. She could kick herself for blabbing. Laura must be having a ball acting deaf and mute to the plea of a female partner.

She'd see to Laura when the other business of this morning was done.

Teal tried to take a calming breath. This is what her years of meditation was meant for. Spicy perfume undercut with a whiff of feces stopped her inhalation short.

"Are you all right?" Teal stood and banged at the stall. "Answer me, Laura!"

Teal dropped back down to her knees and twisted her head to crane further under the door. Sequined straps wrapped a pale ankle.

"Laura!" Impatience quickened Teal's voice.

This close, the scent became a stench. Teal rocked back, a horrible fear taking hold.

Laura Smart, like Emma Browne, had a knack for making enemies. Laura's came from more than flaunting racy shoes or her personal gender bias. The executive secretary had a reputation for turning on anyone if she thought it might advance her agenda. Laura enjoyed the power conferred on her by sleeping with the partner in charge. And she'd been known to use it. Teal could not understand why Kathy liked the woman, but Kathy said she did.

So had Julia Clarke.

No. What Teal was thinking could not be true. She kicked off her own rather too high-heeled, blue kid shoes and mounted the toilet in the abutting stall. Her five foot seven frame cleared the partition. She pressed a hand to her nose and looked.

The twisted head rested against the back wall. Hands with nails painted the color of a bruise lay on the lap of a skirt hugged to her hips like a girdle.

"Yesterday's outfit," Teal whispered.

She turned her head to gasp a breath inside her palm. She tried to smell the lingering odor of institutional soap, but the truth snapped her head around. The woman's clouded eyes met her own.

Violet eye shadow topped each lid and smeared each brow. Powdered rouge streaked a warm apricot glow from temples to chin. *Laura always wore too much makeup,* Teal thought. Teal set her hands on the partition and pressed to leverage herself higher for a closer look down.

The lips sporting the Mona Lisa smile would never kiss and tell. And the woman leering up at the ceiling never had been Laura Smart.

FIVE

Sixteen pairs of eyes fixed on her entrance to the conference room, fifteen curious Clayborne Whittier partners and the firm's outside counsel. Teal registered only one.

She did not hear Don Clarke chide her for being tardy.

She did not see Frank Sweeny making confetti of his styrofoam cup.

She did not reach to take the agenda Ted Grey held out.

Roger blinked, and the spell broke.

"Teal, will you please—"

"I'm sorry, Don, I had to call the police. Detective Malley would prefer everyone to wait for him here." Teal heard her voice, and it wasn't coming out right.

She wanted to forget the ribbon of blood streaking the wall and the clotted mat at the back of the head, but the image clung in her mind. The gore had provoked a flash of déjà vu. Yesterday, a homeless woman's lined and painted eyes had lifted, as sightless, from under a hat as thick with brain and blood.

Teal wanted to forget something else. She wanted to forget what she had seen wedged behind the toilet.

"What are you saying?" Ted's voice yanked Teal to attention. He waved the agenda. "I'm expected out at MicroAnswer in two hours. We need to get started."

Teal turned her thoughts from the dead to the living.

"And Roger," Ted smacked his hand to the polished wood, "you're coming with me."

"But he can't. You can't," Teal objected.

Don Clarke pushed out from the table and stood and every head swiveled in attention to the partner in charge.

"What has come over you?" He glared at Teal.

"It isn't me." Teal didn't know what to do with her hands. One had curled into her chest on "me." "It's her, in the women's room——"

"Who?" Three or more voices chorused.

"Emma Browne."

The heads had swung back to Teal until a third voice made them spin around.

"We aren't waiting for her," the firm's lawyer said. He nodded, as if to a slow child. "The issue confronting us is that she isn't one of you. Before they take Don's deposition, I thought we could——"

Roger's sudden snicker ricocheted around the room.

"That's not what Teal meant."

Now everyone stared at him.

"Teal meant that Emma is dead," Roger squeezed out before he gasped for a breath.

"Honestly!" Ted bellowed. "We got into this mess because of you and——"

"Gentlemen. Please," the attorney intervened, alert now. "May I advise discretion? Ms. Stewart, please clarify what you do mean."

Teal sank into the chair set out for her. Roger was right. Emma sat on that toilet dead. Dead as a doornail. In the instant Teal had first realized the fact, she'd registered the tiniest flicker of relief. She wouldn't have to decide between the truth or a lie to prove loyalty.

"Emma Browne has been murdered," Teal said.

For a moment, the last note of her voice held the room.

The silence slid away with rustles of uneasy movement. Toes tapped and jittered up and down to rattle the legs of the custom-made table. It was a beautiful table, solid cherry and hand-carved. Styrofoam squeaked as two of the tax department partners joined Frank in picking and tearing their cups to shreds. The management consultants whispered, heads in, away from the larger crowd of tax and audit partners.

Papers rattled in hands that shook. Roger no longer tittered but stared at his shoes, back hunched, head down. If a special bond existed among the partners, it did not show now. Teal considered how she would describe the scene to her friend, Detective Daniel Malley. Every man for himself would do fine. And except for her, it was true. Worried men in sober suits filled the Clayborne Whittier conference room.

"This Emma Browne was bringing a gender-bias suit against each of you?" Dan Malley motioned to the group.

"Against the entire United States partnership," the firm's attorney clarified.

"How can we help?" came from Dan's right.

"And y-y-you are?" Dan asked.

"Ted Grey, the Palo Alto office. I'm in Boston to visit a client and need to be out there in about an hour."

Ted rose and extended his hand. His tie and shirt cost what Dan Malley might spend on clothes in a year. The statement was as true of Teal Stewart's sleek dress and coordinated shoes. Dan took in the hand-rubbed wood paneling, the vase of fresh-cut lilacs, the crystal chandelier.

Nothing here to remind him of the Boston Police Department, even after remodeling, or the interior of the Suffolk County courthouse. The people here were the kind who did not understand shabby courtrooms or that quadruple bunking made a mockery of penal justice. No, this was the crowd that screamed the loudest for law and order and voted against funding for schools and services and institutions necessary to maintain an intact community. Their kids went to private schools and saw private psychiatrists when Mommy found the pot. Their kids were shipped off to adventure camps instead of let loose on the streets. The subject depressed his reserve of goodwill.

"Sometimes people get what they deserve," muttered the man at Dan's left.

"And your name, sir?" Dan asked.

Frank Sweeny took his baby finger away from reaming wax in his right ear. He scraped a pencil point through the tan crust as his narrow face mottled with pink splotches.

"I think what our partner Frank Sweeny meant to say is that Emma Browne could be a difficult woman." Don Clarke raised his hands.

The gesture of conciliation affected Dan like the subtle barrier Don Clarke most likely meant to create. Clarke had made it evident who ran the show, and at Clayborne Whittier it wasn't a servant of the public.

"You haven't said, Detective—"

Dan felt Clarke's eyes, active and alert as Clarke finished his question.

"—how Emma died. Was Teal right? Was it murder?"

Every face lifted to watch Don.

"Would she have deserved it?" Teal's voice punctured the quiet.

"I think there's your answer, Don," Ted said.

Dan turned to catch Teal's eye, but she was frowning at Clarke.

"Let's wait for the police investigation before we jump to conclusions," Clarke said, his voice mild. He nodded to Dan. "Detective, I am relieved to see an old friend assigned to us. Now, what can we do to help?"

"Old friend" is stretching the truth, Dan thought. Clayborne Whittier had lent Teal Stewart to the Boston police a few years before to help him on a case where financial expertise counted, and, yes, he had married her secretary. That's where his contact with the firm ended.

"Before I get down to s-s-speaking with each of you alone, I'd like to ask if anyone can identify this?" Dan Malley raised the clear plastic bag by a corner.

He watched Teal wince as a gasp united the larger group.

"The murder weapon, I presume?" Roger Singer's voice cracked from a fit of nerves.

"It was not me!" Roger repeated back in his office.

Teal's expression made him uneasy.

"That's what everyone wants to think," he said, seeing her staring at him. Anxiety knotted his bowels.

"I doubt it," Teal said.

He noticed she did not quite meet his eye.

Labored breathing made him wheeze. Yesterday he thought he'd been so smart, letting her go on and on about the mortgage and about the rumor and Laura Smart.

"I was joking. You know, because of your history with dead bodies." He worked up a shrug. "Don't you believe me? Jesus, what am I supposed to do? I told the truth. It was my tombstone."

"Are you okay?" Teal asked.

Roger stopped vibrating his crossed leg.

"You're the only partner in Boston who worked on the MicroAnswer offering, Roger. You had to tell the truth."

"Someone used that stupid piece of rock to lay Emma's murder on me!" Roger shouted.

"Malley won't fall for a trick. He isn't stupid," Teal said.

Roger was back to normal breathing.

"Any one of us could have done it."

"You're right," Teal said, but it did not reassure him.

"But I can't tell Barbara," he whispered. "She'll leave me."

He'd never intended it to get to this.

"Then don't," Teal suggested.

"Barbara loves the perks of being a partner's wife—"

"Not more than she loves you, Roger," Teal said.

"Sure." Roger fidgeted with the metal cap covering the eraser of the mechanical pencil he picked off his desk. "Come on Teal, what did you see?"

"I can't. Dan asked—"

"Forget your stupid detective and think about me! Why did you have to leave my offering trophy behind for the police?"

"Don't be ridiculous. I couldn't exactly walk in, push her body aside and remove evidence. I never thought you killed her and neither will he."

"Everyone isn't you. Half the office must think I'm guilty, and the other half just hasn't heard." Roger squeezed the metal until the circle narrowed to an oval. It would not fit back over the eraser. "Help me," he said.

"There's no need to worry."

"Where's your loyalty?" he pushed.

"Good question," Teal muttered. "Okay, but this is against my better judgment."

Roger tried to smile.

"She looked horrible, you know," Teal said.

Roger wanted to shake the words out of her.

"That's it? She looked horrible? You expected death to bring improvement?" His voice squeaked.

"Do you remember telling me about Laura Smart?" Teal asked.

He stared at the pencil. The MicroAnswer logo adorned the pocket clip. Laura Smart was delicate ground.

"What about Laura?" he said.

"Remember you told me she leaves her work outfits in her desk overnight sometimes? Julia Clarke asked me about the same story yesterday," Teal said.

"So?"

"So Emma was dressed in Laura's clothes."

He clicked so hard the graphite spit a streak of black

dust across his desk. It looked like mushroom spore. He laid the pencil down.

"And she was made up like a parody of Laura," Teal finished.

Roger tried to lift his shoulders as if nothing was new, but they wouldn't move.

"Laura told Kathy about the list of partners tagged to be transitioned out."

"So?" Roger worked up the shrug.

"She said you were on it."

"You told me all that yesterday," Roger snapped. He regained his composure. "You didn't tell the police, did you?"

"Why would you be fired? It doesn't make sense," Teal mused. "I don't care what you said to Emma, you're our technical guru. No way Don or the firm would let go of you."

"But the police will hear the rumor and think I wanted Emma dead because the partnership blamed me for her lawsuit." Roger swallowed. "I can't believe I got myself into this."

"What are you talking about? You aren't the only person with a reason to wish ill of Emma," Teal said.

"No kidding. Tell me something new. Emma was out for Don. She didn't plan to spare you—"

"Or Frank or Ted—"

"Or your little protégé," Roger said. He rubbed his tongue over his teeth.

"Amy Firestone? Amy organized the underground campaign in support of Emma. *SUE*—Stand Up for Emma—it's pretty dumb, but Amy, at least, is a true believer," Teal said.

"Whatever you want to think."

"I think someone who knew about the list decided to divert suspicion to you," Teal concluded.

Roger wondered if she could see his heart pounding.

"Maybe," he managed to get out, and prepared to confess.

Six

"I think someone who cares about the law is not to drop everything to work," Teal concluded.

Teal wondered if she spoke the truth, the words sounded false in her own ears. But she pushed forward despite the doubt.

"What are you talking about?"

Teal whipped around. Roger popped up.

"Amy!" Roger exclaimed.

"What are you talking about?" Amy Firestone repeated, and stepped into the room.

"Nothing to concern you," Roger said.

Amy did not look convinced and opened her mouth as if there was more she planned to say.

"What is it, Amy?" Teal interjected.

"Actually, I'm waiting for you," Amy said.

"Damn." Teal fought the impulse to cast her eyes at her watch. How could she be late the second time in as many days? "Excuse us, Roger."

He did not protest, and Teal let Amy lead the way down the hall.

"Okay, so what's this list you were discussing?" Amy asked once they were out of Roger's earshot.

"Some things are confidential in a partnership, sorry," Teal said.

Amy chortled. The direct reaction suited the short, compact woman. All of Amy's reactions were direct. Her hazel eyes registered profound doubt, but she walked the rest of the way in silence. Teal stepped faster to keep up.

"So, it's all straightened out?" Amy said before they entered Teal's office.

"Not exactly," Teal hedged.

"Well, did you agree to let me? If I can work for him now in Boston, it could give me an important vote this—"

"We ended up not meeting. I'm sorry, Amy, Ted had to cancel yesterday when I came back a few minutes late."

"You think he's a pain, don't you?"

Amy did not spare anyone, Teal decided, and grinned.

"Well, what do you think of him?" Amy pressed.

Teal hesitated. Clayborne Whittier tradition held some things to be sacred among the partners—like voicing candid opinions of each other to staff, even to a senior manager as promising as Amy, when Amy behaved. Teal realized her acceptance of these institutional inhibitions marked a shift in conduct.

Hunt had commented on the change. All she had to do was close her eyes to see his disgust across the breakfast table.

"You're losing your grip on reality if you can tell me Frank Sweeny is good for practice development and keep a straight face. Next thing, you'll be saying Roger Singer's a pro at handling stress. What is this? Admission mutes you from speaking the truth? Or blinds you?"

She could remember every word. Funny the memory should make her miss him. She wondered if he would return her calls.

"Ted Grey's not the pain," Amy interrupted. "My problem is your friend Roger."

"Your bigger problem is going to be me if we can't straighten out your schedule, and that takes Ted," Teal said.

Amy spun around. "Let's go."

Teal sighed. Amy enjoyed confrontation. Emma Browne could not have had a more effective ally. Teal stopped, suddenly aware that Amy knew nothing of what had happened this morning.

"You just drove in from MicroAnswer?" Teal asked.

Amy inclined her head. Her eyes shifted from Teal's face. It was an unexpected evasion.

"Then you haven't heard," Teal said.

"Heard?" Amy asked, her attention to the floor.

Teal hardly noticed, caught as she was in her thoughts. All it would be for Amy was hearing. Amy wouldn't smell the smell, see the plain face mocked with garish paint. Amy hadn't found Emma Browne.

"Heard what?" Amy repeated.

"About Emma."

Teal watched the outspoken, independent Clayborne Whittier manager jump like a cat tapped with an electric prod. Amy retracted her hand from the doorknob and began a sudden show of picking lint. Teal paid attention now.

"What about her?" Amy asked, head bent to the task.

Amy rolled a loose thread into a tiny ball between thumb and index finger. She dropped that tangle and started worrying a length still attached to her tailored jacket.

"I found Emma this morning," Teal said.

The linen strand vibrated, taut.

"I found her in the women's room. She was dead."

The linen snapped and with it a button spun to the floor. Teal and Amy knelt to the carpet, head to head.

"What happened?" Amy whispered.

"Someone bashed in her head."

Amy plucked up the button.

"I've got it," she said.

They stood, an unusual tension between them. In the matter of Emma Browne, Amy Firestone had taken a stand and risked her career at Clayborne Whittier. Teal had preferred to dodge. It couldn't make her look like a heroine.

"I'm terribly sorry," Teal said.

"Can we talk about things tomorrow?" Amy suggested, and took off before Teal could respond.

Amy wanted to scream, but the churn of masticated salad and lunch bile made her jam a fist against her throat and run. She did not see the yellow tape or "Out of Order" sign but made it to a stall just in time. A minute later she pushed off her quivering arms and raised a wad of toilet paper to her mouth.

That's when she saw the streak of blood and realized what she had done.

Teal turned to the window. Bright spring sunlight flared off the mansard roof of the old Federal Reserve on the other side of the park at Post Office Square. The handsome building had been redesigned on the inside to house a Meridien Hotel while the ongoing Federal Reserve Bank of Boston was located in an aluminum tower across from South Station. Teal laid her forehead against the cool glass and stared down.

She had never called Emma to give a word of support, had never said "I can imagine what you've been going through," had never offered to help. Receipt of the subpoena for her deposition had sent her straight to Don Clarke, who had turned her over to the firm's lawyer for instruction in the party line. She had not even called Emma to ask why.

It was never easy to see someone work hard to become a partner and come up short, but that's what happened to Emma, Teal had decided. Surely her own career put the lie to any argument of gender bias, she had told herself. She had made it, after all. Clayborne Whittier admitted individuals on the basis of merit. Emma had not made the cut, pure and simple. The rationalization had satisfied her until yesterday, when the idea of repeating it to Hunt had made a mockery of her hypocrisy.

Tiny people formed a human mosaic in the park. Teal watched a group of three cross the street. Two others disappeared underground into the garage. The elevators would be piping in classical music, elegant and cultivated. A sharp rap on her door interrupted her thoughts. She straightened. Grieving the loss of her integrity was of no use to Emma now.

Don Clarke did not wait to be invited but charged in.

"Your friend Malley wants to see you," he said.

Don's transformation of the last six months had taken him from a sloucher with a gut to a tall man with a thick middle, but right now, pasty skin did not aid the overall impression of his health. He looked dreadful.

"I've set him up in the conference room. The police are finished with . . . with . . ."

"Emma?" Teal assisted.

Don swallowed the name like a bitter pill. "Yes. And with the restroom, but we need to have it cleaned. Did you know that?"

"Know what?" Teal asked.

"We're responsible for washing up the remains . . ." Don snorted. "Emma was a pro at making a mess."

Teal wanted to sit in shocked silence, but she couldn't make herself feel the shock. Don was right. Emma had set the partnership on edge and made a mess.

Don reached out to thump her shoulder, and Teal worked not to cringe.

"You had lunch with my wife yesterday," he said. "She's very fond of you."

His hand dropped to his side and he directed his gaze to her face. *Don can look you right in the eye and reveal nothing of himself,* Teal thought. She held her eyes as steadily on his. He shifted his weight.

"I'll bet she even tells you the kinds of things she would never admit to me." His "ha-ha" came out flat.

Teal tried to smile back, but the message conveyed was no joke. A handy quip about gender solidarity died in her throat.

"I don't think so," Teal offered. "We've been busy with the CCF raffle. I'm flattered Julia thought to invite me—"

"Word of advice, Teal. It's hard being a partner's wife— ah, spouse. All these years and Julia still can't understand my hours." Don spoke like he and Teal were confidants. "You know, she runs late herself sometimes with this CCF business. Take last night. She's a great gal to have put up with me all these years. I'm a lucky man."

"You are," Teal murmured.

She didn't say, "And how is Laura today?" No. She held her lips in a wan smile.

"I should get on to Detective Malley," she suggested.

Teal noticed the sheen of damp on Don's forehead. He cleared his throat as she moved for the door.

"I heard something about Emma being dressed like . . . ah . . . like—"

"Laura?" Teal suggested.

Like a parody of a real girl, in makeup and a tight little skirt? Like a perversion of what the admissions committee had advised? Would that be closer to the truth?

"And that's how she, the body, looked to you? Like Laura?" Don said.

"Well, sort of."

"Laura isn't in today." Don fidgeted with a book on Teal's desk. "You will consider what you say to the police?"

"Yes," Teal agreed. She would consider what she said.

"Good."

Don walked out to the corridor first. He slowed to give her another short thump on the back before he walked past her turn for the conference room. Don's comment about Julia didn't register until she had stepped inside, but Julia had not been at the CCF meeting last night. Teal spun around to catch Don, but he was gone.

"How was the interrogation?" Kathy asked.

Teal shrugged. "Same old, same old. I'm not sure I was much help."

"He thinks you are," Kathy said with the confidence of someone who admired both parties, her detective husband and her partner boss.

64

Teal imagined Kathy's loyalties wouldn't be so undivided if Kathy knew Teal had spent the hour telling Dan less than the whole truth.

"Well, speaking of same old, same old, guess who called?" Kathy asked.

Kathy lifted a deceptively innocent face for someone so able and shrewd. She had managed to pry Dan away from his mother's hold without causing a bitter family feud. In fact, the elder Mrs. Malley claimed to love Kathy, too. Teal wondered when there'd be a baby, adding another Malley to the group. The honor of being godmother would be nice.

"Come on, guess who called," Kathy prompted, and brought Teal back to the moment.

"Probably Roger."

He would expect a word-by-word on her encounter with Malley.

Kathy rotated her head no. Good humor lit her green eyes. The heart shape of her face tightened with the strain of holding the secret.

Teal couldn't imagine it was Amy, not after the manner of the senior manager's earlier departure.

Kathy's face began to drop to disappointment. "You can't be thinking straight. Same old, same old, Teal!"

Teal's brain went blank. She wasn't thinking straight or any other way, her mind mostly full of pictures of Emma slumped on the toilet. Emma, dead. Emma, murdered.

Dan Malley had pounded on one idea over and over, the similarity of the blows. Emma and the homeless woman—each one had died from the impact of a blunt object cracking their heads open. Teal could imagine the homeless woman with her bright penny dye once had been beautiful. Not so Emma.

"Teal!" Kathy snapped. "Listen. He called you. Here."

Kathy thrust the pink message slip into Teal's inert hand.

"Isn't this what you said you wanted?"

SEVEN

Hunt relaxed his thumb and index finger where they squeezed the fat drafting pen. He stared past the top of his drawing board for the third time in the last half hour. He could see BG at the other end of the floor leaning over the shoulder of the young associate their firm, Huntington BG Associates, had hired a few months before. BG's drift of blond hair contrasted well with the young Japanese-American's plumb straight, black bowl cut. She lifted an alert and attentive face to respond to BG.

Renewed pressure forced the point of Hunt's pen to snap in a shower of ink across his rendering of the new sports megaplex.

"Shit!"

Black ink dripped from his hand to the white paper. One blot feathered into a dark medallion which started on the *H* and bled through *untington,* leaving *BG Associates* readable in the legend box. Hunt rolled his wet thumb across the *BG.* The print whirls obliterated his partner and curved toward the *A.*

"Should I watch my back, buddy-ola?"

Hunt turned up to encounter BG's tight grin.

"Your front is more to the point." Hunt couldn't quite get the feel of a joke into his tone.

"Ah-ha! Am I hearing the sound of a jealous male? Our Midori is lovely." BG nodded in her direction.

Ginger eyebrows knit in studied innocence above canny eyes. Full lips pouted like those of a curious child. Hunt squirmed.

"And how *is* your sex life?" BG asked.

"We're on company time," Hunt said, his jaw muscles in a knot.

BG's lips flattened. "I stopped by to say the lovely Ms. Stewart returned your call—"

"Yes?" Hunt rose from the drafting chair.

"And she promised to stop by on her way home from work this evening."

"Fine," Hunt said to end the conversation.

"It's been a long time since I've seen our Teal." BG did not move. "I imagine I'm the excuse you used."

Hunt raised a hand in protest, but BG just winked.

"Don't say I never did anything for you."

The entrance to the MBTA subway at Park and Tremont was packed. Teal dodged the panhandlers standing inside the swinging door and joined the crush descending the littered, metal steps. One man called out for money to buy a cup of coffee and a pastry. She grinned at the impulse to demand more than the minimum in life.

The line to buy tokens edged down to the kiosk. Teal shouted to the attendant through the metal circle cut in the barrier of glass between them and raised a finger to indicate a single token. One would take her to Hunt's office. She'd walk home.

The day's heat was trapped in the station along with the smell of popcorn exploding out of the metal popper in the vendor's cart on the inbound platform. She waited on the other side to go outbound. An E train pulled up. The E could take her to Symphony Hall, the Huntington Theater, Northeastern University, the Museum of Fine Arts, The Isabella Stewart Gardner Museum, or hospitals on Longwood, but it turned left after Copley Square Station and could not take her to Hunt's new office at the funky end of Newbury Street.

Two more trains screeched into Park Street. Passengers elbowed on and off. More commuters crowded the platform. Teal wished Hunt's office had remained on Commercial Street where he and BG had started.

She had cut up and across Cobbs Hill hundreds of trips before the first time she stopped to look around. So many slate headstones in the colonial cemetery had been carved with the winged skull of the angel of death, a grim *memento mori* did more to chastise the living than cherish the memory of the dead. Most of the stones showed their age, with shattered shards fallen to the ground. Huntington BG Associates was visible from the hill. The firm rented the top floor of a building which had been painted with the legend "FRUITS & VEGETABLES" on the exposed side.

Teal used to wave at their window from the top of the granite steps before descending to the park. Once she'd been buzzed into their building, she would climb the distance she'd just come down on the outside.

On days as hot as she felt now, the three of them would

go across the street to the Metropolitan District Commission public pool and take a swim. Teal had enjoyed turning heads, but it had been BG who won the stares there. He'd worn an Italian bathing suit that summer. Dressed in the ribbon of lycra no bigger than a G-string, he had made the teenage girls try anything to get his attention.

Huntington BG Associates' success had prompted the move from the North End to the tonier edge of town in the Back Bay.

Teal shifted in the thickening crowd and itched with a fine sweat. She wished she could free her hair from the tight chignon. But Hunt's message had said to meet him at his office. The request would not have been strange for the middle of the day, or if he had mentioned a project keeping him late, but Teal recognized that it represented another change. He wasn't asking her to his home on South Street for a casual visit where she could undo her hair and throw on the old sweats left in his drawer.

She sighed. Nothing in the relationship seemed to remain but a history of knowing one another.

A briefcase slammed her shin.

"Lady, I am sorry," the hefty businessman said.

She returned a wan smile. A wave of people pushing for the tracks pulled them apart. The station vibrated with the rumble of a coming train.

Teal let momentum lift her up through the open doors. The Boylston and Arlington Street stops added at least nine bodies to the mix. Copley might have been an even exchange at thirteen. Teal counted to counter her urge to scream. She hated rush hour on the T. Claustrophobia constricted her throat and unsettled her stomach. Finally, the train arrived at ICA/Hynes. Teal reinforced a polite "excuse me" with her elbows to climb off against the shoving tide.

She stepped across the Huntington BG Associates' threshold tired and testy.

Hunt watched Argyle lift his head from his snooze and shake off the stupor of sleep to run for the door. The nails of the old Scottish deerhound made a wonderful click as they hit the hardwood floor. Argyle never understood that Teal was not returning home.

Her voice came to Hunt from around the corner.

"Argyle," she said in her most melodious tone, and Hunt could imagine her dropping down to scratch the big guy's head and nuzzle her own in his furry side.

Everything about Teal remained familiar, even as everything had become foreign. Hunt sighed.

"Too much work?" Teal asked as she came closer.

She bent over his drawing.

"The convention and sports megaplex? My, my. So, do you think I'll get season tickets to the Celtics now that they have their new Boston Garden?" she said, betraying her parochial interest.

"The Shawmut Center," Hunt corrected her, and they laughed.

The new home of the Celtics and Bruins was likely to remain the New Garden, however much the Shawmut Bank had paid to change the name.

He had put her on the basketball team's season ticket waiting list, with a promise to pay for the first season, before she'd made partner. Since then, ticket prices had increased, even with the team in the rebuilding phase, as the euphemism went, and still the Celtics' front office told him she was nowhere near getting a good seat.

"BG's behind you," Hunt said, but it was too late.

His partner had Teal spinning into his arms for a hug and kiss.

"We've been missing you," BG said. "He's been a big-time pain in the ass."

"Occasionally, so are you," Teal said and squeezed harder.

Her smile lit the gray right out of her blue eyes, and Hunt felt the old pangs. But it hadn't worked, and at the end, nothing either one of them did seemed right. BG spoke the truth, however. Hunt did miss her.

"Still breaking hearts?" Teal teased. "What wife are we on? Number four or—"

"Five. And she's already out the door." BG wriggled his face into an exaggerated frown. "I'll leave you two."

"That's all right," Hunt said. He turned to Teal. "I thought we might go for coffee."

"Oh, you want to talk about me." BG wagged his brows up and down. "Don't believe a word he says."

"I won't," Teal promised.

The Massachusetts Avenue end of Newbury Street pulsed to a twenty-something beat of Tower Records customers and Berkeley School of Music students. The Coffee Connection was a few doors down. Some of the customers offered living proof punk would never go out of style.

Teal set her frappuccino on a tiny table. Hunt joined her with an iced espresso and the offer of a biscotti.

"Thanks."

He didn't know where to start.

"You called me," she prodded.

Someone jostled Hunt's chair. The terrible cafe design made the architect in him want to start rearranging the counters.

"Well?" Teal said.

She ripped the paper from a straw and stuck it into the cup of khaki slush. Hunt sat, tongue-tied. He had thought it would be easy. He cleared his throat.

"Tell me about Emma Browne's suit," he said.

"What?"

She knew she was making that face, the one he hated, the one that said, you tiresome dolt. She took a deep breath.

"You want me to tell you about Emma Browne's lawsuit?" she repeated.

He nodded. She spooned a load of milled coffee ice to her mouth. It was deliciously sweet and sharp with flavor and cold.

"May I ask why?" she said.

Hunt could not know Emma had been murdered, hit on the back of the head with Roger's tombstone.

She understood Hunt well enough to read tension in his black Irish eyes. *Repressed anger at me, most likely,* she thought. *But why is his jaw in a knot over Emma Browne?*

"I want to get some familiarity with sexual harassment suits—the grounds, the defenses—"

"She didn't claim sexual harassment," Teal exploded. "Gender bias, Hunt. Clayborne Whittier judges women by quite a different standard from men, at least that was the gist of her argument."

She watched him concentrate on the circles he smeared

around the table top from the condensation on his cup. He hadn't taken a sip of his drink.

"This isn't what you want to hear?" Teal asked.

Anger at something else, the year of silence between them, made her shrill. Hunt stopped fiddling.

"You know how BG can act childish, a little—"

"Like he's ruled by his libido? Yes," Teal said. She enjoyed BG, a lot actually, but she had been waiting for this.

"It's not exactly that," Hunt countered.

"I don't understand you, Hunt. BG's screwed around before and you never said a thing—"

"He's my partner, Teal. He's a good landscape architect, a genius, maybe. And he can act immature, but . . ." He lost the struggle for words.

She glared at his unhappy face.

"He's my partner," she mimicked. "What's this, a little go-along-to-get-along behavior to keep the peace at Huntington BG Associates? Seems to me, that's the reaction that made you get so high and mighty about Clayborne—"

"You're right! Okay? You were right and I never should have called you!"

They both stood and glared. Half the room turned to watch, the other half paying no attention to the public display.

"You should be talking to him, not me," Teal said as calmly as she could.

Hunt dropped back to his chair.

"I'm sorry. When I try, BG weasels out of any serious discussion with snide remarks about me and male jealousy. You know his reaction to criticism is not good—"

"Explains why he's up to wife number five," Teal said.

She offered half the biscotti to Hunt.

"Huntington BG Associates can't afford to split apart, not with the megaplex," he said.

"And he is your friend." She nodded, unsure of what to say. "Someone sent Frank Sweeny to Funsters."

Hunt's eyes opened wider.

"Really, and it wasn't me, but I'm afraid it was my best staff and now I'm stuck with the problem of confronting her. Like you with Beej—"

Hunt's howls of laughter drowned out the analogy. He slapped the table. Then she began to giggle. Frank Sweeny was narrow-minded and a rube. It was almost impossible to picture him walking into the wildest gay bar in town.

"So, what happened?" he asked when he could speak.

The question stopped her cold.

"I don't know. He went yesterday, and when I saw him this morning there were other things on my mind."

Then she told Hunt about finding Emma Browne.

He realized how much he had missed her as they stood outside, the late sun turning her hair to the color of burning wood. She could be as annoying as anyone he had ever known, but she could also be more wonderful, more incisive, and more fun. He kept her talking about her work and her house and her last year because he did not want to let her go.

"I think you should speak with BG before he makes any real trouble for himself . . . and the firm," she said.

She made a move to turn.

"You aren't coming back to the office with me? Give me more advice?" he asked too quickly.

"I'm tired. I'm hungry. And I live that way." She pointed in the other direction.

"Argyle will be disappointed," he said.

"He's been disappointed before."

"Your briefcase looks heavy—"

"It's my shoes, Hunt. I never carry work home, you know that," Teal's voice rose.

"How about you come home with me and I pull out a nice bottle of Australian red and we throw together some pasta and garlic and olive oil with cheese?"

She inspected everything from his uncontrolled, curly, black hair to the scuff marks on his shoes, but her eyes retreated with a wariness he could not read.

"How about I say no. I'm not sure it's that easy—"

"To forgive me?" Hunt held his breath.

"To leave your house if I go," she said.

"I promise to have you home by ten," he whispered.

One o'clock in the morning came closer.

She tiptoed up the stairs of the townhouse she owned. She didn't want to disturb her tenants on the first or second and third floors. Her unit had been converted from what once had been quarters for the help on the fourth and fifth floors. Hunt's design had opened the cramped rooms to capture air and light and space. She dropped her keys on the hall table and headed for the library.

Moon glittered off the surface of the Charles River across Storrow Drive out the window. Teal laid a cheek to the glass. So Hunt had called her worried about BG, nothing to do with her. Not hope or habit or loyalty. But BG wasn't why

Hunt had asked her home. She smiled into the shadows of a city night.

The telephone ring did not turn her around. Anyone calling at this hour deserved the machine.

"You may leave Teal a message after the beep."

At first, she heard only breathing.

"Teal? Are you there?" The pause sighed with hope deflating. "It's Laura Smart. Look, I need to talk. You can call when you get in. Nothing's too late for me. I'm just home myself and it's—" Teal heard a rustle, "like after one, okay?"

The connection ended. Teal turned around to consider the blinking red *one* on her machine. She reached a hand for the receiver but let it fall back to her side. Laura Smart could wait until the morning.

WEDNESDAY

EIGHT

Laura hadn't expected a machine.

Her lungs squeezed the air out in bursts as the crest of the adrenaline surge set her heart jumping around in her chest. All the debating whether or not to call, all the obsessing and look what she'd got—a recorded voice on an audio chip. Laura wouldn't work for a woman. But Kathy said Teal was okay, and Laura thought it was time to talk to someone, plant the seed with someone she could trust, someone who might see her point and offer a little insurance.

Laura unwrapped a piece of gum and pressed dents into the fat stick with the tip of a curved fingernail. The nail sported a little golden mock-up of the Clayborne Whittier logo. It reminded her that he loved that. He loved a lot of things she did. No other woman let him do it where she did. No other woman fed his greed quite like she did. But the loving might be coming to a dead end.

Laura shivered.

One in the morning brought a cool breeze to stir a draft in the close apartment. Usually, she liked living on the first floor, no nosy neighbors to listen to her comings and goings, and the heat of the day rising to fry them, not her. She didn't feel so comfortable tonight though.

He had hated her three dumpy rooms at the start, but she'd told him flat out not to think so suburban. She'd grown up in Chelsea, gateway to Revere, or Revee-ya as she used to say. Until he came into her life, the town of Somerville had looked like Beverly Hills.

Growing up on welfare corn flakes for dinner and a father her mother couldn't name hadn't thwarted her intelligence. Laura Smart held a steady eye on where she wanted to go and it might as well be as high as Beverly Hills. She looked at it this way—he'd raised her sights.

Laura realized she still gripped the phone. She uncurled her palm to let the handset drop. The contact broke the stillness with a bang. She did not like silent nights, but she could not bring herself to slip on earphones. The idea of not being able to hear made her nervous. Sometimes he needed to come back. Mr. More, More, More.

But not lately.

Laura frowned and decided to think about what she wanted to say.

She could say too much and make a mistake. She could say too little and Teal Stewart would appraise her with cool eyes and conclude she was crazy. Or trying to make trouble, which is what Teal would think anyway. Which was true.

Laura smiled. Trouble could be so useful when you slept with the partner in charge.

She realized she was shaking. The translucent robe offered no warmth to her naked body. She dropped her gaze to appreciate the rosebud nipple stiffened to a blunt point from her soft, sweet breast. Pathetic how even a drop in temperature aroused her so much more than him, not that she planned to let him know. She sighed. The hunger in her body went to waste under his dumb hand. She only took it the way she did to protect herself from facing him when he brandished the ugly thing.

He had power, though, and realizing that got her juices flowing. He could make things happen. Elevate someone to the partnership or lay them low. Get them in trouble or get them a raise. She'd recognized that fact at once. Then Emma Browne had come to mess things up.

Laura ground her teeth. It wasn't a pretty sound.

What would titillate the aloof Ms. Stewart? Laura had worried the issue all yesterday morning before Kathy's call.

"Have you heard?" Kathy had asked, not even bothering to question why Laura was home. Laura had said she felt a little sick. Kathy already had told her most of what she'd wanted to know.

She had listened without a word. Emma Browne deserved to be dead. Emma Browne was the type of woman Laura really hated.

It made Laura nervous about the clothes, but she did not let Kathy know. The idea of Emma Browne in red spandex had struck Laura as revolting. Laura cackled out loud. She might have to stop wearing red spandex for a while. She liked these thoughts. The echo of her laugh made the old dump of an apartment less isolated. Then a car backfired as it rounded the corner.

Laura about left the thin robe behind as she jumped from the couch. She gulped to regain her composure as she sat back down and hugged tense arms around raised knees.

Why didn't Teal fucking answer her phone? she thought.

———

Julia Clarke rubbed her eyes as she drove. She couldn't decide when she had slept and when she'd just stared into the dark. She knew she had cried most of the night. One bad dream woke her with tears leaking around her closed eyes.

Failure to thrive. The diagnosis applied to more than the newborns she held in her arms whenever the CCF board visited a special-care hospital ward. Don never understood her willingness to take sick babies against her heart and kiss the fuzzy soft spots at the top of their heads. If his own kids had found him undemonstrative, why did she expect him to change when offered a baby with AIDS?

She wondered if the Valium and Xanax her doctor prescribed every three months could ever properly address a case of failure to thrive.

Her grandmother used to sit in the carved, high-backed ebony chair she and Don now kept in the living room and stroke Julia's small, golden head. Squeezing her eyes closed, she recalled the imperious tenor in her grandmother's voice.

"Marion," Nana had instructed Julia's mother, "this girl is a perfect lady."

And I won't have it any other way, had come across to the beribboned little girl. She had learned at her grandmother's knee to pour tea and make social talk and understand duty and obligation to family. Her grandmother had prepared Julia to be a credit to the clan, a regular churchgoer, a perfect corporate wife.

And then the world had changed.

Julia sighed. The pale drab of first dawn penetrated the side windows. Neither her grandmother nor four years as a legacy at her mother and grandmother's liberal arts college beside the lake in Michigan had prepared her for women like Emma Browne. Younger women like Emma snubbed the sphere Julia had been trained to dominate. They expected to achieve independent of a spouse. These were the women who had turned the Hillegonds College campus upside down. Julia had heard the stories. In her day, boys had been permitted to eat in the dining rooms dirty from sports, but girls were required to dress. Ten years later, the Emma Brownes had refused. They had upset a standard Julia never would have thought to question.

Complacency had its price.

The first time Don had come home and told her Clayborne Whittier had assigned a female to his out-of-town job, she had wanted to refuse to let him go and actually thought about calling the then partner in charge. Don had gone, of course, and so had the woman, long since departed from the firm. Now Don ran the office and Teal Stewart and other women had been admitted as his partners.

Julia tried to make sense of this different universe, but she remained her grandmother's granddaughter, the perfect lady and the perfect wife. And Laura Smart was her reward?

No. No, that's not right.

She straightened to see out the car window. The squat triple decker remained obscure in the dark. No lights glowed from the house. Julia knew one thing for sure: Don could not be inside.

She tested her legs. Pins and needles pierced her feet. She flapped her arms and lolled her head around on her neck. The movement caught a reflection of her perfect smile framed in the rear view mirror, the tense smirk of a woman who had never challenged the status quo.

Her smile bared her teeth. Wouldn't Don be surprised at his good little wife?

Surprise had not described her reaction when he crept into their bedroom at half past midnight. She had not stirred, having chosen to accept the agreed pretense. He had warned her duty called on him to work late into the night and she had nodded a perfect wife's understanding to the cold telephone.

"And I volunteered for the early, early shift at the hospital in the morning," she had said into the mouthpiece. "I'm afraid you'll have to get your own breakfast tomorrow."

He wasn't shocked. She chose hours most CCF volunteers despised. Babies, heavy with sleep, snug and accepting in her arms, compensated the inconvenience of any hour. Of course, she had not been honest about today.

The notion that Laura Smart had once been a baby pierced Julia's thoughts. She could imagine it too easily. Laura was young enough to be her own child, young enough to have been held in Julia's arms, kissed on that fuzzy soft spot by Julia's mouth.

Hysterical snickering clouded the windows of her closed car. That Don had held Laura Smart, kissed her mouth and done—Julia broke down. She refused to think of what her husband and his secretary might have done. Had done. Had done before midnight last night?

Perhaps she should take a Xanax and depart, drive home, leave Laura to God. Many people had it so much worse. Illness, poverty, abuse, illiteracy—she tried to string out the list, but other people's sorrows in life did nothing to diminish her own. They only added company.

She should have asked Teal outright, put her on the spot,

but Emma Browne's voice over the line had told Julia all she needed from anyone other than Laura Smart. She had a hard time remembering how much she had disliked Emma Browne. Death did that, let you forget, rewrite history. Forgive and forget was easy with some people when they were dead. It was feeling easy with Emma Browne.

The churchgoer in Julia liked to forgive and forget. She'd managed with Emma. Now she was about to do the trick with Laura Smart.

Laura resisted the urge to come fully awake. She settled back into the dream, but the images dissolved as the compulsion to pee became immediate. She knew the way by heart and left the bed with half-closed eyes.

The bathroom glowed with a night light. She brushed her teeth when she was done. She always brushed her teeth when she woke, sometimes more than once in a night. He didn't know that. A grin curled her mouth. He didn't know she wore T-shirts to bed when he wasn't around, either.

Pajamas. He'd wear pajamas at home, she decided. PJs with piping. Her grin widened. He wouldn't have been caught dead in pajamas with her. No, they both pretended to spend their nocturnal hours in the nude. Sometimes she wondered why she'd ever let it get started. Vanity, no doubt. Vanity and the thrill of another flaunting of her own power, a brush of her tit across his arm at work, the day she sat on his desk wearing a black silk garter under her skirt and nothing else.

He had noticed.

She giggled. Men, the ultimate fools. She wasn't a bit political, but she'd never forget how a penis and the press could bring a man down. She was glad she wasn't ruled by anything as fickle as a dick.

She left the bathroom to prowl the living room. No cars moved on the street. Not quite six was too early for the neighborhood brats to aim for her window in their endless game of street hockey. No more breeze stirred, either, and she flushed up hot. The covers lay in a tangle beside the bed, and she left them on the floor.

She did not sink back to sleep, but swayed and dipped close to dropping off, only to regain her consciousness with a jolt. Almost and not quite, almost and not quite, until the effort had her exhausted. She didn't question the knock.

She never focused through the peep hole, with her attention on yanking up her shorts as she swung open the back door.

NINE

Impulse made Teal grab the home address list for the employees of the Clayborne Whittier Boston office before she headed out of her house. No traffic yet clogged Storrow Drive and she was about to turn up the ramp to I93 and head north when curiosity made her spin the steering wheel around. She toured Leverett Circle and back to Storrow to take the Longfellow Bridge into Cambridge. Outside of Kendall Square she took a right in the direction of Somerville, where Laura Smart lived according to the list.

Laura's message surprised Teal more in the morning. She'd listened to it again after the alarm radio had dragged her awake with the news from National Public Radio on WBUR. She couldn't imagine what Don's troublesome secretary wanted. Laura had never expressed a particular affection or respect for her. But if Laura wanted to talk, Teal wanted to listen. There were benefits to knowing the office gossip. She could stop by Laura's and still make it to the audit committee meeting in Nashua, New Hampshire, by nine, with a little fast driving.

Teal enjoyed the periodic ride to her one client in the

Granite State. Her lovely dowager of the highway, a 1959 Mercedes 190SL sportster, benefited from the long miles driven to the speed limit, according to her mechanic. He should know. Recently her dowager had spent too much time in the shop.

Most of Teal's clients were near Route 128, the famed "technology highway" circling Boston, which had brought traffic gridlock and suburban isolation to eastern Massachusetts. Now highway-access malls replaced town centers as the heart of commerce.

Teal pulled over in Davis Square and fished for the book of local maps she kept by the back seat. Study revealed that Laura lived three blocks up and two over. One-way restrictions added ten minutes to a two-minute ride.

She made the last turn and slowed to squint at the front of each house for a hint at the street number. Single-minded concentration almost made her sideswipe Julia Clarke. She swerved the Mercedes wide just in time.

Julia, leaning out the window of her black Lexus, binoculars to her eyes, did not react. Teal realized the magnification must have made her blind to the 190SL in the foreground.

Teal pulled a U-turn at the end of the street and parked behind a van and under a tree one door up on Laura's side. She hunched down in the well-worn red leather seat to keep an eye on Laura's house.

She had learned about surveillance from her first Clayborne Whittier client, Stratton Security. As a new staff, she'd been so eager to follow the firm's dictate to "understand the client's business" that she had sat in on operative training classes. Today she and Julia had both failed the first rule—don't drive an expensive or distinctive car. But Julia was also parked on the wrong side of the road, easily visible across from Laura. Anyone in the triple decker could see the luxury Japanese automobile and its conspicuous driver.

Teal observed Julia while Julia stayed fixated on the house. *Who does she expect to see come out?* Teal wondered. *Don, no doubt.*

Julia's little show had fooled Teal at Monday's lunch, what with calling Laura "dear" and soliciting Teal for advice. Julia must have known about the affair over every bite. An uncomfortable chill rippled Teal's arms. She was about to call on the woman making a fool of the wife of the partner in charge, and him as well, at this too intimate hour. It would not do to have Julia Clarke watch her saunter down that walk.

Every minute dragged like an hour. Teal willed Julia to move off. Julia rearranged her binoculars, withdrew her head, poked it back out, but she did not leave. No one entered or exited from Laura's door. If Julia didn't drive away soon, Teal would not have a chance to speak with Laura this morning.

She was so busy wishing Julia gone she did not register the Lexus vacate its space until seconds later. When she did, Teal locked the 190SL and sprinted up Laura's walk.

The house was typical of a Boston triple decker, each apartment stacked one atop the other, each fronted with a square porch. The wooden shingles were painted an unattractive brown and the trim a dying moss. Laura's name labeled the buzzer for apartment number one. Teal rang, then inspected the detail of the Victorian balustrade while she waited. Two columns were settling into the ground where the porch floorboards showed rot. The landlord deserved a code warning.

Laura did not answer, and Teal turned to try the common front door. She expected resistance, but the hinges squealed open. Laura's unit faced Teal from the end of the hall.

Hard knocking brought no more result than the buzzer. Teal caught sight of her watch and her fist dropped. If she expected to be in Nashua by nine, she needed to get going.

The discussion in Nashua ran late, but Teal pulled into the FNEB garage in time to make her one o'clock with Ted Grey and Amy Firestone. Frank Sweeny was getting out of his Cadillac from his usual spot as Teal slammed her door.

"Still driving that thing?" he said.

His expression was one of contempt, the kind a man who had never been to a ballet or visited a museum or owned a house over five years old or driven any car but a Cadillac could have for the things she loved.

She grinned. "You bet."

"What will you do when you have kids?" he asked as they turned together for the elevator.

"Gee, I don't know. Leave them at the house with my spouse like you do yours, I guess."

She stretched her grin wider. Frank did not approve of women, except in the form of the Virgin Mary above the altar or taking care of him and his at home. He detested Teal. She knew because his secretary had told Kathy all about his reaction when she'd been admitted to the partnership, and Kathy had told all to Teal. The story had made

Teal take the seat right next to him at her first partners' meeting.

A part of her wished she had been the one to send him to Funsters.

"I understand you may be bringing us a new client," she said in a voice as clear of malice as glass. "Roger mentioned something about you rushing off the other morning."

Frank colored to a dull scarlet as the razor burn plaguing his face glowed. His hands twitched.

"Very funny, I'm sure," he snarled as they exited the elevator. "I hope you are still laughing when I make my report on that sick stunt to Don Clarke."

Teal managed a pleasant nod.

Frank slammed his briefcase down on his desk. He hated the bitch. He'd hated Emma Browne, and she got what she deserved. Death in a single blow, and just like that, the lawsuit ended. Someone should have thought of it before.

His mouth twisted. He couldn't help it. Emma Browne dressed like Laura Smart, that was rich.

Laura Smart—the name snapped him to a frown. She was another one kicking up trouble.

"We're putting Amy in the middle," Teal said.

Ted let his expression say this wasn't new at Clayborne Whittier. Every professional on the staff had found himself in the middle, torn between competing seniors as a staff, managers as a senior, and partners as a manager. It had happened to Ted. It had happened to Teal. Amy would survive.

"Amy will survive." He stared at the young senior manager. She stood back, quick and sharp. He returned his attention to Teal. "You're trying to make life easy for yourself—"

"And what about you?" Teal said, her palms flung up and open.

Her tone was half mad and half joking, like who's kidding whom.

Ted spread his hands and grinned. "You're right."

"So where does the wisdom of Solomon lie?" Amy asked. "Cut me in two?"

"Three, actually," Ted said.

He watched Teal. She had the intellect, negotiating skills, and ambition to become a powerful force at the firm if she watched herself. He knew he already counted among those aimed for the top, but why turn this discussion into a fight? No one had ever accused Edwin Darwin Grey of being shortsighted.

His mother hadn't been wrong in her choice of name for her only child. She had stood behind him all her life, and Ted had rewarded her devotion. He had done better than survive.

Teal faced him, expectation in her eyes. Canny, sapphire eyes in this light. She was a good addition to Clayborne Whittier's partnership. Ted dropped his hands to gesture peace.

"I get her tomorrow and Friday for MicroAnswer. You get her at your . . . what?"

"BiMedics," Teal offered.

"Your BiMedics Monday and Tuesday, then she joins Roger at the MicroAnswer subsidiary in Michigan for the rest of next week." He turned to Amy and scrutinized her expression. "Agreed?"

"Like I can disagree." Amy sucked her lips together. "Okay, fine," she said after a pause just shy of too long.

"You don't look fine," Teal said. "Sure you can manage?"

"I guess I have to."

"I guess you do," Ted said.

He didn't waste a lot of his time persuading subordinates. He liked Amy. She knew she was likely to get his support if she performed. And she knew it beat the alternative. No one who worked for him came out on middle ground. Amy would be a lot more fun to support than Emma Browne. And he expected to be more successful this time around.

Ted liked that thought. Of course Emma had been a brilliant manager. Difficult, but a genius. She should have been made a partner. He hadn't liked losing that battle. He wouldn't lose the next time he championed a talented female or minority staff. The other partners might not see it, but he understood the future of the firm.

"What are you chuckling at—getting the best of me?" Teal asked, laughing herself.

"I wouldn't say that. I came into this meeting with no intention of giving up even a day of Ms. Firestone's time."

"So I heard," Teal said. "But you did."

She stood.

Ted wondered how she had gotten to the partnership wearing dresses that hardly made her look like an accountant. There was something that unbalanced him in her style. Something a little too independent for digestion by Clayborne Whittier. He remembered the discussions, now, about whether or not she should be admitted. No one disputed her ability, or her skill in working with clients, but the rumor on Teal Stewart was that she would not give up her life to be a partner. Don Clarke had pressed them to vote her in, as hard as he had pressed to keep Emma out.

Ted shifted in the conference-room chair and frowned.

"You knew I didn't plan to give up any of Amy's time in this meeting? Who said?"

Teal shook her head. "You may be hot stuff in California, but you can't expect me to tell you the secrets I need to get me where I want to go—"

"Are we done arranging my work life?" Amy interrupted. "I need to talk with Teal about BiMedics before I go out to MicroAnswer."

Ted rose from the chair to his full six feet.

"Be my guest, ladies," he said, and left the room.

"I can't decide if he's trouble or damned funny and nice, but he will be back in our lives," Teal said. "So, what's up about BiMedics?"

"Nothing. Look, I'm sorry about the other day, I—"

"Don't explain. Emma's death hit all of us, if for different reasons," Teal said.

Amy felt her throat tighten. Teal jumped so quickly to the wrong conclusion. Amy did not know if she wanted to set her mentor right.

"I guess," she said to buy time.

"The strangest part is that Emma's death will work to your benefit," Teal said.

Amy stopped breathing.

"I'm not accusing you." Teal looked startled at the reaction to her remark.

Amy tried to smile. Her lungs were working, her blood still circulating. She'd be fine.

"I'm stating the terrible but obvious," Teal continued. "The partners hated the trouble Emma was causing and her underground of supporters."

Amy fiddled with her silk tie under the bore of Teal's eyes. A hangnail snagged on the smooth fabric.

"Your SUE wasn't winning any friends," she continued. "But now the boys will fall over themselves to let some number of women in before some one of us tries another suit. Since you're up next summer, Emma's demise should help you. Grim but true."

"Do you think I figured all that out and decided to bash in her skull?" Amy tried to say it with humor, picking at a cuticle.

"I'm not making an accusation." Teal's voice had sharpened. "Now what can I do for you?"

What can you indeed? Amy wondered and swallowed hard. She decided to say "nothing," but the truth blurted out.

"I need help."

Ten

Amy studied the grain in the table top. She stared at her feet. The size five, sensibly flat shoes went with her cotton-twill suit. Teal's narrow and high calf pumps, on the other hand, seemed foolish, but Teal was not, Amy reminded herself.

"How can I help if you don't talk?" Teal asked. She leaned forward.

"This is really hard for me," Amy said.

Teal was her partner counselor, responsible to act as her champion within the firm, but she was more as well. Amy trusted her, or had until Teal's cautions not to become too involved with SUE had stuck in Amy's craw. But it looked like Teal advised her well after all. She hadn't listened, of course.

Amy bit at her cheek to block the memory of Emma's screaming face, the invective spitting from the woman's colorless mouth. Never having been treated that way, she had reacted on instinct, that's one thing she should explain.

"I'm waiting," Teal prompted.

Amy heard impatience, but couldn't make herself say

Emma's name. Thin lines of moisture beaded in her palm. Her fingers cramped. Would she be questioned by Teal's cop?

"You and Ted aren't my only problem. There's Roger," Amy pressed out of her mouth. The words tasted wrong.

Teal did not pull back or look puzzled. Amy experimented. She could breathe.

"MicroAnswer can't be much fun right now with two bosses," Teal said.

"It's more than that."

Teal had not wanted to be Amy's counselor. She had not warmed to the small, vigorous woman who dressed in clones of man-tailored suits. Amy even wore the silly silk bow flopping at her throat that other women in business had discarded years before. But Don Clarke accepted no exceptions and no excuses. He had fought for Teal to become his first female audit partner, and he expected her to accept being used. He had transferred Clayborne Whittier's most senior and talented female staff to Teal as partner counselor. Amy rated at the top.

The Clayborne Whittier conference room struck Teal as a poor choice for the intimacy of a post-meeting unburdening. She considered a relocation to her office, but Amy did not appear to share her sensitivity to the artificial opulence of the room. It wasn't surprising in someone who could wear such awful shoes.

Teal smiled to contain her urge to chuckle.

"It isn't exactly funny!"

Amy sounded stern, a good word to describe the determined and ambitious manager, Teal decided. Smart as anyone at Clayborne Whittier, a technical stickler and an activist for equality of treatment for women in the firm, Amy had made enemies in minutes. But Teal had come to respect her.

"No," Teal agreed.

Half of counseling was patience, the other half an ability to craft advice appropriate to the individual and within the rules of the firm. Any always challenged Teal's skill with the delicate balance.

"Roger may be your friend, but he's a pain on MicroAnswer," the senior manager said after another stretch of silence.

"Conflicts with Ted?" Teal asked.

She wished Amy would get to the point. She wanted to see Laura Smart and find out why she'd called in the middle of the night.

"Can I have your full attention?" Amy broke in.

Teal raised her eyes. Amy had guts to direct a partner like this. Other times she could be unyielding and stubborn.

"Sorry," Teal murmured.

"I was saying it isn't Roger and Ted, at least not yet, but his refusing to listen to me. I've told him I think something isn't right at MicroAnswer. Ten shipping records in our test sample don't jive with what's recorded—"

"Ten out of . . ."

"Sixty sales transactions selected from shipping and invoice logs. You know how clients get crazy after they go public. Some will do anything to make their target number," Amy concluded.

"No kidding," Teal said.

She and Amy had seen that reaction at BiMedics when management had lost perspective after their initial public offering. Decisions hung on one issue—the effect on earnings—not what made sense for the business, and this at a company investors expected to record losses. Biotechnology stocks sold on the hope and hype of coming up with miracle drugs, but, like most of the competition, none of BiMedics' products yet had moved from the laboratory into commercial production.

Fortunately, management's perspective had returned before any damage was done to their reputation, or Clayborne Whittier's. BiMedics adopted a conservative set of accounting policies and left the glamor moves to other biotech stocks, making BiMedics a less volatile investment than most companies in their sector. Still, it was a risky stock.

MicroAnswer operated in a different industry. The market expectations for computer software did not give MicroAnswer any excuse to end the year with a net loss. Teal wondered if auditing might be easier in Japan, then pushed away the irrelevant thought.

Amy left unsaid what hung in the air between them. Some accountants would do almost anything to aid a client in reaching the target number. Teal could not imagine such an accusation seriously leveled at Roger.

"What does the Massachusetts facility represent? Forty percent of consolidated sales? Has Ted said anything about results in California?" Teal asked.

She disliked the implicit request to judge her colleague and friend. Roger enjoyed a reputation as one of the firm's best accountants. The recent internal Clayborne Whittier review of the Boston office had rated his jobs properly decided and well documented, although Roger himself could be a difficult boss. Teal knew these confidential results through Kathy's pipeline from Laura.

Teal had yet to be subject to an internal review herself as a partner. She had considered asking Frank about the drill since he had just headed a team out in California. There was something ludicrous in the thought of Frank judging another professional's skill, but the firm had taken the precaution of placing good people on his team. This was the story of careers like Frank's—the worse an admission mistake, the bigger the effort to cover up. She wondered if things would change now with all the talk of firings.

"Teal!" Amy's voice rose. "You aren't listening."

"Sorry."

But her attention slipped to a moment's wondering what awful things Laura could say about Frank. Laura was privy to all the files.

"Teal! I said I have no idea what Ted would say because Roger refuses to let me talk to him on this. Roger says he wants to take care of it in his own way." Amy settled back in her chair with what seemed a spiteful smirk.

"No easy decision for you," Teal said. "Going straight to Ted will alienate Roger, and Roger will be on Boston's admissions committee when Ted is back in California. He can't do you much good from there unless you make the cut in Boston first."

"But if someone is playing around with MicroAnswer, I'm worse off saying nothing to Ted, right?" Amy suggested.

"You need Roger's active support," Teal countered.

"Not if he's been—what's the firm's word?—transitioned out."

Teal couldn't believe what she'd heard.

"Who said that to you?"

The senior manager plucked at a chip in her left thumbnail, defiance showing around her mouth.

"Has your secretary been talking to Laura Smart?" Teal asked.

Amy raised her head with an open mouth.

"Secretary? I've shared four secretaries with two managers in the last year and I don't have a clue who they talk with for the brief time they—"

Teal raised her hands in self-defense. There was no use getting Amy started on the administrative blunders of the office. Teal appreciated her good luck in being assigned to Kathy from day one as a manager. Amy, with her different treatment, appeared ready to kill.

Amy hoped Teal could not see the pulse banging at her throat. She had come too close to blurting out the truth about Emma Browne. She found it hard enough herself, now, to accept her idealistic passion for Emma's cause before she had met her.

The memory of the first meeting burned in Amy's chest. And their last—that horrible battle. She choked.

"Are you all right?" Teal leaned forward in a gesture of comfort, but Amy shrank back.

"I'm fine. Just give me some clue of what to do," she said.

"You don't think it's that easy—"

"It should be," Amy rasped.

Emma's voice still raged inside her head about the politics of partners' power. Amy caught her lip between her teeth. The snap of pain cleared Emma away.

"I can't answer for you. You've worked with Roger on MicroAnswer for years."

"Roger doesn't deserve my blind loyalty," Amy said, the worm of doubt making her voice back down.

She could see Teal losing her patience like Emma had lost hers. Then Emma had grabbed Amy's shoulder. Amy knew she should explain to Teal about the fight, about Roger. She couldn't open her mouth.

"Then my advice is to extend your testing of sales and get better proof to take to Roger. But don't go around him to Ted." Teal stood. "Is anything else troubling you?"

Amy took a moment to decide. She'd already lied, and Teal seemed impatient as she edged for the door.

Amy decided. "No," she said.

Teal couldn't think of anywhere else to look for Laura. The partner in charge's executive wing, the lunch room, the library and the hall all were exhausted. She started for her office.

Clayborne Whittier was a model of calm. Padded, cream-colored wool muted any sound. Thick carpeting overlaid with an occasional well-placed accent rug muffled every footfall. A careful mix of modern and traditional art engaged the eye that strayed from the panorama of Boston outside the floor-to-ceiling windows.

Staff cubicles wrapped around the interior core of access to elevators, administrative services, and bathrooms. Managers and senior managers were rewarded with small exterior-wall offices. Partners rated the large corner lots. The space had been taken on a thirty-year lease before the real estate boom and bust or the subsequent emphasis on downsizing.

Teal could not have survived in the competitor CPA firm that had received press for the use of a concept called "hoteling," which involved available desks being assigned at random to staff not on site at a client. No one under senior manager had a permanent spot in the office. Teal wondered how anyone there achieved a sense of control. It was a feeling impossible to gain from the work, that was for sure. She grinned.

"You and Ted settle Amy's schedule?" Don Clarke boomed from down the hall.

"About," Teal said.

"He's the coming guy, Teal," Don said.

"Like you a few years ago?" Teal teased.

Don guffawed and waved her off as he turned in at Roger's office.

"She called you?" Kathy said.

Laura hadn't told Kathy anything about wanting to talk to Teal. The omission irked Kathy.

"Do you have any idea of what it's about?" Teal asked.

Teal leaned on the half partition of teak that gave some privacy to the chaos on Kathy's desk.

This could be awkward, Kathy decided. Laura told her all sorts of things. Laura liked to demonstrate her power and Kathy didn't object. She wasn't a detective's wife for nothing. She knew how to listen, Laura how to talk. But only some things were right to pass on.

'Perhaps this discussion would be more comfortable in my office," Teal suggested and Kathy agreed.

Kathy settled into a chair. She loved what Teal's room said about its occupant. The other partners had used the firm decorator and ended up with the standard antique or neutral corporate look. Not this partner. Teal had used Hunt. Her three-part, black desk from Roche-Bobois angled and curved away from the inside wall. Two upright and right-angled leather chairs invited guests to sit. The modern art rug displayed a big red bow. The combination of strength and femininity held uncommon grace.

"What has she been saying?" Teal asked.

Kathy wrinkled up her face. "I guess Don Clarke really was upset about Emma Browne. Yesterday he called his own attorney."

"You mean, independent of the firm's counsel?" Teal asked.

"Um-hum. But only after Emma was dead."

Teal looked surprised.

"Laura says she doesn't mind working for Ted, but I think two people telling her what to do is driving her nuts. Laura prefers to be in control of everything," Kathy said.

Laura had even thought she could take control of Kathy's new condition. It hadn't worked, of course.

"Like poor Amy," Teal murmured.

"Oh yeah." Kathy paused. Teal might not know, and she should, being Amy's counselor and all. "About Amy. She and Emma had this huge fight."

Teal whipped her head up from scanning the messages Kathy had set on the desk.

"This was when?" Teal asked.

Kathy never used the word "murdered," it belonged in her husband's world.

"The other night. The night Emma died," she said instead.

THURSDAY

Eleven

Hot air boiled off the asphalt and bubbled in through the open windows of the 190SL. Heat from the engine wrapped around Teal's feet. She ran her palm back and forth on the steering wheel and fought the urge to scream the stalled traffic into motion. Why did she always overlook when baseball season started? Probably because she didn't care about the sport until she'd hit her first game traffic.

Storrow Drive hadn't slowed to a crawl coming up to Kenmore Square, it had stopped. Her side of the road resembled a parking lot, and she was past the last chance to exit before getting caught in the mess. She had never been to Fenway Park, not even with Hunt. She had convinced him to take his father each invitation, instead. He hadn't asked her in years, so she didn't have to come up with any more excuses to dodge baseball.

The thought made her smile. Their break-up hadn't been all bad.

No, that wasn't true. She had forgotten how it felt, was all. She, who had made the suggestion first. That night had been almost as hot as now. She'd come home early to surprise

Hunt for his birthday, but he had worked late, until her buttercream frosting had become a melted heap on the plate. "Happy" had not started her greeting when he'd walked through the door.

"This isn't working for either of us, is it? Not anymore," she'd said after the immediate anger had been spent.

The hardest part to acknowledge was how easily he'd agreed. No hesitation, no "doll, I don't think you're right." Just coal-black eyes registering no hint of surprise and the slightest nod. She could still see the giant shadows of his dark, Irish curls bounce on the kitchen wall.

"I think you're probably right," he had said.

She'd moved out a month later. In three months he'd been showing off a bottle blonde. BG had given it four weeks and had turned out wrong by one. This many years later Hunt was left with Argyle, and she was left with what?

A horn blasted behind her.

Teal raised her hands in a gesture of surrender and rolled the three feet between the Mercedes and the rear end of the car in front. The classic roadster charm wore a little thin when the weather turned this hot. She could have popped off the hard top and replaced it with the soft one. She never did. She didn't like the wind to tangle her hair or dirt to fly in her face and never had, not even when the convertible option had pleased Hunt.

Today didn't feel like early June but late July, and she was going to arrive at the CCF raffle meeting sagging with sweat. Already she had to pull her dress and slip from where they stuck to her ribs.

Nothing moved a foot further forward, and she returned

to inspecting the thought, *and she was left with what?* Her career.

Hunt had said he deserved some credit for her promotion because he hadn't been around to mount a campaign of resistance—and if they'd stayed together, she never would have thrown herself so far into her job. She had to laugh. That wasn't what most Clayborne Whittier partners thought. They thought a more traditional life would do her good. Frank had been stupid enough to say she should be home having babies, but she, unlike Emma Browne, had seen no future in bringing suit.

Emma brought Amy Firestone to mind. Teal bounced her fist on the horn. She didn't like knowing something Amy had not told her directly, certainly not this, but Kathy's words stuck. Why hadn't Amy been the one to reveal the fight with Emma?

Other horns blew and, like pushing a string, the traffic inched forward. At this rate, Teal would arrive at the meeting half an hour late. She was surprised she hadn't heard from Julia Clarke today. Julia's habit was to call before each meeting to ask Teal to prepare a comparison on ticket sales by site for this and the prior year. Julia loved to demonstrate the results her committee had achieved.

Teal had brought along her Powerbook to run the data. She hoped Julia would ask and give her the excuse to stay busy. She preferred number crunching to worrying what Julia had been doing outside of Laura's house yesterday morning.

Nothing innocent, Teal had forced herself to conclude. Nothing she hadn't thought of herself.

She remembered her reaction to Hunt's blonde. She'd

wanted to tell the woman to lay off, to call and hang up in the middle of the night to see if she could hear Hunt's breathing at the woman's side. It hadn't been a question of wanting him back but of wanting to know. Or maybe it was like poking a bruise. She'd never acted on her impulse but had learned to let Hunt lead his life and to lead her own. But how much worse must a wife feel when she discovers her husband has a lover? A young lover, half the wife's age—

A long honk set Teal upright, eyes on the road. The driver behind her was right, her line of cars moved, if slowly. She made it off Storrow and onto Commonwealth Avenue while drivers turning for Fenway still fumed. Her increased speed created a false breeze, and the temperature in the car decreased maybe three degrees. Tendrils of damp hair dried enough to lift from Teal's neck. She forgot grousing about driving her grand old car.

The elation of movement lasted exactly half the distance to Massachusetts Avenue. The Clutch did not seize at once but fought her downshift to second from third. She tried to find neutral at the light, but the stick refused to budge. The cream and gray sports car jumped forward as she eased off the pedal on green.

Her mechanic had been right. She should have replaced more than the fluid, but what good was hindsight? She made the next light in time to turn up Mass. Ave., and her luck held at the extension of Newbury Street running parallel to the turnpike. One more right spun her past the parking attendant behind the Harvard Club.

"Okay, darling," Teal said as she lifted her foot off the gas without being able to disengage the clutch.

She hated the sound of her car stalling to a halt, but the maneuver proved effective. The engine rattled to a stop.

"Problem, Ms. Stewart?"

The handsome young attendant sometimes flirted and sometimes gave her flack. Tonight he showed professional concern.

"Never ignore your mechanic's advice, Kwame. I think the transmission is shot," Teal said. "Any chance I can leave her here for the night?"

Kwame grinned. "Mr. Houston sure is good to let you use his club number. If I'd say yes to him, I better say yes to you. Might make sense to push her out of the way. You steer."

They managed to ease the 190SL to a side of the lot.

"What's Mr. Houston going to say?" Kwame looked dour.

Kwame had fixed notions about the proper relationship for women and men.

"What he always does—I should buy a new car."

Kwame grinned with renewed hope. "Sell her to me?"

"Not on your life," Teal laughed. "Not to you or anybody."

"A lady who knows what she likes. All right!" Kwame said. "My mama calls loyalty a virtue."

Teal knew that mamas weren't always right. Loyalty could exact a high price. Inconvenience, for one. She had to be out at BiMedics tomorrow morning.

Roger squeezed closed his eyes and cocked the phone from his ear. Barbara's voice came across smaller, but he heard the words.

"Why? Why do you have to go? Tell Don no. For this once would you please tell him no? What about me? Clayborne Whittier doesn't—"

Roger laid his right thumb over the holes punched in the plastic telephone that let her voice out. Barbara went dead. He did a slow count to thirty.

"Are you listening? Roger? Roger?" Barbara clamored, but thinly, weakly.

"Uh . . . of course," he said.

"Well, are you going to say what I said?" she asked.

He twirled a pencil on its lead. The point broke as it fell. "Roger?"

He hated the nasal tone, the whine as her inflection rose at the end of his name. He wished he could repeat hers in the same voice. He couldn't. That had been the advice from the divorce attorney Monday morning. "Don't provoke a fight." Roger rounded his shoulders forward. He wondered if he should pay another visit to Laura Smart. He jingled a hand in his pocket, rattling the change.

"I'll try," he said. "But honey, I think I should go out to Michigan—"

"Why?" she screamed. "Let some other partner go! You know how I hate being left with the kids, and they miss you, too." She had softened her voice, made it imploring.

She liked to throw Rebecca and Samuel in his face. Five and three years old. Barbara said they loved him, wanted to spend more time with Daddy. When he was home, one of them always cried or picked a fight or begged for Mummy.

Why did she want this new house? Was she crazy? Was he, going across the street? Seeing Laura Smart? The throb in his head began to feel like the other night, Barbara's shrill "why" sounding like Emma Browne. His breath came in short pants. No, he reminded himself. This demanding voice belonged to his wife.

Outside his window day had turned to night.

He pulled the stack of papers into the middle of his desk and lined up the corners. Teal thought he had been across the street to sign the mortgage. He should have told her the truth about the attorney, about Laura.

His fingers closed around the pack of gum left behind after his talk with Laura Monday morning. He eased a piece out and pushed it back in again. Barbara was screaming something else into the phone. Tension knocked his toe against the trunk by his desk. It was full of more work to get done. He hurled the gum pack into the trash.

"Honey? Got to go," he said. He eyed the big trunk and reached into his wastebasket to fish the pack back.

Teal depressed the phone cut-off button. Rental car company number four was sold out for tomorrow.

"Everything in the city is, like, taken by a convention or something at the Hynes Center," the clerk had said.

"Which one?" Teal had asked.

"Bouchercon or something."

Teal could hear the shrug.

"But it's, like, had us totally booked for months."

"Thanks," Teal had said and hung up.

The CCF board secretary motioned from the other side of the glass conference-room wall. Teal waved a "one minute" finger.

Maybe he was still in the office.

Teal prayed for success and tapped out the number.

The direct line picked up on the first ring.

"This is Roger Singer. Please leave a message and I will get back to you as soon as possible. Thank you."

She waited for the beep.

"Hi Roger, it's Teal and I guess you must be on your phone. Any chance I can borrow your car tomorrow morning if you're in town? I need to get out to BiMedics and the 190SL just died. I know, I know, you and Hunt kept telling me. Anyway, give my home machine a call, I'm heading into a meeting. I hope you can because there isn't a rental available. Some damned convention. Thanks."

"I think it makes me uneasy," Kathy said.

She set the pot roast in the middle of the kitchen table and turned for the bread. She made a point of preparing his favorites on his off nights. She enjoyed the cooking and he enjoyed the eating, not that he looked it. His mother complained that Kathy had to be starving "her poor baby." But Mrs. Malley could be all right, Kathy kept reminding herself.

"What makes you uneasy?" Dan asked.

She looked at her husband. She loved his smile, with its little crook at the end of the left side of his mouth. The smile made him seem less tired. She thought him the most handsome man alive, with the most beautiful, luminous eyes. She settled at the table and held out a plate as he carved.

"What makes you uneasy?" Dan repeated.

"That you're assigned to the Emma Browne case," Kathy replied.

She added carrots and mashed potatoes beside her meat.

"You think Teal did it?" Dan asked.

She had to look hard before she realized it was a tease. She never caught him first off on that.

"No," she said as if he'd meant to ask. "I just don't like being in the middle. And don't tease me."

Dan set down the carving knife and fork and added vegetables to his plate.

"You aren't in the middle," he said.

"I am, sort of. I work there, don't I? And I knew about Emma Browne. Everyone hated her, at least the partners."

"Does everyone include Teal?" Dan asked.

"Of course not."

"So you don't know every one of the partners hated her because you know at least one who didn't." Dan chewed a piece of roast. "Wonderful," he said.

Kathy hadn't lifted her fork.

"Is that detective work?" she asked.

"Is what detective work?"

"Picking apart what I said to make it precise."

"S-s-sort of," Dan said.

"And that's why the chief thinks you're so good, because you're so picky?" Kathy couldn't swallow her mirth fast enough.

"Now you're doing the teasing."

They ate in enjoyment of the food and each other.

"Laura Smart is the one you should talk to," Kathy said with her plate empty. She pushed her chair back. "Dessert?"

Dan nodded. "Why is Laura Smart the one I should talk to?"

"It's applesauce cake," Kathy said, but he didn't pay attention. "Okay, because Laura always knows the dirty secrets along with everything else in the office. Since you have to be

117

on this case, I'd just as soon you solve it. You love applesauce cake."

"And you." Dan grinned. "So, I promise to visit your Laura in the morning."

TWELVE

Laura Smart curved around the guard's shoulder and let her breath disturb his ear as he ran her security card across the reading beam. She squinted at the information displayed on his small screen.

"Wow. And you understand what it means?" she asked.

She rested her hand on his arm just enough to make him sense the touch. The green data pulsed and flickered.

"So which one is me?" she asked.

He pointed with a dusky black finger highlighted by the pink skin under his nail at the tip. "Right here at the top. You came in last."

"And who is the one before?" Laura asked.

He shrugged. "Someone at the advertising company on seven."

"How can you tell?" she asked.

"See these first three numbers?"

She nodded.

"They belong to the advertising company. Clayborne Whittier starts with 923, see, like yours."

"So can you tell me who's upstairs? My boss, maybe?" Laura giggled.

The young Haitian guard laughed with her. "No. I have to know the company code for security reasons, but the other numbers mean nothing to me."

"Oh." Laura lifted her hand and straightened with her disappointment.

"Your card," the guard said with a shy grin.

She nodded scant thanks and watched his happiness erode. Laura didn't care about his frustration. She had her own. She stepped into the elevator, ready to get off at forty-one and play a game of hide and seek. He deserved a little of her kind of fun.

She smirked at her distorted reflection in the metal doors. Yesterday morning she had not expected the knock on her door. She didn't like to be caught off guard. Tonight would be her surprise!

Teal shuffled her notes. The meeting was running late, like every meeting at CCF. The collaborative culture of the organization gave encouragement to every committee member to speak, no matter how off-point, and all views would be heard until the group reached a consensus. The director said the process fostered "buy-in." Teal was not as sure. She had participated in more than one decision simply out of exhaustion.

She wanted to scream but forced a patient expression of engaged participation on her face.

"Work and kids and God knows what keeps life busy," one committee member offered in the discussion on how to get every board member to support the raffle effort.

"People feel the event runs itself," another said.

"But how can they, when we're always begging for more participation by board members at every meeting," said yet another.

"I wonder if we're right to depend on board meetings to get everyone excited about our fundraising events when attendance is so low?" asked another.

Teal had made a few suggestions to improve attendance in the past. She considered plugging her fingers in her ears as the oldest CCF lament set in motion. *How could the organization make board members feel welcome and important?* Teal didn't remind the group that no one had been forced to join the board.

The first speaker suggested pot luck.

"Pot luck?" Teal heard herself repeat.

"Sure," replied the other. "We could each bring a favorite dish and spend time getting to know each other better before the formal meeting."

"You're joking?" Teal said.

The woman was not, and the group devoted the next half hour to an exploration of pot luck versus rescheduling the monthly board meetings to a different day or hour. Teal realized she could be trapped at CCF for the rest of her life.

"Let's just ask people who aren't interested enough in coming to resign and create openings for individuals more actively committed to our mission," she offered in her best collaborative voice, while her reorganization of a stack of papers was intended to signal that this discussion was over.

Mouths gaped around the table. One or two snapped closed.

"Now, to business," Teal said and prepared to elicit

every opinion on the car raffle, no matter how off point, if it took all night.

She missed Julia's hand in guiding the group to agreement, but she wasn't surprised to find Julia a no-show, not after discovering her in front of Laura's house. Teal wished she didn't know about this particular love triangle. The behavior of the partner in charge upset office morale and had her caught between fidelity to a boss and affection for his spouse.

Julia must feel miserable tonight.

The young Haitian guard grinned. He liked this lady who always asked after his business studies at the university. Unlike the flirt, this one respected his position and remained where she should.

"Good evening, Jean," the woman said, giving his name the French pronunciation. "How is it going at Northeastern?"

"Fine, thank you, ma'am." He reached out his hand for a card.

"You remember me," she said. "My husband runs the Clayborne Whittier office, Don—"

"Mr. Clarke." Jean nodded.

"Yes, but remember, I don't work upstairs. I don't have a security card."

The kind face held concern.

"I can call your husband for authorization," Jean suggested.

Jean did not see the woman twist the strap of her pocketbook to a tangle behind her back as he typed up the tenant directory on the computer and dialed.

"He is not answering. Do you want to leave a message?"

The woman blinked and struggled with her mouth. He did not like it when ladies cried.

"No, I need to find him. Perhaps you will let me just run up?" she suggested.

"But how will you get in without the card?" Jean asked.

"Forty-seven still has the old security punch pad beside the door from before Clayborne Whittier went magnetic."

He thought her smile was beautiful. She was like his mother, a real lady.

"I'd be so grateful," she said. "And I don't need to mention your kindness to a soul."

He dipped his head and whispered. "Go."

Frank leaned against the wall, his heart jumping in his chest. Someone else was rifling the papers on Laura Smart's desk. He concentrated on not moving an inch and thought about how he had been going through Laura's things when he'd heard the footfalls coming down the hall. He had made it through the connecting door just in time.

Don and Laura used this anteroom between their two offices to store confidential partner records. Frank tried to stop his breathing. He stood behind the door, his knees weak at the thought that it might open. The light in Laura's office snapped off. No one had discovered him. He relaxed and refocused his mini-flashlight beam on the white page and skimmed the memorandum he had pulled free from under her blotter.

He read the name twice, looking hard at the type. Something was not right; this copy had been altered.

He considered the files against the wall, glad that his

partners had approved a standard system when the office manager had listed the benefits of avoiding mistaken lockouts. Frank's key would open all the drawers in the office. Laura should have secured the anteroom door at her end with its special combination lock, but she never bothered.

One twist and a tug and the heavy bin slipped forward on silent runners. He found the original under "Sweeny" and lost his caution.

Noise from Don's office on the other side gave Frank a start, and he dropped the altered memo across the top of the drawer before he banged it closed. He dashed to Laura's office, then he realized he could not storm into the hall with the original memorandum. He hesitated until he heard the voice. He jammed the dreadful paper under her blotter and made it out to the corridor as the light in Don's office switched on.

Frank focused on what he had tried to avoid. He had to finish this business with Laura Smart.

Roger played Teal's message twice, his face twisted with worry. No one could ever guess his age right. The truth would have sounded like a lie. Thirty-eight did not fit with the fatigue rimming Roger's eyes, adding lines around his mouth.

Which is better, he wondered, *to die over time or in a single, fatal stroke?* He couldn't keep the thoughts roiling his brain in order. Him, Mr. Careful. Mr. Play the Game and Don't Rock the Boat. What a mess.

He wondered if he would ever tell Barbara, the one who should be able to see right through him, his spouse. He wanted to laugh, except for how uneasy he felt.

Teal borrowing his car might be all right. It meant he wouldn't have to risk bringing anything home. Who would be looking in the parking lot? He reached for the train schedule in his top right drawer and decided he could get into the office before Teal in the morning and take care of what he planned to leave behind.

He dialed home. No answer, no mechanical voice. Barbara had to be very angry to ignore the phone.

Teal, at least, made the transaction easy. She responded by machine.

The *beep* scattered his thoughts. He collected them to speak.

"Teal? Roger here. I've left the keys on my desk. You can take the car in the morning."

Amy jerked back her hand from the handle at the intrusion of the guard's voice.

"Evening, miss. You're working late." He gestured at the closed office.

"Thinking about it," Amy said.

She didn't have the kind of mind to come up with the quick lie.

"Not too hard, I hope," he joked.

The guard was well past middle age, but Amy imagined he could take care of himself in a fight. He looked like a retired cop. Her plan seemed less and less a good idea. She stepped away from the door.

"Change your mind?" he asked.

She nodded.

"You won't be unhappy," he said.

He waited for her to move forward, and they walked together for the elevators. She stopped in front of the women's room.

"I'm just going in here before I leave."

The guard seemed to be stalling.

"Don't wait for me," she said, and pushed the door.

"Well, you have a good night now," the guard said.

The empty restroom echoed with her footfall. She spent a minute flushing a toilet and washing her face, enough noise to prove the purpose of her mission, enough time for him to give up on waiting to take the ride down with her. She'd had another change of mind.

Julia had no luck in Laura's office. She hesitated outside Don's door. *The little tart,* she thought. She could not bring herself to knock.

She'd tried being polite with Emma Browne, and look where it had got her.

Rage tore at her head, made her crazy jealous. *Dead might be the best,* turned over and over in her mind.

Laura jumped and whirred around. She'd never expected this. But the face that could have been angry smiled.

"What a pleasant surprise."

Laura didn't say, "What are you doing here?" or "I didn't think we had anything to say to each other." She never made excuses.

"Please, you look uncomfortable. Maybe we should sit down."

Laura worked up enthusiasm with her grin and dropped to the couch.

"Gum?"

She reached for the wrapped stick without thinking twice, slid the gum out, and pressed it into her mouth. The grain of the powdery sugar coating was a surprise, but she needn't have worried. The bad taste which followed did not last any longer than her life.

THIRTEEN

Amy hunched to hold the telephone. Her hair swung forward to hide her face. Three rings preceded the recorded voice on the fourth.

"You may leave Teal a message after the beep."

"Teal? Teal are you there? Can you answer me, please?" Amy whispered.

Amy pulled the bow loose from her neck, but her shaking fingers stuck in the knot. Then she remembered if she remained silent for too long, Teal's machine would cut the line. Amy rushed to speak.

"I know I should have explained things earlier today. Anyway, I need to talk and am——"

Amy stopped her lips from curling up with "in" or pulling back to "the" or finishing rounded to "office."

"I'm home." She hurried the receiver to the cradle.

The next problem would be getting her awkward cargo out of the building unnoticed.

Frank fingered one of his thinning hairs and plucked. *Ping. Ping. Pop.* They all thought he was so funny, and they didn't mean funny ha-ha. Well, wouldn't they just see.

He pulled out another one.

Teal Stewart was behind it. Feminists made him sick, pushing their ambitions into his face. They couldn't get a man to look at them twice, that was their problem. A bunch of screwed up old maids. No normal man would give them the time of day. Look at Emma Browne. Frank grinned. All the makeup sure hadn't helped.

He rammed a fist to his mouth. He must never say that, even to himself. No, better to remember Teal at the annual dinner dance with her date.

Guy had to be a fairy with that hair. Hunt. What a fruit name.

Frank fumbled for the paper bag he carried in his briefcase. The thought of homosexuals was making him hyperventilate.

Funsters. Remembering brought bile to his throat. He never would have gone in from the look of the place if his secretary hadn't warned him there was a problem with the management committee's assessment of his performance.

Frank held the bag to his mouth.

"Who told you?" Frank had asked his secretary.

"Laura Smart." The motherly woman had regarded him with pity.

"What's the problem?" he had asked, demeaning himself.

His secretary had raised her shoulders. "I don't know. You could ask Laura, but I think she made a mistake, letting it slip. Then again, maybe I heard wrong with the talk about Roger Singer."

Frank had hated the glow of compassion on the woman's

face. It said, maybe you are both getting fired. He had wanted to believe Laura was mistaken. But he couldn't now. Tonight he had found the confidential management committee memorandum to Don Clarke.

> Frank was promoted to bring in emerging business clients. His nonperformance in this, or any, area suggests he be the partner for Boston to transition out.

His blood pressure began to rise. *Laura Smart—Laura Smart—getting into her pants is no art,* drummed through his mind. He couldn't remember which of his partners had authored the ditty. *Not Don Clarke, the fool.*

To be a fool no more thanks to Frank. Frank's hand trembled.

He wished he could have cleaned up right, but he'd take care of that when he had the time. He tugged another hair from its root and laid it on the desk. He had only to take his revenge for Funsters. He punched on the speaker phone and tapped out her number.

Teal's machine voice filled his office. *God, she sounds smug,* he thought.

"It's Frank. I don't want to ruin your evening, but I think we need to have a talk about your Amy Firestone."

Julia's head stormed with the migraine. She wanted to get out fast. She needed to do one thing first to cover her tracks. Make the call.

Teal answered on the third ring, but Julia realized the voice was on Teal's machine. She forced her brain to compose a message while she listened.

"Teal, dear? It's Julia Clarke. I've made the most foolish mistake. I thought tonight was the library council, so I drove out to an empty building and now it's too late to make the CCF meeting. I am so sorry. Please call me with a report tomorrow. I'm sure you handled my duties brilliantly, thank you."

Julia looked around the office. She hoped dumping off her burden would be as easy.

Ted looked up to see the guard.

"Making rounds?" he said.

"Yes, sir. Everything okay?"

"Fine. Just fine, except for finding myself in the office at this hour." Ted glanced at his watch. "Will you leave the copy machine going?"

"Sure thing, sir," the guard agreed.

Ted watched him leave. The Boston office ran pretty well. He'd been transferred through enough different cities as he'd moved up in his career to see that Don Clarke was one smart partner in charge, except for his blind spot over Laura Smart. Ted considered that information very interesting. Useful, perhaps, when Don made the management committee.

Ted felt confident Don had forgiven him their disagreement over Emma Browne. She should have been admitted, and Ted had fought hard. Too hard, according to the informative Laura Smart. Ted had made a point to rectify the situation. It wouldn't do to be in the doghouse with the man he hoped to follow in Boston.

Ted considered Boston a fine office to run. It wasn't the biggest in the firm, but it was among the most profitable, and prestigious. He'd get used to winter, a season he had come to loathe over his college experience of lake effect snow outside of Chicago. He grinned. This worrying about the seasons was getting a little ahead of the curve.

He read the job schedule in front of him and raised a knuckle to his chin, wondering if he had been wise to compromise with Teal Stewart on Army Firestone. He twisted his mouth in a smile. He had seven years on Teal. She'd be a comer, like himself, once the great firm decided how to handle women. Still, he wasn't unhappy not to be competing with her now. He wondered how safe Roger Singer felt, not that it mattered if Roger was the one to be out.

Ted had decided to win Teal's loyalty from the start. Amy Firestone's schedule was tight, but he could offer Teal an additional half day of Amy's time. MicroAnswer would be fine.

He debated using the speaker phone and decided not to. *Why play that game?* he thought.

He got her machine.

"Hi Teal, Ted Grey. I'm thinking I might be able to ease up Amy's schedule to give you a few extra hours. Stop in to negotiate when you get to the office tomorrow."

He dropped a tape of dictation on Laura's desk for the morning, then collected his things and headed out.

Hunt stroked Argyle's head and raised the glass of Penfold's 1987 Bin 389 Cabernet/Shiraz. He knew Teal would like the Australian wine and considered inviting her over but decided against it at this hour. It was another difference between them. He liked late nights, she preferred morning.

Hunt growled and Argyle raised his head like Hunt was

crazy. Maybe he was. Maybe the last year had been better than the other way, always confused about what they wanted from each other, what to say.

He missed her.

He looked around the big, open loft in the building he had purchased after the break-up. South Street wasn't hot or cold back then, just the leftover of a more industrial Boston. Leather manufacturers, window display provisioning firms, and a few small jobbers still retained addresses on the street, but times and tax laws and shifting demographics had changed its profile.

His building had been big enough to convert and still make a small profit in the co-op sale of the units below his. He let his top floor remain with everything exposed and open, a deliberate departure from his work for others. He refused to live in a space too imprinted by his mind.

She had made her mark, though, even not living with him. He could see it now in the Motherwell and Frankenthaler prints, which gave a slight definition between the living and eating spaces; in the roof garden, where she had taught him to manage pest control on his own; in the Australian wine.

Which made more sense—to call or be haunted?

He flipped open the telephone.

The answering machine did a credible job catching the velvet in her voice, but like Teal on a bad day, it gave no opportunity for an even exchange. He left his message after the beep.

"Comment ça va ce soir, Jean?" Teal asked.

He grinned.

"Is my French nothing like you speak in Haiti?"

"Is like my family speaks. Spoke." Jean stopped.

"I'm sorry," Teal said.

She could have kicked herself. His parents had been among the island's elite, and their support of an upstart president priest had been considered a betrayal. Jean, at school in Boston the day they were killed, had remained away from the island. The assassination of his family made Jean take the United States as his permanent home. He worked at FNEB to support his schooling and himself.

"No. No, no," he exclaimed. "You are nice to use my old language."

Teal smiled. "Here's my card."

She hadn't been sure about the change from keys and laminated picture IDs to this one-piece wafer of security. The thin, blue plastic rectangle with no writing or magnetic stripe on the outside could log her in as she entered and log her out as she departed. The system had uses not available with the old keys and ID. Big Brother could watch her tonight.

"You work too much," Jean said. "Everyone else is gone home."

"I won't be long," she said.

She meant it, wanting only to pick up what she'd need for BiMedics the next morning and leave. In the elevator, she rubbed the back of her neck to massage out the tension. The prolonged CCF meeting had left her feeling less than charitable.

She stopped in the hall when she saw her office was not dark and the door hung wide open. Fear clogged her throat.

"Ain't you got no place to go?" the thickset woman

boomed as she straightened from behind Teal's desk with a wastebasket. She dumped the trash into her big, rolling barrel. "Scared you, didn't I!"

"You did, Martha." Teal heard her own relief. "And what about you? Isn't this a little late to be cleaning?"

Teal stepped up to collect the draft financial statements off her desk.

"I'm a-slowing or you folks is making a bigger mess," Martha groused.

"Is Roger still in?" Teal asked.

"He better keep out of sight, the way he left his place. I wouldn't have anything to do with him right now." Martha sniffed.

"I need to borrow his car," Teal said as if to justify the friendship.

Martha had that effect on her.

Martha's disapproval grew louder. "I hope for your sake his wife's the one keeps his car clean. Papers every which way on the floor. You shouldn't be here so late. What's wrong? You about live in this place, girl."

Martha's satisfied chuckle accompanied her departure. She stopped to give a last piece of advice.

"Honey, you need to get a life."

Teal tiptoed past the first floor. Those tenants had a new baby. She hurried by the duplex on two and three. On four, she pushed her key in the door and relaxed, glad to be home.

She dropped everything on the foyer table and kicked off her Keds. The pantyhose and dress were stripped by the time she entered her bedroom. Hunt's old Harvard T-shirt slipped on like she'd never left.

Comfortable, she padded on bare feet to the kitchen. Car lights made streaks of white and red on Storrow Drive, but otherwise Boston slept. The neon triangle flashing "Citgo" in Kenmore Square was dark. She loved that piece of unintended urban art. She poured iced spring water and rolled the cool glass against her forehead.

She hoped her mechanic and Roger had called, and she wouldn't mind hearing from Laura Smart.

The numeral in the call register of the answering machine in the study read 7. Teal relaxed in the desk chair and pressed play.

"Hi, it's Jack. I've got the 190SL dragged into the shop and should be able to report more soon. You sure you don't want me to sell it before the rust gets going? Or do you just love to see me?"

Too true, Teal agreed. The grand old car had been acting up a lot, and she would have considered an affair with Jack except for the fact of his happy marriage.

"Teal? Roger Singer here. I've left the keys on my desk. You can take the car in the morning."

Good, Teal nodded. She had a car.

"I know I should have explained things earlier today. Anyway, I need to talk and am—" Hesitation. "I'm home."

Amy Firestone. The machine kept going.

"It's Frank. I don't want to ruin your evening, but I think we need to talk about your Amy Firestone."

Damn. He must suspect Amy had something to do with the Funsters stunt. She made a note to stop by his office.

"Teal, dear? It's Julia Clarke. I've made the most foolish mistake. I thought tonight was the library council, so I drove out to an empty building and now it's too late to make the CCF meeting. I am so sorry. Please call me with a report tomorrow. I'm sure you handled my duties brilliantly, thank you."

So that was her excuse. Teal added "call Julia" to her list.

"Hi Teal, Ted Grey. I'm thinking I might be able to ease up Amy's schedule to give you a few extra hours. Stop in to negotiate when you get to the office tomorrow."

Task number three. The next message began to play.

"Argyle misses you and so do I. The *Globe* Jazz Festival starts in three days with Ray Charles on the Esplanade. I promise we can leave the minute the crowds make you crazy. Call me in the office tomorrow if you want to go."

Teal smiled. She missed Argyle, too. The counter looped back up to flash 7, with no word from Laura Smart, which was odd, but not odd enough to make her call Laura at this hour.

FRIDAY

FOURTEEN

Teal loved the hush of a city dawn, before the rush of commuters and commerce. Most mornings, she jogged or walked the path beside the Charles and across the Mass. Ave. bridge into Cambridge and back over the Longfellow in a three mile loop. Today, up at 5:00 A.M. and uneasy about Laura Smart, she skipped the exercise routine and headed straight for the shower.

The hot, pounding water did nothing to help.

She considered the problem as she twisted her damp hair into a tight chignon. The style Hunt had suggested for Clayborne Whittier still suited her work hours.

But she was more interested in Laura Smart. Laura enjoyed the power gained through her affair with Don Clarke too much, Teal decided. Corporate secrets could make one indiscreet and vicious with knowledge. Don seemed to think he had concealed the affair. Wouldn't he be surprised to face the truth and consequences with his spouse?

Julia's excuse for missing last night's meeting rang pretty false. Julia must be furious at her self-deluding husband, the conniving secretary, and herself. And there was

Laura's rumor about Roger being fired. Laura would be in a position to know, but Roger's reaction continued to strike Teal as false. He would never gamble on taking out a mortgage if he really had known he was about to lose his job. Roger could have lied to her to disguise his shock, Teal decided.

She wondered what Laura wanted. "Approach with caution" should have been posted on Laura's door, but Teal could not ignore the request to talk. She respected Laura's power.

Teal loved breakfast best of all meals, whether a slice of toasted sourdough spread with jam or bananas in a bowl of steel-cut oatmeal, but today Laura had her too curious to eat. She'd save the time and stop in Somerville for another try on her way to BiMedics.

Two pairs of swans, freed from their acclimation pen this week, graced the Public Garden lagoon. The swan boats, flat mini-barges with a giant, fiberglass rendition of the bird at the back where young athletes sat to supply pedal power, were lashed together in the middle of the water like a white, feathered island. Their benches would be filled by midday with children and grownups throwing bread and peanuts to the swans and flotillas of mallard ducks.

The security guard in the FNEB lobby had changed from Jean last night. Teal greeted the woman as she handed over her card. Off the elevator at Clayborne Whittier, she saw no one else on forty-eight.

Teal noticed nothing to have caused Martha's distress when she picked the keys off Roger's desk. She stopped in her office for the box of reference books she had promised BiMedics' new chief financial officer. The heavy load made an uncomfortable cargo as she lugged it down the hall. The freight elevator, which could take her directly to the garage, would at least make the trip easier.

Roger's car, a new black Mercedes, was in its usual spot. Teal curled her lips in disapproval. Like all the new ones, this was an automatic. She raised the box to one knee as she angled her hand to reach for the trunk lock with the key.

"Need help, Miss?" The short and wiry garage attendant came up beside her. "Can I open it for you?"

Teal nodded and jingled the keys. He took them from her trapped hand. She straightened as he bent.

"Actually, no," she amended before he popped the lock. "It may be easier for me to get these out of the back seat. Just help me open that door if you could, please."

She wasn't keen on involving herself with Roger's trunk. She hoped no one ever opened hers uninvited. The mini-version of her life, the odd bits and parts, wasn't that appetizing—a seldom-used beach chair, Argyle's old collar, and the T-shirt-jeans-toothbrush kit for emergencies like the time she'd been snowed in at a client.

The attendant shrugged and loaded the box in the back.

Traffic remained light through the city and over the Longfellow. Bostonians called it the "salt and pepper" bridge because the four stone turrets which graced the arch looked like giant condiment shakers. Teal never confused owning a house on the flat of Beacon Hill with the life-credentials of a native, but she, too, had come to say "the salt and pepper" and to call the private park halfway up Beacon Hill with a flat, English pronunciation of the "Louis" in Louisburg Square.

Neither Julia Clarke nor her Lexus was in front of the

triple decker house. Roger believed in car phones and, at this moment, and at this moment only, Teal agreed. She scanned the Boston office list and punched in Laura's number.

Two rings.

"Ooo-eee baby! Leave that message for me" Laura's disembodied voice enthused before the beep.

Teal clicked her tongue to the top of her mouth. Her plan wasn't exactly working out. Laura either wasn't answering or wasn't home. There was one way to find out.

She tried the front door with the buzzer and a series of hard knocks. This time she tried the back door, too, but with no better luck. The conversation with Laura would have to wait, again.

Teal wasn't good at patience. She remembered the visit she and Hunt had made to an astrologer up in Glouchester.

"The biggest difference?" the astrologer had repeated Hunt's question. "You want to know what will always stand between you?"

They had nodded in unison, trying not to show how much. Already, things had been breaking apart.

"For you," the woman jabbed a blunt finger at a circle of symbols representing Teal, "thought is action. For him," the finger speared Hunt's annotated disk, "thought is thought."

Thought is action versus thought is thought. And still true. Teal thought about Laura this morning, and here she was outside Laura's house. Not that her proclivity for doing had brought success.

Teal wondered if Julia had ever discovered what she had sought in watching Laura's door.

She turned the key and automatically reached to press a starter button that was not in Roger's car. This was a new

Mercedes, she reminded herself and laughed. It even had a digital clock to show her she had time for one more unscheduled stop.

She could as good as hear Hunt's voice.

"Curiosity killed the cat," he said.

"But satisfaction brought her back," Teal countered out loud.

Julia didn't miss her children, not like everyone said she would. All of those articles about empty nest syndrome did not mesh with the reality of her life. She had expected a great hole when the last left for college, but it just wasn't so, not like when an infant was taken from her arms. She loved the newly discovered freedom from her children's demands. She loved the peace and calm and had come to resent the vacations when they stayed home too long.

The surprise had been Don. He had taken their departure harder. Did a son following the old man's footsteps at Don's alma mater make him feel old? Julia didn't know, but Don had groused a lot about the rattling house, his added weight, the touch of gray she found distinguished and he so hated. And then came Laura Smart.

Julia now realized Laura was the inspiration for his new commitment to the in-town gym and his move from the old barber to a stylist. Ever so briefly, she had imagined him wanting to reclaim her younger ardor, have that second wind of passion some couples bragged about. Foolish delusion.

She laughed, a not at all pleasant sound.

"Did you say something?" Don stepped out of his closet, a tie draped over each hand. "Pick the best one."

"Best for what, dear?" Julia asked.

That should have been the other clue, Don coming home with suits and ties from Armani. Armani for the partner in charge of the Boston office of Clayborne Whittier? For a man who couldn't distinguish between an American and European cut? But she hadn't figured it out. Not then.

"The best with this suit," he said.

"Oh, I thought you meant best for impressing the girls. Isn't that what all you middle-aged men want?" She smiled like an angel.

"Honestly, Julia!" he snapped.

Why hadn't she noticed the other signs, she wondered as she watched him choose his own tie. His convoluted excuses for working late, as though long hours at Clayborne Whittier were something new, something to apologize about. The number of times Laura Smart had called him at the house on the slimmest pretext. That thought made her smile.

Little Laura wouldn't be calling him at home anymore.

Teal turned in the drive. The Clarke residence fooled managers and new partners into thinking one day they, too, could own such an estate. *Not likely,* Teal thought. *Not with the competition up and collectable fees down and malpractice insurance premiums going so high.*

One negligence suit, settled out of court, had cost another audit firm over 40 million dollars. Every time Teal signed "Clayborne Whittier" to an annual report, she prayed. And she prayed doubly hard if the report, as BiMedics' had last year, followed an initial public offering.

Teal knew the stories—companies like MiniScribe investigated by the Securities and Exchange Commission on allegations of shipping bricks to book as software sales. She knew about shareholder lawsuits. Accounting firms, with their deep pockets and close relationships with client companies, made good targets.

Teal didn't imagine her partnership shares would ever afford her a home like this. She grinned, happy to live in the city.

"Who's that?" Don complained as he finished tying the knot.

Julia shrugged.

"I'm hardly expecting a visitor at this hour," she said. "Shall I look?"

Teal was in a shadow when the door opened. The German automobile, not her, caught both pairs of eyes.

Don took in a breath fast. Julia grabbed for the dog, but the black Labrador shot out the door.

"Dudley!" she shouted.

"Oh, Teal. It's you," Don said with no pleasure in his voice.

The Labrador circled the Mercedes to the back, where he barked and lunged for the trunk. His claws skittered across the black paint.

"Jesus!" Don exploded.

Julia got to the animal first and took him by the collar. Don dragged the resistant Lab into the house.

"Come in," he said as he passed Teal.

She followed with Julia.

"Isn't that Roger's Mercedes?" Don said as he secured the door.

"Do you think he smelled skunk?" Teal asked.

Julia shrugged. "Who knows with a dog. Dudley's really a good boy."

"He's too damned spoiled," Don said.

Teal stopped rotating her attention from each point of interest—car, woman, dog, man.

"It is Roger's car," she said. "I'm lucky he could give me the loan this morning. Mine's in the shop. Look, I am sorry to barge in so early, but it was an opportunity to leave this stuff for Julia."

Teal held out the CCF meeting notes, then turned to Don.

"And could you tell Laura I've been trying to reach her? I'll be at BiMedics for the morning."

Teal couldn't have gotten more of a reaction if she'd said the office had blown up in a ball of fire.

"You won't find her here," Don bellowed.

"I didn't expect to." Teal drew back.

"She just thought you could speak to Laura, dear, since you'll be in the office first," Julia said in her well-bred voice. The smile never left her face.

Teal admired the woman's pluck. No letting on things were bad in front of the troops. Julia acted the devoted spouse.

Teal had debated the excuse for her intrusion on the drive out. She chose to rely on the obvious—her version of the truth.

FIFTEEN

"What is this, Teal?"

Don sounded angry. Teal swallowed and cleared her throat.

"Laura has been trying to get a hold of me, and we keep missing. I thought you might have better luck since she's your assistant." Teal turned to Julia. "I'm sorry about your mix-up last night, I could have used help. The raffle might run fifty tickets short of—"

"Let's not bore Don," Julia said and pressed Teal forward. "We can talk in here."

Teal flicked a glance at Don. He stared at his wife.

"You told me you were going to a CCF meeting last night," he said, his voice too soft.

Teal did not mistake the tone. No partner at Clayborne Whittier would. Don Clarke could act bluff and hale. He could thump her on the back or grill her on a technical point, his manner concentrated and his speech loud, and she knew where she stood. But when Don turned quiet, her anxiety grew. His manner had the same effect on Julia.

Teal watched Julia's lips flutter up in a smile.

"I can be so foolish. I did have a meeting at CCF, like I told you, but when I got into the car I just . . . well, blanked and headed for the monthly library council. Can you believe me?"

Julia laughed and nodded to prime her husband's agreement. He continued to glare.

"No," he said and turned to Teal. "Don't you have something better to do this morning? Last time I spoke with BiMedics, the president said he hadn't seen enough of you. It's a hard transition, manager to partner on an account."

"So you told me a month ago," Teal replied.

She worked to keep the fury from icing her eyes. When she wasn't careful, her eyes made it difficult for anyone to mistake her mood. Don had said all this in her first job evaluation as a partner.

Why repeat himself? she wondered. *Because he's on edge as Julia this morning.*

"I'm on my way out there now. That's why I thought to stop by, with BiMedics so close," she said.

Don's anger appeared to abate as he waved a hand at the living room.

"Five minutes with Julia, then I want to see you go put in those visible billable hours," he said.

The joke fell flat, but gave them both a way out.

"Of course," Teal agreed.

Tears stung Julia's eyes, and she squeezed the lids tight. Don and Teal wouldn't notice. They were too busy bristling at each other. She had never imagined Teal coming out this morning.

Don would never suspect. Period. And neither would anyone else.

Julia opened her eyes, set her smile, and piloted Teal into the living room.

Teal couldn't decide if her detour had been useful. Black dog hairs peppered her taupe, summer-weight wool dress, and that's about all she had to show for it at the moment. Her outfit reminded her of Julia—well-bred. Cap sleeves, modest neck, mother-of-pearl buttons down the front. But if you looked inside, the careful structure and detailing might be a surprise, also like Julia.

The raffle committee chairwoman gave Teal at least five good ideas for stimulating sales, first among them a special Father's Day mailing. Julia did not say another word about the prior night. She did not mention Laura Smart or the concerns she had voiced at lunch.

Teal tried one other tack before she went out the door. She mentioned Emma Browne.

"You know, I never was deposed with poor Emma Browne. What a horrible way to die."

Julia's face did not move except to let the words out from between her lips.

"Do you ever wonder what you would have said?" she asked. "I don't think I'd want to have been a professional woman at Clayborne Whittier. Not like you or Emma Browne. Of course, it could have been hard to tell the truth."

Teal stumbled in her surprise. Julia, sweet Julia, wasn't giving her any place to hide. Then, as suddenly, Julia smiled and laughed the light tinkle her mother must have taught her. It didn't disturb the skin around her eyes.

"Clayborne Whittier makes so many demands on you partners. I think it must be easier to be someone without all the responsibility, someone like Laura Smart." Julia grasped the dog's collar and opened the front door. "Thank you for stopping."

Julia's comments almost startled Teal into asking Julia about Wednesday morning, but she did not.

BiMedics held another surprise.

Teal swung through the door of the conference room reserved for the Clayborne Whittier audit and skidded to a stop.

"Do I see shock?" Amy Firestone asked.

The other audit staff in the room watched.

"Yes. I didn't expect you here today," Teal said. "Are you trying to get me in trouble with Ted?"

"Don't worry, I'll get to MicroAnswer on time. It's. . . . I need to speak with you. Why don't you guys go find the general ledger?" Amy recommended.

"Like get lost?" the senior suggested.

"Right. Like get lost and let me talk to the partner. But be back in ten minutes."

"Okay," three voices agreed as the group left.

"How are they?" Teal asked.

"They're good."

Amy didn't want to spend a lot of time on the abilities of the staff assigned to the job.

"Remember I told you I was worried about MicroAnswer's sales Wednesday?"

"Yes," Teal said.

"I went to see Roger after we talked. Ted came by with

Laura to straighten out something about our flights to Michigan when I was in the middle of trying to make Roger understand my problem. He got all funny and told me to be quiet. Like shut up!"

"Slow down," Teal said.

"Roger humiliated me in front of the partner responsible for the overall account and a cheap little secretary."

Amy slapped her hand to her mouth. Laura Smart and her cheapness were not at issue, and she'd been laughed at before on the same stupid subject by Emma Browne.

"Do you want me to ask Roger what's going on?" Teal offered.

Amy had the hardest time meeting her partner-counselor's eyes.

"It will probably make more trouble for me," she said.

"Not if I—"

"There's something else," Amy interrupted. "I was in the office last night, and I saw Laura—"

"You did?" Teal jumped in. "I've been looking all over for her."

"Well she was in with Roger," Amy said.

"Why?" Teal asked.

"I don't know why. She acted smug, like he owed her something. You're friends with him, so I thought I should mention it to you before—"

"He does something foolish?" Teal suggested.

Amy had intended to say "before someone else tells you I was hanging around the halls" to cover for herself, but she preferred Teal's interpretation.

"Yes," Amy agreed. "So, I guess I need to get going."

"Before you're found out?" Teal asked.

Amy knew she must have looked alarmed because Teal reached out a hand to her arm.

"I was joking, Amy. Ted was so precise about your schedule Wednesday, but now he's giving me a few more of your hours. Look, maybe you'd help me with the box in my car for the CEO before you leave," Teal said.

"Sure," Amy agreed, glad to drop the subject of last night.

Amy stutter-stepped to a halt in the parking lot. The expression on her face made Teal whip around, but Roger's auto looked fine. No graffiti, no slashed tires. Nothing to cause alarm.

"Amy? Are you all right?"

"That's Roger's—"

"Mercedes. Yes. Mine broke down last night. The books are on the back seat. Hang on, I'll get the lock," Teal said.

She assumed Amy's sigh meant relief.

"What were you thinking? A case of speak of the devil and here he is?" Teal grinned, but she knew Amy's problems with Roger on MicroAnswer might not have a funny ending.

All the rumors she was hearing about Roger were making Teal unhappy—Roger being the one to rile up Emma Browne and set off the lawsuit; Roger slated to be fired; Roger, Mr. Cautious, laughing off Amy's concerns on what could be fraud. And now Amy seeing him in a private meeting with Laura Smart?

Roger could be a royal pain, but he'd been a colleague and friend ever since Teal had started with Clayborne Whittier. The two years they had shared a staff cubicle had taught her a good deal about the difference between men and women, at least in business.

She and Roger both worked hard and smart, both gave the required hours, but Roger loved to mouth the favorite firm lament, that he was "out of control." Teal preferred order. But as a result, Roger was judged willing to sacrifice himself to the great firm while Teal was questioned on her devotion. On thorny accounting issues, Roger had sounded sure while she, with no less knowledge or reasoning, expressed doubt. Roger was regarded as brilliant, she as uncertain. It had made her furious until she'd realized how much his world was limited to Clayborne Whittier. Still, she would have appreciated someone giving Roger's behavior a little scrutiny and hers a little approval.

Teal gave a wry smile. What distinguished her from Roger now, she wondered? Nothing, according to Hunt.

Amy waved a hand in front of her eyes.

"Can you come out of your trance long enough to help?" Amy asked.

Teal's meeting with the CEO finished in under an hour. She was working with the staff when Kathy called.

"Roger's all bent out of shape about needing something out of his trunk," Kathy said. "Maybe you should come back to the office."

"I don't understand," Teal said. "He left the keys for me."

"But I guess he never expected you to leave before he got in this mor—"

"Fine," Teal snapped, fed up with Roger. "I'm on my way."

She spent the thirty mile drive wondering if she should mention Amy's story or let it lie. Twice, her left foot touched the brake going for the nonexistent clutch. She wasn't thinking well.

The FNEB garage sign read "Full," but Clayborne Whittier held permanent spaces as the building's major tenant. Someone was taking Roger's usual spot as she pulled up. She reached for the handle to open the window and yell but found the electric button.

"Hey!" she called out when she was finished fumbling.

Ted Grey spun around.

"Hey yourself—" he said, and stopped as though surprised to see Teal or the car.

"That's Roger's," Teal said, pointing at the place taken by Ted's rental.

"Not according to the attendant. You guys have nineteen spaces, none assigned by specific individual." He craned his neck. "I see an empty next row over."

"Thanks," she said without a bit of grace, but she couldn't fight when the attendant was right on the technicalities.

She had to grin when she saw the open slot. Roger's car in Frank Sweeny's favorite place would set Frank on edge.

Ted waited for her to shut the ignition off. They walked together to the garage elevator. Teal did an about face just after she stepped on.

"What's wrong?" Ted asked.

Teal shook her head. "Nothing, but Kathy said something about Roger needing something out of his trunk. I was gone the longest time, so I might as well be nice and take it up."

Sixteen

Ted pointed to the ramp.

"Are you sure you want to go back?"

Two pairs of eyes watched Frank's Cadillac rumble over the grate. In a moment he would turn into the row with his customary space, the one Teal had taken.

"Right. Maybe later." Teal grinned and repocketed the keys.

"The black Mercedes isn't your car?" Ted asked.

Teal shook her head as she stepped into the elevator.

"You knew that," she said.

"I did?" Ted asked.

Teal watched his mouth twitch. He used a certain flirtatious style with everyone in the office, but this was the first time he'd tried it on her. She found it disconcerting. And she could see he did not believe what she'd said about the Mercedes.

"Yes, you did," Teal said feeling sharp. "I have the old 190SL. I heard you went wild when you heard about my car and ran downstairs to see for yourself."

Ted exaggerated the drop of his jaw. "You!"

"I'm right!" Teal stepped out to the lobby.

They walked over to the Clayborne Whittier elevator bank to share the ride up with a group of staff, who fell silent. Partners had that effect.

Ted did not defend himself until they reached forty-eight.

"Mea culpa," he agreed as they rounded the receptionist's desk. "How could I forget such a fabulous auto belonged to you—"

"Only real men with real balls drive classic cars?"

Teal grinned. She did not hear Don Clarke.

"Teal!" Don hissed from behind them. "Watch that talk!"

"My fault. I goaded her," Ted said.

Teal stood as though she'd been chewed out at school. She held her temper on a four-count beat and held her breath an extra second.

"Sorry," Ted said as Don went on down the hall. "Let me ask you something. How did you know I took a look at your car?"

"Laura told Kathy—"

"And Kathy told you." Ted's laugh held a sour top note.

"A sort of old-girls' network," Teal teased.

Her face darkened as she thought of Emma Browne. Emma's lawsuit had held out the old-boys' networks as institutional barriers in the Clayborne Whittier workplace. For months, no one but Emma's supporters had used the term. Teal realized Ted could take her joke wrong, given the current politics of the firm.

It wouldn't be the first time.

"A more effective network than ours, believe me," Ted said. "You're thinking of Emma."

Teal considered a denial, but Ted held up a hand.

"I agreed with her. I supported Emma," he said.

Now Teal felt the fool. Ted Grey had been an Emma vote against Don's drive to block the promotion. Teal should have remembered the rumors. It wasn't a situation she understood. Don had stood behind her. Why not Emma? She considered Emma's record on new business. It beat hers by millions.

"Speaking of hearsay, I need to find Laura," Teal said.

Ted laughed.

She wondered what Hunt would make of her, jumping at the boss's reprimand, joking in the hall with Ted, enjoying the relief of not having to take a stand on the lawsuit with Emma dead.

"I'll send Laura on to you when she's done with the tape I left for her," Ted said.

Dan Malley read the report for a third time.

The blood and hair on the tombstone matched the victim's. The prints lifted from the marble surface matched Singer's index finger, thumb, and palm; Stewart's index finger and thumb; four other partners; and Singer's secretary's. Smudges might or might not be an indication the killer wore gloves. The cleaning woman for the floor said she wiped the memento with her cloth twice a week.

The pattern of blood and brains splattered on the stall wall confirmed that the victim had died standing where Teal had found her body slumped on the toilet. Other forensic evidence suggested that the Halloween-style makeup had been an afterthought, or at least put on after Browne's soul had departed from the body. Ditto for the clothes.

A messy job, Dan decided. Traces of the victim, clumps of her cellular matter and blood, had been cleared from a sink trap, along with a good deal of other unsavory stuff. The killer had taken plenty of time.

Which meant what?

Nothing! Dan banged his hand to the report. Nineteen audit partners alone had been documented in the security report as in and out of Clayborne Whittier around the suspect hours. Three cleaning workers, two shifts of the building's private guards, and fifty other people between the word-processing late shift and professional staff had come in after or stayed past six that evening. The statistics hadn't surprised Kathy, who worked hard and smart, nine to five, with no ambition to live another kind of life.

Don Clarke had characterized it as a night of business as usual.

Malley flipped to his file on the interviews. No one had made an attempt to disguise the general dislike for Emma Browne. Even the few partners who had voted to admit her called her "difficult" and "hard to warm to" or "a challenge."

Dan dished the manila folder back to the pile. He cracked his knuckles one by one and stared at his desk.

"Theresa Mars," he said aloud. "Reesa. R-R-Reeses pieces. Reesy."

Those had been her nicknames on the street. White female, late thirties, 5'5" bony inches at 110 pounds, copper penny hair dye used to cover a head of pepper gray, topaz eyes. Pretty, clean, and well-groomed for her kind of life, and a smoker with a set of lungs on track for emphysema. The meager possessions at her single, rented room in South Boston offered no clue to a family. She had habitually paid late and short on the rent, but in the last week or so she had been flush according to the landlady.

Reesy had lived her last year in a one hundred square foot space, ironing her dresses and drinking wine and listening to the voices. The landlady had said Reesy swore by them and wasn't a danger to herself or society. An educated, careful drunk, if crazy on the side, had been the summary. The landlady had had no idea where Reesy had come from before the welfare cuts and local counseling center closed by state privatization of the social service budget had pushed her out of her halfway house.

Reesy had taken to panhandling downtown for spending money. The take had never equaled the rent, but something had caught her up right before she died.

According to talk on the street, Reesy Mars had worked the financial district and no place else, moving around between the Boston Harbor Hotel and Downtown Crossing. The landlady had said Reesy's voices told her to exploit business women and men. That was the very word Theresa had used, according to the landlady—"exploit." Just another articulate Boston street person.

Dan didn't want to kid himself, but he could not ignore the two indisputable facts—Theresa Mars, like Emma Browne, had been murdered with a direct blow to the head and the killer had been close by or inside the First New England Bank building. Theresa had died first and on the ground, Emma second and forty-eight flights closer to the clouds.

Frank could not believe his eyes. Roger Singer's car blocked his slot. His hands stuck on the wheel and a pain shot up his left side. *A heart attack,* he told himself. He began to pant.

"Hey! Hey! No standing!"

Frank heard the pounding, saw a palm flatten on the glass. The ache in his side subsided. He nodded to the little man.

He eased his foot from the brake and the automobile rolled forward to where the attendant pointed at a space at the end of the row. An automatic reflex put the car into park and got him outside.

He had been found out. He had been found out. He had been found out.

The thought repeated round and round. His legs felt like ribbons of jelly. *How?* he wondered, thinking he'd been so careful the night before—crazy, maybe, but careful.

"Have you seen Roger?" Kathy asked.

"Uh-uh. Have you seen Laura?" Teal asked.

Kathy made a face. "But I left a message that you wanted to speak with her."

Teal shook her head. "She wanted to talk to me."

"Whatever." Kathy handed over a stack of messages. "Should I run the keys back to Roger?"

Teal flipped through the pink slips—a senior out at one of her jobs, the controller at Fruiers Construction Company, Hunt.

"When did Hunt call?" she asked.

Something brightened in Kathy's eyes.

"First thing this morning. Are you two . . ." Kathy moved her hands together through the air.

"He wants help sorting out a problem with his partner," Teal said.

"And you are seeing him," Kathy suggested.

Teal felt herself tense. "If you mean, are we speaking, yes. Some, I guess. And I'll take these to Roger."

She dangled the keys. They were as good an excuse as any to avoid any more questions about Hunt.

"Barbara, plea—"

"You come in at all hours, jump into the shower, leave this morning before we have a chance to talk, and you want me to act like a happy little wife and mommy? I'm sick of this, Roger, and now I hear from someone else that you might be fired!" Barbara screamed.

Roger twisted his neck back and forth, but the kink did not release. He had expected an epiphany.

"Isn't that what you wanted? Don't you hate Clayborne Whittier? Don't you complain about the firm constantly? That it acts like it owns me and I lie down and let it. That you can't stand—"

"So I'm just supposed to sit there and be humiliated by Margaret Sweeny?"

"Who?" he asked.

"Frank's wife, who do you think I mean?" Barbara shrilled. "And didn't she love saying it to me."

Roger heard a tap and turned to see his door crack open.

"You want these?" Teal mouthed. She jangled his keys.

Ted Grey pushed past Teal.

"Have you forgotten our meeting?" Ted asked.

"Look, honey, I have to go," Roger said.

He heard the faint sound of Barbara's voice as he set down the phone.

"I'm sorry, Ted, my wife. I need a minute to get a file out of my car." He addressed Teal in the doorway. "You didn't tell me you were going to take off so early."

"You didn't tell me——"

"Look. Can you two work this out another time? We need to start, Roger," Ted barked.

"I can run down and get what you need," Teal said.

"No," Roger said and took a step.

"Roger!"

Ted's voice acted like a brake.

"My office please," Ted said.

Roger couldn't do anything but nod and follow.

Teal walked up to the Mercedes.

"You going out?"

The attendant's question made her swing around.

"No," she said.

"Too bad. I need the space. Too much traffic in and out of your place today. Maybe you should buy more spots," he said.

"The building won't let us." Teal shrugged.

The attendant did, too, as he walked away.

She turned the key. One click and the trunk sprang open.

SEVENTEEN

Teal's arm stretched as it held the key sticking from the lock. Her head remained half cocked toward the attendant as he disappeared into the garage office. She had been thinking about her own car when the catch popped. Trapped heat rising to her nose jerked her attention back to the present moment.

A black steamer-type trunk, the kind Clayborne Whittier employees used to transport the supplies and workpapers for an audit, filled the available space in the trunk of Roger's car. A trunk within a trunk. Teal had expected Roger's papers would be easy to find, but she hadn't planned on lugging up a trunk. She reached for the snap shackles and flipped each one. The lid seemed stuck, and she grabbed the lock and jerked her hand up.

She couldn't let go. She couldn't shift her gaze away.

"N-o. O-h n-o!"

Death had not been kind to Laura Smart.

Teal pressed a hand to her mouth.

Goose bumps puckered the skin of her arms. The stench

of death swirled around her like invisible smoke. For the last four hours, she had been in and out of this car.

The Clarke's black Labrador, lunging at the trunk, had known. His hair had gone stiff as he'd stretched his neck to howl. Teal recalled how Julia had worked to restrain him. But she was not going to think about anyone but herself right now.

Teal could not force a second look. One glance had been enough to show her Laura's knees bent back flat like a six-year-old mimicking a frog, the face innocent under the brash makeup and the stiff mouth gaping open. Teal need only close her eyes and this image of Laura would too quickly fill the void.

Horror and irony struck Teal like a blow. While she'd driven to the secretary's home this morning, while she'd knocked on Laura's door, Laura was already with her, neatly tucked into the closed box. Teal pinched her nostrils and took a step back while her fingers found the metal edge. A blind swing slammed the car trunk closed.

Then Teal ran for the garage telephone.

Don Clarke sprang out of his chair.

"No," he repeated. "No."

Teal's voice came back at him with the words she had used before.

"Don, it is Laura. I know. I saw her."

He paced around the curve of his mahogany desk until the length of cord stretched taut.

"How can you be sure?" he said. His mind had stalled.

"This can't be easy for you," Teal murmured, but he sensed she avoided saying what had him worried.

The muscles of his jaw bunched to a knot. His eyes stung. He stumbled where the carpet met the floor. His palm strangled the telephone.

"Thank you for calling," he managed before he hung up.

He pressed the pads of his fingers to make his eyelids stay shut, but the tears leaked between the edges. This was not behavior he could afford to tolerate. Not here, in his office at Clayborne Whittier. His weeping sent a stream down his palms to soak his shirt cuffs.

He had been such a fool.

Teal knew Dan Malley would not approve. She was familiar with the right thing to do. She should have called the police first. The impulse of human compassion had made her dial her boss.

Everyone in the office told stories about Don—his ambitious enterprise from the day he had joined Clayborne Whittier, how he used the political instincts honed smooth from his time at Harvard's business school, where the firm had sponsored his degree. Younger partners were cynical enough to believe he had married Julia Wade for her family money. Old-timers said Don had fallen head-over-sense in love.

Whichever truth one chose, Don had worked on his handicap and joined the best clubs. He'd forgotten some of where he had come from, except for what counted. Teal recognized Don Clarke's power to make and ruin careers. He had made hers and ruined Emma Browne's.

But Don was more than Boston's influential partner in charge. He was human. Laura had been the object of his desire.

Teal's second call brought the police.

Roger couldn't concentrate on Ted's speech. And it was a speech. Something about teamwork. Roger had the distinct impression Ted was waiting for a response, but he didn't care. The distant scream of a siren grew louder. Roger rubbed his temples and pictured Teal at his trunk.

The rush of blood thundering in his ears blocked Ted out. Had Teal found—

"Amy!" Ted smacked his hand to the table and Roger, startled, jumped. "You aren't listening! Let me repeat, Amy Firestone asked to see me this afternoon without you. Do you have any idea what this is all about?"

Ted commanded Roger's attention now. Amy Firestone represented another side of the vice, another Emma Browne. Then there was Laura Smart. He thought he'd been so clever, deceiving Barbara, and look where he'd got—Amy sneaking around behind his back to Ted, Teal downstairs rifling through his trunk. The pulse at his temple throbbed.

Roger blinked his eyes shut to imagine a different life— no Barbara harping on him for both more money and more time, no Clayborne Whittier, no reporting to Ted. He knew he had to focus.

"Amy?" He forced his eyelids up. "She's worried about my judgment on sales at MicroAnswer."

Ted pulled his head back in surprise. Roger thought he'd been pretty smart to take away Amy's power. Then he realized Ted wasn't paying any attention to him but was looking at the door where Detective Malley stood with his badge flipped open.

SATURDAY

Eighteen

Teal lay in bed, seeing Laura's glazed face and listening to the hiss of water spin off the tires of cars going too fast below on Storrow Drive. The week had been hot and the temperature was no different today, except that the heavy humidity had congealed to rain. She rolled over to turn off the alarm before the radio could start.

Her bedroom, still shadowed by her fancy, translucent blinds drawn against the dim western exposure, felt cool at the beginning of the day, but it didn't mean she could sleep. Nor did she want to get up. Not yet. Not with her mind racing through yesterday.

She hadn't told Dan Malley about Laura's call, the late-night message left unreturned. She tensed, her toes cramping and her fists clenched. Her mind knew she was crazy to blame herself, but her heart was not so forgiving. If only she hadn't waited. There would have been something in what Laura said, something to hint at what was wrong, something to save her from an untimely death.

All death was untimely, that's what Hunt had said. All death robs the living, whether the departed was eight or eighty, dearly beloved or dearly hated. The funny thing was, he'd meant the analysis as sympathy and hadn't understood Teal's pain. But then, she hadn't told him the truth.

She squeezed her toes tight and shook out her hands until her feet and fingers went limp. The tendons contracted into a knot as she thought again, *I shouldn't have ignored Laura. I shouldn't have gone to bed. One call, one stupid call was all I had to do.*

The telephone ring did not penetrate to her consciousness at first. Then she thought it was Laura, as though time could be edited and replayed into the other night. But when she reached the receiver, it wasn't Laura she heard on the line.

"Argyle thinks he needs a walk," Hunt said.

"You're coming over tomorrow," Teal objected, unwilling to let go of her dream of redemption. "Ray Charles, remember? I . . . I have errands—"

"Which we can do together. I want to see you, Teal."

It wasn't like Hunt to insist. He, between them, had always been the one who could wait, delay the decision, think something through one more time until any action came too late.

But she didn't care. Perhaps seeing Hunt would push Laura away. She imagined Argyle waiting, eyes on Hunt, ready to leap for the door.

"Okay," she said. "But I have a whole list of things you can do—"

"Starting with pick up scones at Rebecca's, right?" Hunt said.

She could hear his grin. Sometimes it was a comfort to realize someone knew her.

"What a nice idea," she agreed like it had been his. "I'll start the tea in about half an hour."

She was still thinking dog as she rolled out of bed, but it wasn't a lean and lanky Scottish deerhound. A heavily muscled Labrador retriever lunged through her brain and attacked the back of Roger's sedan.

Hunt didn't hurry; he matched Argyle's eager pace. Argyle didn't exactly strain at his leash but maintained a quick clip the length of South Street, past the art galleries and on to Summer, where the quiet end of the financial district gave way to the overt hustle of retail. Downtown Crossing looked tired, with missing bricks in the sidewalk and fast food wrappers caught at the curb and three windows of the old Jordan Marsh department store papered off to hide the changing of the display.

Early shoppers came out of Park Street Station. Hunt checked the steeple clock on the Park Street Church. Not quite eight, which told him Filene's Bargain Basement must be having a special sale. Nothing else could explain the crowd at this hour on Saturday. The Basement racks would be picked clean by ten at the latest. Teal could shop there, but it was an experience he hated.

Heat and rain had brought the grass up lush and green and the trees to full leaf in Boston Common. Argyle set as straight a course as the paths allowed across the park. The shallow wading pool was drained of water, except where puddles had formed. He never understood why the ugly, cement cut-out was called the Frog Pond, unless it waited for the kiss of a princess. Man and dog hurried across the unofficial softball field and past a reconstructed entrance to the Common garage.

He had to laugh at Teal's making partner the year she lost her under-Common parking spot. Shot with luck was what he called it. Her admission as good as underwrote her purchase of a condominium space at the Brimmer Street Garage.

And people expected him to enjoy the luck of the Irish.

Deluca's Market on the first Beacon Hill block of Charles Street had the awning down and their trestle tables heavy with a display of too early and imported summer fruit. Argyle ignored the toy poodle tied to the lamppost by the door. The deerhound waited, unshackled, at the curb while Hunt ran in for the orange juice.

Whatever else might be said about Deluca's, and there was a lot, the juice they squeezed in the back of the shop was worth the ransom Hunt had to pay.

Rebecca's take-out took a ridiculous amount of time considering only four people preceded Hunt in line. The inefficiency would have sent him in a U-turn out the door if he hadn't wanted a golden raisin-studded scone as much as Teal. The other truth was, he wanted to buy himself time.

He had pushed her to see him this morning, and now he dawdled as he drew near, while Argyle paced outside, restless to sprint for Brimmer Street and Teal.

It had seemed so important to Hunt. All he could think of was that he must talk to Teal about the problem with his partner. The tension had flared again last night when BG had pressed an after-work drink on Midori. Hunt had tagged along despite BG's glaring. BG had bared more than the bottom of two bottles of wine. Midori had made pretty excuses and small gestures and escaped early, but not before her eyes had glistened with panic as BG had reached for a hug. After she'd fled, BG had turned to Hunt.

"Little pecker's gone dead," he had said, watching Midori's retreat.

Alarm had strangled Hunt's throat. "Not with Mi—"

"Midori?" BG had slugged back the wine. "Worried about a hostile work environment, boss?"

Hunt had wanted to smack his partner then, slap some sense into his foolish head.

"What about feeling something for me? Your old buddy, your old friend?" BG had whined.

"Get up, Beej," Hunt had instructed. "You're drunk."

"Hey, I'm baring my soul to my best pal—"

"Save it," Hunt had advised, hauling his partner to his feet.

He had managed to navigate BG out of the bar and dump him in a taxi. That part hadn't been hard or easy, only a necessary chore. The worst of it was he had never asked BG to justify his behavior. Hunt's unwillingness to recognize a problem had almost been taken out on Midori. Hunt understood, that for the sake of Huntington BG Associates, he needed to know more.

This morning the thought of asking Teal to talk with Midori had seemed a stroke of genius.

Now Hunt wondered if he was as crazy in his own way as BG.

"Next? Next?" The woman behind the counter raised her voice.

Hunt hurried to place his scone order.

Argyle could have guided Hunt blindfolded to Teal's

door. The elegant hound stood on the front stoop and whined at the sound of her footsteps as she came down. He had been trained never to jump up. She kneeled to meet his excited bark.

"Is this how a child of divorce feels?" Teal asked, lifting her face to Hunt from Argyle's mist of fur. "Confused?"

He could read defensiveness in her voice as she stood.

"So, what's so important you had to see me a day early?"

"Impotence," Teal said, careful to keep her voice void of a judgment.

She coasted a full mug across the granite counter to Hunt and considered the subject. Impotence could be tricky, bringing back memories of the time right before she and Hunt had moved apart, the period when anger had been their repressed emotion and Hunt couldn't help but let it show.

"Happens to the best of us," Hunt said.

She looked up from fussing with the warmed scones and into his burnt brown eyes.

"I know," she said and forgave him their spat of a year ago. They had invested too much to let Clayborne Whittier make her deny his importance.

"I think this fifth divorce . . . anyway, BG's bringing his emotional problems into the office," Hunt said. He broke off a corner of scone and tossed it into his mouth. "Yum."

"This is new?" Teal avoided shaking her head, but she couldn't help the disbelieving shrug.

It was weird, talking about BG as though Laura hadn't died, as though if she didn't tell Hunt it wouldn't be true. She listened to Hunt detail BG's pursuit of Midori—the uncomfortable tension created in the office, Midori's vulnerability as a new member of the firm, her difficulty knowing how to react from her background in a different culture, Hunt's concern for BG and fear of a lawsuit. Hunt finished the plate of scones without noticing Teal hadn't eaten one.

"Look where Emma Browne's treatment got you," he said.

"Clayborne Whittier," Teal said. "Not me."

"You're a partner. You are Clayborne Whittier. What affects the firm affects—"

"Laura Smart," Teal blurted out.

Hunt shut his mouth and Teal felt his startled eyes on her.

"I found Laura Smart yesterday in Roger's trunk. I'd borrowed his car because—"

"Laura in the trunk of the car?" Hunt asked.

"Dead." Teal couldn't help herself. She laughed. "Murdered even." She didn't mean to act flip. Murder was an insult to humanity. The temptation to hysteria made her throat itch, and she swallowed. Hard. "I think Emma had something to do with Laura, but I can't get it to make sense."

"Puts impotence in perspective," Hunt said.

"Small," Teal said and giggled.

Her body shook with the horror and pain. She knew Hunt was doing the best he could, holding her close, murmuring reassurance. He couldn't know what she had seen in Emma Browne, in Laura Smart, in the poor homeless woman—her future, every future. But death by murder was worse than any other cause.

Argyle laid his head in her lap and rumbled in his throat.

She came out of the storm of grief in fits and starts. Finally, she could hear Hunt's voice and understand the words.

"Emma Browne. Laura Smart." Hunt paused. "The police don't think it has anything to do with you?"

Teal hadn't thought of what the police might believe, but she shook her head.

"No," she said. "I do."

"You do? What do you mean, you do?" Hunt asked.

"Laura called me this week. The night we . . . the night I went to your place and got home so late. Laura called and I stood and listened while she left a message. I considered her rude to try me at such an hour. I thought it could wait. I thought . . . nothing good enough to have it end this way."

"Hey. Hey, doll. Calm down." Hunt stroked her head to his chest. "You didn't kill Laura Smart. You could have taken that call and talked all night and she'd still be dead."

"I'm not so sure," Teal said.

She could hear the beat of Hunt's heart, feel the heat of contact with him. Laura would be as cold as leftovers in the fridge by now, where she waited in a morgue drawer.

"Laura had never, ever called me at home. She hardly knew me, didn't want to. I can't believe she didn't have something important to tell me, even if she hoped to use me. And if I'd answered and heard what she had to say, I could have done something—"

"Hush. Hush," Hunt said and stroked her hair.

The hurt didn't start or stop anywhere but set her mind and body aching. She tried to catch the guilt but it skittered and slid through her brain, pumped through her veins. Hunt's gentle hand felt like a rake, and her mind flamed with self-loathing. She should have answered that telephone.

"It isn't just Laura," Teal whispered.

"What is it?" Hunt asked, his voice gentle as he bent to her ear.

"I'm worried."

"The police will catch the killer. Your friend Malley knows what he's doing," Hunt said.

He voiced her worst fear. Dan Malley did know what he was doing. He might look young, and was, but he was not naive or stupid.

"I know who Dan thinks killed Emma and Laura, and I don't want to." Hunt's shirt muffled her words and soaked up the spill of tears.

"You know?" Hunt repeated.

Teal nodded in the conflicting motion that was as much denial as confirmation.

"Who?" Hunt said.

Teal squirmed from his arms and groaned.

It isn't just because I read whodunits."

"Maybe it's right, sweet, but she's got a gentle way of poking it in."

I grunted.

"So you're all ready to take your friend Hollis over what she found, sergeant."

"I asked her where the Hollis did that take her?" said Craig. He was hunched a little, his eyes on her own desk.

"I know what Hollis killed Conlin and Lewis and ... may be. That's what I called Joe Hollis and looked at a sort of way.

"You know," Hollis began.

"I wanted to ask something about that was as much as I saw it conclusions."

"Yes," Hollis said.

"And that was easy to answer," I ground.

SUNDAY

NINETEEN

Hunt asked again on Sunday morning, "Who does Malley think killed them?"

Teal turned a strand of hair around her finger. The curl did not last.

"You aren't going to say."

"No," Teal agreed.

"Loyalty?"

"Maybe."

It wasn't easy not telling Hunt, but she couldn't, not without real proof. Mostly, she wanted to believe Malley wouldn't come to the same conclusion.

"We don't have to go, you know," Hunt said.

She didn't correct his misinterpretation of her sigh. She did want to hear Ray Charles at the Hatch Shell on the Esplanade later in the day.

Argyle's nails clicked a circle around the bed. He nosed a shoe Teal had dropped to the floor in the haste of last night's first intimate moment. There had followed a second this morning, acts so private Teal wasn't sure she had the words to describe them.

She narrowed her eyes to inspect Hunt on the bed. He looked almost too much at home, pillows propped behind his head, one arm stretched out as his fingers stroked her collarbone. The other hand started on a different, more delicate course. The languid sound which escaped her mouth was no tense groan. If he asked now, she'd tell him anything.

He didn't ask, of course, but shifted her full attention to the pleasures of special moment number three.

"I'm exhausted," Teal murmured.

They looked at each other as Argyle wailed from the front hall.

"He's your dog," they said in unison.

His baying moved them from the bed.

They went together, Argyle bounding down to the street, Hunt stumbling on the leash. Teal followed slowly as she adjusted a pair of sunglasses to hide her unprepared and kiss-blurred face. How could the day have slipped to afternoon?

The last person she ever expected to run into was exiting a Charles Street antique store.

"Teal!" exclaimed Margaret Sweeny. "I haven't seen you in ages, dear."

Margaret was as gracious and lovely as her husband was a rube and a bore. Teal often wondered about such women and the marriages they must have made when young. Very young, with the Sweeny offspring up to a count of nine and Margaret just brushing at her late forties. *Nine children,* Teal thought, *and the youngest born three years before.* The statistics described an unimaginable life.

Margaret eyed Hunt, where he waited half a block ahead. "I didn't know," she said.

Teal grinned. She had forgotten her indiscretions after last summer's spat with Hunt. Margaret's face made Teal remember she'd told anyone who would listen exactly what she thought of Boston's most controversial architect. Not a complimentary word, that was for sure.

Margaret had been all sympathy, expressing worry about the emotional lives of professional women like Teal. The concern had been neither offensive nor phony. Margaret's reaction had made Teal consider the possibility that Frank Sweeny's wife actually liked the man and her status as his wife. It had been hard to picture since Teal considered Frank an ass, but she came to see that Margaret harbored a different view of her husband. Margaret loved him. She was more than he deserved.

"Where's Frank?" Teal asked.

Distress clouded Margaret's fine face. Her dark eyebrows arched over fixed eyes.

"The office. Where else?" she said. "I don't know how you partners do it."

"I think it must be easier on us than a spouse," Teal offered in an effort to hide her confusion.

Frank Sweeny was not a partner who worked weekends or stayed late of a weekday. Surely Margaret considered this new behavior. But her "where else" sounded like she expected no doubt from Teal.

"How's the antique—" Teal started, but Margaret broke in without listening.

"I'm worried about him, Teal. He's not acting a bit like himself. Not since that dreadful woman died."

Teal didn't ask which dreadful woman. Both Emma and Laura had appalled Margaret.

Margaret didn't ask if it was awful finding a body. But her hands were quivering where she held them bunched at her side.

"It's turned into such a terrible year. Little Sean, Frank's schedule, now this . . . this mess." Margaret's voice cracked and broke.

Teal had forgotten about the diagnosis of the second from last Sweeny child. Autism. Sean was almost four when the doctors' hesitant verdict had come down. Autistic spectrum disorder must have left Margaret and Frank reeling. And where on the mysterious spectrum would little Sean fall? That was the worst question, the unknown.

Shame burned Teal's cheeks with the memory of her laughing with Roger as Frank had chased off to Funsters on Monday. And this after Teal had discovered the vagrant woman with her skull crushed.

"He's not himself, Teal." Margaret's hand brushed at her coat, and she did not meet Teal's eye. "Don't be too hard on him, please, for me."

The request left Teal speechless.

"So, what was all that with Margaret Sweeny? And what did you say to explain me?" Hunt asked.

They were settled back at Teal's house, another two plates of weekend scones, *The Sunday Globe,* and a pot of tea between them.

"You're not listening," Hunt said. He poked her.

"No," Teal murmured. "I'm reading." She shook the paper to settle the fold. "Look."

"PRESTIGE AT YOUR PERIL? Clayborne Whittier Joins Ranks of America's Best Firms in Letting Partners Go," Hunt read. *"In a change for one of the most conservative of the Big Six—"*

"I don't need to hear it," Teal said.

"You?" Hunt asked as he raised his eyes from the paper to her face, shock in his voice.

"No!" Teal snapped.

"Sorry."

"It's . . . The rumor is that Roger Singer has been asked to leave."

"Your buddy?" Hunt said. "I can't believe it. Roger makes you look lazy. He about kills himself from what you told me." Hunt stopped to stare at Teal. "Does he know?"

Teal inclined her head. "I guess."

"He about killed himself to be a partner." Hunt paused to purse his lips as he held his eyes on her face. "You're worried he killed someone else with the party about to be over. Someone like Emma and Laura, maybe?"

Teal managed to shrug, but she couldn't raise her voice above a whisper. "I don't know."

"But the thought has you worried," Hunt pressed.

"Yes." Teal cleared her throat.

"It's not much fun in corporate America these days," Hunt said.

"No," Teal agreed.

Roger Singer had knocked himself out to be admitted, had done the firm's bidding and left his wife and kids at the front door each morning unsure when he would find time to return home, except that it would never be early enough to read the kids a story and tuck them into bed or to converse with Barbara, though she did learn to spend the money. Roger lived a life without the luxury of even an hour a week for himself alone.

Roger had made the sacrifice, and now he was about to be pushed out, left on his own. He never had questioned the bargain of his personal sacrifices or that he'd have a lifetime of security. The change in business practice couldn't be easy for him or Barbara or anyone else at the firm. But internal upheaval did not make Roger a murderer.

"You have to go to Malley," Hunt said.

They stood on the Fiedler Bridge, the thick twist of salmon-painted concrete coated with a jam of humanity. Ray Charles, the big draw, was not in evidence as a warm-up group struggled to divert the restless crowd. Hunt eased them forward. They could see to the elegant, open-air stage of the Hatch Shell.

"I don't think I can make it," Teal said.

She didn't have to explain, one advantage of being with an old flame. Hunt understood about her claustrophobia, understood when she wanted to go and when she grew anxious and afraid. Some of the people on the bridge were in worse shape, holding dogs and children in their arms.

Teal looked ahead. People. She looked down to the street. Storrow Drive had been blocked off, but a gridlock of bodies compressed in the road.

"Your roof deck," Hunt suggested.

Teal nodded. He had said it earlier, but something in her had insisted today wouldn't be like every other. It was, of course, with the press of flesh against her own making her skin crawl, the kick and stomp of other people's feet on hers driving her insane. But when it came right down to it, there wasn't the room to go crazy.

Something clicked in her brain. Bodies took up a lot of space. Discarding one could not be easy. After Laura had been hoisted into Roger's car, what would have been the next step? A cement block and a long drop into the Charles River? An evening spent feeding a wood chipper? She didn't mean to be crude or gory, but what had the killer planned for the body?

Disposal had to be a major drawback of turning to murder.

Hunt tightened his grip on her arm as the headliner was announced. The crowd roared and surged.

Teal clung to the pedestrian bridge until she could edge herself against the tide. It took ten minutes to make it the few yards to the in-town side. Off the ramp they could walk with a normal stride.

"Did you hear me before?" Hunt asked. "I said you have to go to Malley. And you do, don't you, since you think you know?"

"But I don't," Teal said, and meant it.

"This is a great view."

Hunt leaned forward in the deck chair and started to count the motorboats tied up on the Charles River. Music echoed off the water. Teal's roof was by far the better way to handle the crowd.

"I have a favor to ask," he said.

Teal turned from the wrought-iron rail. "Which is?"

"Talk to Midori for me."

She was already shaking her head no and he hadn't even

explained. Hunt felt his jaw go tight. At least he was willing to ask for help, which was more than she could say with her close-mouthed suspicions about poor Roger. He knew it was Roger she was so worried about.

"Why not?"

He must have sounded as mad as he felt because Argyle sat up like he'd been caught doing something he didn't understand was wrong.

"I don't really know her. What can I say? 'Is BG causing a problem? Oh, don't mind him, he's just confused and takes out his anxieties in an unsuitable manner? And, as an aside, please don't bring suit?' Honestly, Hunt, no!"

"I'm worried about her—"

"You're worried about Huntington BG Associates and yourself. You're worried your sophomoric partner is going to embarrass you or worse. And okay, okay, you have feeling for her, too, but that's not why you're asking for help today, or not the first reason."

"You're using that 'you're like all the rest' tone and I don't find it amusing."

He found it infuriating, actually, that she had spoken so much of the truth. But he did care about Midori.

"Talk to her yourself. It would be much the better way," Teal said. "She'll be appreciative you noticed she needs support. But first talk to BG and straighten him out. He's your partner, for God's sake."

"Easy for you to sound so virtuous," Hunt groused.

But he knew he should have demanded more of his partner's behavior years ago. Turning a blind eye to what did not concern the firm was a poor excuse.

"When did you ever sit down for a heart to heart with

your partner Frank Sweeny?" he challenged Teal, mad at himself.

The jibe must have hit the target. Teal glared, but she didn't protest.

"Time for me to fire up the grill?" Hunt asked.

"I think you've about worn your welcome out." Teal's mouth was stiff.

Argyle looked from one to the other of them like an unhappy child. Hunt didn't want the weekend to end on this.

"Forget Midori," he said. "You're right, I should handle the problem myself. So, what were you and Margaret Sweeny going on about?"

Teal bit her lips.

"I'm not sure I know," she said.

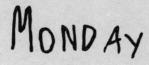

TWENTY

Margaret Sweeny used to love these morning meetings for the Clayborne Whittier spouses. Clayborne Coffees had started in the 1950s when partners were men and spouses were wives and no one used the gender neutral term. *Spouse,* she thought. *How ridiculous when the coffees remained all wives, the poor women partners being single or as good as divorced the way they led their lives. Look at Teal Stewart. Not a hope she'll find someone without putting her ambition in under-drive and getting rid of Hunt,* (a man Margaret had pegged for a lifetime bachelor). Margaret wished Teal would find someone nice, then maybe Teal would ease up on Frank.

The Funsters escapade had been no joke—Frank upset for the week, getting short with the children, and bubbling out in hives whenever she'd asked him to trust her and confide. He'd said something about Funsters being a bar and an affront to his pride, but she didn't understand how he could be so upset by a bar. He'd spent enough time in them himself. Too much time these days. Margaret's coffee cup rattled as she set it down.

"Julia, how nice to see you," Margaret said as she stood.

"I just said to Frank we should visit with you and Don more. The old guard, we need to stick together."

Margaret hoped she conveyed sincerity with her tone. She inclined her head a fraction toward Barbara Singer as if to say, "there's the new guard." Julia smiled back, but then she'd smile if you told her all her children had drowned. Julia patted Margaret's arm.

"I'm not sure now is the right time," Julia said, her smile a shade lighter.

Julia's fingers trailed along the silk sleeve of Margaret's dress as she stepped away. Margaret felt funny, like she'd been brushed by a hot poker. What did it mean, "I'm not sure now is the right time?" What had Don said to his wife about Frank? The heat twisted up Margaret's chest and threatened to wash her face with the nervous flush she never had learned to control.

"Hot flash?" Barbara Singer asked.

The question set Margaret on edge. *Doesn't she know enough not to discuss the personal in public?* she thought.

In the moment of silence between them, words from a conversation one cluster over filled the room.

"—and then I had the most god-awful pain and the doctor told me I had to have the hysterectomy, you know. Well, after the trauma of Billy's birth—I told you about that didn't I—"

Fortunately, other voices resumed and the discussion of Billy's birth, which Margaret had endured at least four times before from the mouth of a tax department wife, was drowned out. The interlude reduced Barbara's well-meant query to a mild privacy invasion.

"No," Margaret murmured in response. "I'm a tad hot standing, that's all."

"Well, sit," Barbara said and dropped onto the couch.

Margaret gave in to Barbara's insistent hand tugging her down.

"I've been wanting to speak to you for a week. I know you're going to find this hard to believe, but Roger had nothing to do with that terrible Funsters joke, and I want to tell you how sorry I am Frank had to go through—"

"What?" Margaret asked. "Go through what?"

Maybe she had raised her voice because all the chatter in the room hushed to a stop.

"Funsters." Barbara dropped her voice like the word meant something Margaret should know, like it was a code.

Margaret wished someone would tell her what the funny looks were all about. She saw her husband with a pretty clear eye. He might not be anyone else's idea of a prize, but she loved him and he loved her and they both loved the children. Frank Sweeny never minded that he wasn't the handsomest or the most talented or the smartest. He worked hard to provide and had done better than any expectation—an amiable, if limited, guy.

Margaret wanted no more. Experience had taught that the handsomest and most talented and smartest were the first to leave you in the dirt. She had seen enough of that in her mother's unhappy life. It was not for her.

"You don't know what Funsters is all about, do you?" Barbara asked.

Margaret heard the woman's voice raise as if appalled.

"It's the most outrageous gay bar in town for picking up pretty boys or meeting the leather crowd," Barbara said.

"That's why she——" Barbara snapped her mouth closed and looked chagrined.

Someone had sent Frank to a bar where men dated men? Margaret could imagine his reaction. She hoped he would never find out about their oldest son.

"She?" Margaret forced out of her mouth.

Margaret watched Barbara's elaborate shrug.

"I don't really know," Barbara said too quickly.

Margaret made herself think about Barbara. She bet Barbara was thinking about the other evening with the wives and all the talk about Clayborne Whittier's new policy to transition out targeted partners, all the wives on edge trying to guess who in Boston would be fired. Margaret had been herself, but when she'd noticed Barbara Singer's ashen face, she had tried to help out, made some comment about everyone worried for themselves and someone being right.

It would be an understatement to say her attempt at kindness had backfired. Barbara had responded with tight-faced fury, as though Margaret had really meant to confirm that Roger was the target. Margaret, being older or simply wiser, knew all the spouses felt the same insecurity. All but Julia Clarke.

Julia looked over at Margaret. She wondered if she should rescue her from Barbara Singer. Not that Barbara wasn't an energetic young wife, but she could become quite tiresome with all her talk of buying the new house, her decorating problems, and her constant harping on Roger's contributions to the partnership. She must be worried.

This ridiculous transitioning out mess had everyone in a state, Julia thought. Everyone but herself. Or at least not about Don being forced to leave Clayborne Whittier.

Thinking of Don made Julia smile, she could feel the corners of her mouth going up. She'd never forget the cast of his face when he had come home Friday night, puffed and rubbed raw. He'd used the excuse of a terrible cold and had insisted on sleeping in the other room the past three nights. Each one of them, he'd cried till all hours. Julia knew. She had listened at the door.

All over that little—Julia stopped herself. She wasn't going to think about her, wasn't going to let the departed have that kind of power, not now with the little whore out of the way, dead and buried.

Buried. Julia wondered if Laura Smart had been buried yet. The police had arrived to question Don at the house Saturday. She hadn't liked the visit. It had made her feel uncomfortable. Everyone would be better off to get the girl underground and forgotten.

She realized she'd been doing too much thinking and too little talking.

"Barbara. You look lovely dear. How are you enjoying the hospitality committee?" she said as she laid a hand on Barbara's arm.

Julia decided she still liked the perquisites of the wife of the partner in charge. How much, she could not decide.

"You did a wonderful job with the annual Clayborne Whittier dinner dance," Julia said.

Barbara rolled her quick, tiger eyes and shook her head.

"I don't know how we ever did it in that terrible space. I'm trying to tell the committee the hotel is too small for us and to invite everyone in the office, the professional staff and admin—next year we can't do it in a Boston hotel is all . . ." Barbara went on talking but Julia had stopped listening.

199

She watched Barbara tick her fingers off item by item. Somewhere around eight Julia registered "valet parking." These new partner wives drove her crazy. They didn't know when to stop, when to act gracious or forgive the mistakes of an older generation. She narrowed her smile.

Barbara was closer to Laura Smart's than Julia's own age. Barbara must have thought Roger's admission to the partnership two years ago had meant she'd arrived. She didn't get it. That admission was only the bottom rung on the career ladder at Clayborne Whittier. Maybe the last for Roger.

Julia had heard the rumors. Perhaps once she'd been as naive herself.

"What do you think?" Barbara was asking.

Now Barbara's hand was tugging at Julia's arm. Julia stepped back and away. Barbara noticed, Julia could tell by the blush of anger flaming across her face.

"I think you are doing a wonderful job and working so hard. How do you manage, what with Ted's dinner coming up and plans for a new house?" Julia said, solicitation filling every pear-shaped vowel.

"It's Roger," Barbara enthused. "He really supports me, just like I'm sure Don does you."

Julia pressed her smile higher and wider. What a transparent bit of flattery and how widely off the mark. Support her? Don hardly noticed her these days. Funny thing was, this weekend changed that tune. Only the tiniest bit, but he had paced hurt and lost around their kitchen after the police had departed. He'd stayed to be close to her, Julia had realized. Her perfectly competent and successful husband, lonely and frightened. The moment had not lasted long, but long enough for Julia to decide she had not done wrong, not if it brought him back to her.

"Can't live with them and can't live without them, can we?" The cliché slid from Julia's mouth. "You are fortunate in Roger."

She watched Barbara's face illuminate and was reminded of a fox. She wondered if it was Barbara's pointed face and sharp red hair, or something that ran deeper, to Barbara's instinctive ability to go after the poor rabbit. And she had been the rabbit today. Barbara was worried about Roger.

Well, aren't we all worried about our husbands, Julia thought as she looked around the room.

Are. That's how Julia had said it. Barbara repeated the line to herself. *You are fortunate in Roger.*

Not *were,* but *are.* But Julia was talking about her, Barbara, not Clayborne Whittier. The question Barbara wanted answered was if Clayborne Whittier was fortunate in having Roger.

What did Margaret Sweeny know? She wasn't looking all that confident herself today, Frank being sent off to Funsters and she not even getting it. Barbara chuckled low in her throat. It wouldn't do to laugh out loud. Not at one of these deadly coffees.

Clayborne Coffees for spouses! Were they serious? What male would be caught dead with this crowd? What male was there to catch? Women like Teal had better watch out or they would be going on the long march alone.

That's what Barbara's mother always said, life was no more than a long march to the wooden box.

Her mother had done a good job getting her husband into an early grave, dead of a heart attack two years into retirement. Now her mother was in Arizona, set to outlive them all, Barbara and her siblings. It made Barbara sick when she could have used her mother's help with the kids. But her mother wasn't a bit interested in Barbara's problems. In fact, her mother was eager for Roger to slip up, couldn't wait to say *I told you so* to her own daughter.

Barbara ground her teeth.

"Aren't these cookies yummy?" a perky voice said.

It was a management consulting partner's wife. Barbara swallowed to conform to the pretense of eating.

"Isn't it awful? Two women in this office day-ed."

The consulting partner had transferred up from somewhere down south, Barbara remembered.

"I love these coffees. I think they are the most gracious thang."

Barbara nodded. The woman leaned her face into Barbara's. She smelled like expensive perfume and tic-tacs. Her makeup was flawless.

"Do any of y'all know what happened to that poor girl?" she asked in a breathless voice.

"Laura Smart?"

Barbara hadn't thought of Laura as "that poor girl." Laura had been shrewd and smart and dangerous. Roger had finally admitted there was a story going around that he would be the one transitioned out when Barbara had pressed him after Margaret Sweeny's slip, but he'd denied it was true.

"And that other woman dressed up all funny. Why ever did she want to cause so much fuss?"

The woman stuck to Barbara's side.

"I don't know," Barbara said.

"It's the immorality," the consulting partner's wife said. "TV. I will not let my daughter turn it on to see women as aggressive and foul-mouthed as men. My husband said the first day-ed woman swore like a trooper. He repeated thangs that—I had to cover my ears."

"Emma Browne," Barbara said, "swore no better or more than half the partners."

She didn't know why. She certainly didn't have a second of sympathy for Emma. Emma had planned to make Roger's life at Clayborne Whittier as miserable as hell. She had planned to destroy his career. Barbara knew because in Emma's position that's what she would have done. Of course she wasn't in Emma's position, and she was glad Emma lay six feet under.

"Emma. What a pretty name for a terrible," the woman leaned right to Barbara's ear, "dyke." She straightened. "I shouldn't say that, I know I shouldn't say that and wash my mouth with soap, but that's what a woman like that is."

"Was," Barbara said.

"She was?"

"No, I meant she's dead. Past tense. Was."

"Well I know that. I thought you meant she really was a . . . you know."

Barbara stared at the pouf of hair curving up and away from the woman's head. She looked at the eager, open face. She felt like she was looking into some kind of perverse, fun-house mirror.

"Do you work?" Barbara asked.

The woman's pebble eyes blinked and blinked.

"Outside the home, that is?" Barbara clarified.

"Why Lord no, why would I when my husband is a partner? It's the girls can't attract a man who have to work, poor thangs."

The woman was no longer leaning in but away. She found her escape in the wife of the head of the tax practice.

"You will excuse me, I hope," she said to Barbara as she edged away.

Barbara stood alone and remembered the first years of her marriage when she'd still worked. She had left the software company as second in charge of sales. She'd been the one who'd wanted to quit. Odd to remember now that it hadn't been at Roger's insistence. The reverse, actually.

Would this week have gone this way if I still worked and had a life of my own?

Scarlet O'Hara had a point about tomorrow. All Barbara needed was a little more time and everything would be just fine.

TWENTY-ONE

Dan Malley expected Teal to be unhappy. He hadn't expected fury.

"I can't help," she insisted.

Kathy had explained the relationship to him, how Teal and Roger had been friends from the start of her career at Clayborne Whittier. But it was more than that, Kathy had said. They had a history as colleagues. They'd supported each other through the bad jobs, argued the worth of new Financial Accounting Standards Board pronouncements over lunch hours, and schemed to beat the Clayborne Whittier odds. They'd done pretty well both being partners now, Kathy had reminded Dan.

"I'm not s-s-ure it's a question of help." Dan addressed Teal's blazing blue eyes, which, he noticed, she now cast down. "You know these folks in a way I don't."

The hair around her temples caught the stream of sunlight from the windows beside her desk. She looked stubborn and lit with righteousness.

Dan set his expression in a hard line. "I'm not offering

you a choice. I'm not asking you as a f-f-riend. This is a police investigation."

The look Teal flashed held anger and resentment.

"Fine," she said from set lips. "Please, do sit."

The chair was quite an upgrade from her old senior manager's office where they'd first met two years before to discuss another untimely death. This pair of graceful, modern Italian seats signaled the change in her status. One familiar carry-over remained—the oil painting by the famous artist, Nancy Vandenburg, Teal's college roommate and friend.

"We know how Laura died," Dan said.

Teal tried to resist with all of her will, but the word flew out of her mouth.

"How?" she asked and leaned forward.

She could see Laura's body, angled to fit the audit trunk, a coffin, Roger's car the hearse.

"Cyanide."

She hated the pull of Dan's gaze. It was clear and full of intelligence. Her friend the cop could have been a professor in a different life, but the Malley family had a tradition of offering their sons to the force. Dedicated, dogged and smart—that's what had her worried.

"Suicide?" Teal asked. She understood women preferred poison.

"Before or after she jumped into that trunk?" Dan said without humor. "She have any habits you know of?"

"What do you mean, habits?" Teal asked. Of course, it couldn't have been suicide. But suicide would have made her feel better and lifted Roger off the hook.

"Pick her teeth, bite her nails—"

"Chew gum." Teal squeezed her eyes shut.

"Who knew?"

"Everyone. Laura liked to snap it—pop, pop, pop—in your ear. She wasn't shy about getting in your face when she wanted something. The gum drove most of us nuts, and she knew it. Do you think it was the gum?"

Dan nodded.

"Cute."

"Meaning?"

"Someone must have been having fun with pure hate to watch her put a stick in her mouth and wait for her to drop." Teal shuddered.

"And if you're right, who felt that strongly about Laura Smart?" Dan asked.

Who didn't, Teal thought. Laura's enemies about filled the office. The Janus face of Emma Browne.

"Kathy liked Laura," Teal said trying to sort out Laura's few friends. "I'm not sure how I felt. Wary, maybe. Laura wielded a lot of power by sleeping with the boss and she wasn't exactly crazy about me. I'm a professional problem in her book."

"So, I shouldn't book my wife or you for the murder." Dan didn't make it sound funny. "Who wasn't like Kathy or you? Who did hate her?"

"Who didn't? I mean, just about all of us hated her at one time or another. But murder?"

Dan inclined his head. "Murder."

There was loyalty to a friend and loyalty to the facts and loyalty to her belief that any lie would be caught out and hurt Roger worse. Teal wasn't her mother or father's daughter by mistake, however much she had tried to resist. E. Teal Stewart had been raised to tell the truth.

"There's been a rumor going around about the firm's new policy, the plan to transition out certain partners—"

"Fire?" Dan said.

"Fire," Teal agreed. "But Clayborne Whittier doesn't use that word. Conflicts with our self-image, you know. Admission to the partnership once represented a life tenure, no matter the quality of your subsequent performance, or previous some of the time. There was always a distant office where mistakes could be transferred and buried. It's not like that anymore."

"Downsizing the great firm," Dan said.

"Kathy's told you?"

"Yes."

"Anyway, no one around here knows who's on first, which measuring stick counts, and what counts you out."

"But you aren't worried?" Dan said.

"No."

"Your name never came up as someone tagged to go," Dan said.

"No." Teal knew what to expect next.

"Whose did?" Dan leaned back in his chair.

She saw he understood she would help, however she felt. "Roger's."

Dan surprised her. He did not pounce.

"How about Frank Sweeny's name?" he suggested.

Teal spread her long fingers in a gesture of quizzical surrender. "Yes and no, I guess. I mean, anyone with half a brain bet on Frank. It's not that he's a total loser for the firm, just sort of. But Laura kept the files, and she said Roger was going to be kicked out. Ask Kathy. She saw the memo."

"Why Roger?" Dan asked.

"Because of his part in creating the Emma Browne mess, I guess. The 'loose lips sink ships' rule. He broke it."

Teal enjoyed no rush of conscience rewarded. She did not like pointing a finger.

"Emma B-B-Browne." Dan leaned forward. "Head smashed in with Roger's ghoulish toy. It's not making sense."

Teal gave him an opportunity to say more, but Dan studied his hands like he was fighting the urge to crack his knuckles.

"What doesn't make sense?" she prompted.

"The partner to be put out? It wasn't your friend Roger. It was the one I mentioned."

"Frank Sweeny? But Laura told Kathy—"

"A whopping lie."

"It doesn't make sense."

"No," Dan agreed.

Relief fought with confusion in her mind. Cyanide poisoning as a cause of death made it worse for Roger. She once had helped with an inventory at a company in the metals industry. She and other staff had counted well-marked containers of cyanide powder. That company had become Roger's client as a partner. Teal decided to withhold this information from Detective Malley.

She thought about Roger and Emma. Emma's lawsuit had been the one reason people had believed the rumor that Roger, and not Frank, would be fired. Emma had represented trouble for the man whose memento had struck the fatal blow.

She realized Dan had not discussed his suspicions. Were two murderers walking around? Or three?

"Dan, what's happening on the woman I found downstairs?" she asked.

"Nothing," Dan said and stood. "D-d-damned nothing."

Kathy cornered her husband waiting for the elevator.

"Well?" she said.

"Well what?" Dan replied.

The marriage had been easy from the start for Kathy except for two things, Dan's detective precision and his straight-faced ribbing.

"Do you think Roger killed Laura?" Kathy asked.

"You know I can't tell you," Dan said.

"I showed you what I found. Don't you want information like that anymore?" Kathy wheedled.

She had gone into Laura's auxiliary office this morning when Don Clarke had asked her to pull a file. The double gang, metal drawers weren't exactly Laura's, which is why the cops had not known to rope them off. The cabinets were along the wall of the ante-room between Don Clarke's and Laura's offices. Files held all the partner information and evaluations and a few more sensitive documents related to the most senior managers.

Kathy had found a memo from the Clayborne Whittier management committee laying inside on top of the bottom drawer as if Laura had shoved it in to wait to be filed. The directive from the management committee in New York instructed Boston to terminate Roger. Kathy had seen it before. She took the sheet to her husband.

"Roger Singer?" Dan had said and turned from Laura's desk with a similar document pulled from under the blotter.

Before he'd caught her reading, Kathy had recognized a different name under the instruction to terminate. Frank Sweeny's.

"Who killed Laura? Frank or Roger?" Kathy persisted now.

"I don't know," Dan said. "Time we both get back to work."

Kathy turned her face up for a kiss just like she did at home in the morning. Dan bent his lanky frame to oblige.

"Detective?"

"Officer?" Dan said, snapping upright.

Kathy did her best not to grin, but she knew there was amusement in her eyes. Precious eyes was what Dan called them. Jewels.

"E-E-Excuse me, Katherine, I have to be going," Dan said to reclaim his dignity.

She waved as Dan stepped into the elevator with his subordinate officer. Julia Clarke came off. Kathy wondered how Julia felt about her husband, but this was not a subject available for discussion between a secretary and the wife of the big boss.

Teal sorted the stacks on her desk into logical piles—draft financial statements in one, audit workpapers in another, unanswered correspondence in a third. The busy work made her feel productive while her mind worked on murder.

Emma Browne had been dressed to mimic Laura Smart. Teal closed her eyes to recall the contorted body askew on the toilet—smears of makeup distorting Emma's face and the lycra skirt stretched near to bursting across her hips, blood matted to her head, pupils staring sightless and emptied of life.

Teal had first believed the vulgar charade was meant to be an ugly comment on Emma's unpopular cause. The central claim of the Browne gender bias suit—that the Clayborne Whittier partnership did not judge a professional woman on her merits and that this failure was demonstrated in their advice to change her dress and makeup—fueled this interpretation.

But what if Emma's bizarre outfit had more to do with Laura?

What if someone was sending a message? *Don't fool around with ill-earned power or you, too, could end up dead.* Maybe Laura didn't get the point.

So, who had been the sender?

Roger? He satisfied a lot of preconceived notions about accountants, with his white shirts, blue suits, and striped ties. He still carried the accordion leather bag he had been issued as a staff, finding the partner model inadequate for the volume of papers he chose to haul. He was inept at almost any conversation not related to business or golf.

Roger might be driven to commit murder. He might even work out and execute a methodical plan to offer cyanide gum to Laura, but Teal could not see him bent over with color and a brush to adorn Emma's dead face. Nor could she see him stripping her body and dressing it in those clothes. And there was the manner in which the killer had disposed of Laura's body. Forget wood chippers. Teal realized that the murderer was done when Laura had been dropped into

Roger's trunk. That placement had been deliberate, intended to trap her colleague.

The telephone interrupted Teal's silent eureka of relief.

"Teal?" Don said. "Could you stop by my office?"

It wasn't an invitation.

TWENTY-TWO

She never expected to run into Julia Clarke.

"Teal!" Julia's lips stretched into a smile.

There followed a moment of awkward silence.

"I should let you go in," Julia said. "I'm so sorry you had to find that girl—"

"Laura." Teal said.

"There you are." Ted came up from down the hall.

Teal was not sure if Ted had seen Roger following on his heels.

"Julia," Ted said when he stopped. "What brings you to town?"

He knew how to light his glance with a grin to melt an older heart, Teal decided as she observed the exchange. Partners' wives presented something of a challenge, and the wife of the partner in charge often brought out the worst fawning. But Ted demonstrated nothing crass or obvious in his attention to Don's spouse.

Julia responded in kind, warmth illuminating her deep caramel eyes to the color of pulled taffy.

"Our quarterly Clayborne Coffee for the distaff side. Oh dear, sorry Teal," she amended. "It does remain the wives."

Teal thought the coffees foolish and had said so more than once to Don.

"We should go in to Don," Ted said with a wink and a wave. He pushed open the solid door.

Teal turned back to Julia before she stepped in. "You'll be at the CCF meeting tonight? I'm not sure I can manage to go it alone twice."

"Oh." Julia tapped her forehead. "Glad you reminded me. There's so much on my mind. Yes, of course. Fine."

"What was that all about? Getting in good with the big guy's wife?" Teal heard Amy from behind.

Teal spun to face the senior manager. The comment could have come from Hunt. Either way, it wasn't true. She truly liked Julia.

"What are you doing here?" Teal asked.

Amy wrinkled up her forehead. "I don't know. Just lucky, I guess. I got called."

"Great," Teal muttered. She hoped Don hadn't heard about the Funsters joke.

Don and Ted were beside Don's desk when Teal and Amy entered. Roger hunched by the window and ignored the view of Boston below. The smile he gave Teal was tense.

"Ted alerted me to our problem with Roger going to Michigan with Amy this Wednesday," Don said in a sober voice.

Everyone turned and dipped their heads in uncomfortable assent, except for Amy. The weight in Teal's chest unknotted. This wasn't about Funsters after all.

"Why?" Amy asked.

Don looked like he had not expected to offer an explanation.

"Later, Amy," Teal murmured.

"No, Teal, really. I don't mind." Roger straightened. "The police prefer I not leave . . . the state," he clarified.

Amy formed a question, but let it drop when she caught Teal's eye.

Don cleared his throat. "I asked your detective friend, Teal," he said. "He has no problem with you traveling out to Oostown."

Teal swung her gaze from Don to Ted to Roger to Amy.

"I'm not on the MicroAnswer account."

"I know you're not," Don said, irritation cracking in his throat.

Teal realized Roger wasn't the only one in the room under stress. Don had many annoying habits, but he was a gracious, politic host in his office or at his home, and now here was the second time he did not act in keeping with what she expected. The first had been the other morning.

Everyone waited, uneasy and restless.

"It's a simple site review for the audit, since the Oostown division reports to the Massachusetts subsidiary," Ted said. "The client insists we send a partner. I had scheduled Roger, but you'll do fine."

"Why don't you come out?" Amy Firestone suggested.

She had a voice that carried clear as a bell, and Teal could feel the ring go round the room and land back at Ted.

"I'm scheduled to meet here with local management," Ted said, his voice mild.

Teal turned to Ted. "I'll miss your dinner."

He grinned. "Nice try."

216

"I'm going, right?"

"Right," Ted agreed.

"Well, good," Don said. "That's decided. Talk to Ted or," he motioned with a weak hand flip, "Roger if you need help, Teal. There's nothing else—"

"Except my exact status." The words came strained and high out of Roger's mouth.

"Confined to barracks, I'd say, Rog." Ted laughed as if to remove the sting and shepherded the group to the door.

"A minute, Teal?" Don said before she'd made her escape.

"Sure," Teal said.

Amy walked behind Don's back, making a face which looked like a lap dog's fervent lick. Teal wanted to reach out and give her a shake.

"You understand this is all very bad for the firm," Don said in a close voice once the group had departed.

Teal didn't need a translation. "This" was the combination of Emma and Laura and Roger receiving attention from the police. "Very bad for the firm" meant that Clayborne Whittier's impeccable, near century-old reputation for probity and trustworthiness could be on the line. But Don communicated something else.

He was not feeling all that well about events himself.

Frank could feel the sweat in his crotch. His face began to blister with hives. Margaret held him in the grip of her eyes.

"Where were you Thursday night?" she asked.

"I told you," he whined.

"Then tell me again," his wife said in the voice she used with their youngest as she shut his office door.

He didn't want to tell. He didn't want to admit he'd made a terrible mistake with Laura. How long had he known that Roger never had been the one targeted for transitioning out? From the first rumor he didn't have a doubt, not from the feeling he'd had in his gut. He knew he'd been the rabbit scented by the hounds. So why was Roger the partner most talked about? Frank couldn't figure that out. That's why he'd gone into her office Thursday night and found his proof—the memorandum to Don Clarke from the management committee in New York on Frank Sweeny's termination. But he had found something else—that second copy under the blotter with Roger's name where he expected "Frank Sweeny" to have been typed in. He'd had time only to stuff the memo about Roger into the file and the one naming him under the blotter, but he didn't want to get ahead of himself. He continued to spread the false rumor like everyone else.

Why shouldn't it be Roger, Frank thought, *after Roger's messing up with Emma Browne?*

Frank reached down to scratch the itch. He'd made something of a mess himself, with sticking the stupid memo with the clumsy change in Laura's special file. The police were sure to find out, then he'd have to come up with another lie and another and another until there was no way out.

"Frank!"

He wrenched his neck sitting up.

Margaret never raised her voice with him or the kids. He didn't know how she managed. He loved Margaret for not understanding how he'd been considered a mistake of the Clayborne Whittier system, but he had outwitted his brighter competition and been admitted. Margaret deserved to enjoy life with him as a partner.

He wondered if he should say anything to Roger but decided he had other fish to fry. *Fry,* he smiled. Like Emma Browne in hell. Like Laura Smart. And they thought he wasn't smart.

"Frank!" Margaret shook his shoulder. "Tell me what is going on. The tension upstairs at the coffee, you could have cut it with a knife."

Ted Grey shook his head as he drummed his fingers on his desk.

Amy rolled her lips into an angry pinch. "I did everything I should have done. I showed our test results to Roger—"

"Right. You did the right thing." Ted let his fingers smooth a paper on top of the pile. "But Roger doesn't think MicroAnswer has been shipping bricks?"

"But something's going on," Amy affirmed, her chin thrust out.

Anxiety clutched his gut. Amy's sharp, alert face began to blur as he tried to figure out the meaning of her discovery. Bricks.

"Not before the offering?" he managed. This must be what her cute comment about his going to Michigan must have been all about.

Amy understood, he saw from her expression. "No. I don't think so. This is the first time I saw anything funny."

"Well, at least we won't be hauled in front of the SEC over the financials in the offering prospectus." Ted laughed with relief.

"Don't we have to inform the MicroAnswer board of directors, at least, and then maybe the SEC?" Amy asked.

"Let's take it in steps," Ted said. It was not a suggestion. "Extend the audit tests in sales, look at how material the misshipment is—"

"There's no materiality test for fraud," Amy said.

Ted disliked the too righteous intonation, but she was on to something. "Too right. But common sense, Amy. Before I go running to MicroAnswer's board, I need to know if we're talking about the whole company or some ambitious bastard here in Massachusetts trying to make his division look good. Not every situation requires a full-blown SEC report."

She didn't look convinced. "We should at least talk with Don."

Ted pulled himself loose of the soft chair. "Good suggestion."

Teal did not like finding herself caught in the middle.

"It's wrong how he acted!" Amy said, indignation lifting her voice. "Don stood there and agreed with everything Ted said. I felt like I was part of a cover-up or something. I mean, we're certified public accountants, not company clerks, so why aren't we going right to the SEC—"

"Amy," Teal broke in. "I'm not sure things would be any different if you'd come to me on BiMedics. Clayborne Whittier has a responsibility to get the facts—"

"Which are that MicroAnswer is shipping bricks to make the numbers everyone expects now that it's a public company." Amy agitated the button on her jacket.

"You may be right," Teal began, and hesitated.

It wouldn't help for Teal to step into the middle of a controversy on another partner's job, with Ted having overall responsibility for MicroAnswer.

"You're wimping out because of Roger," Amy said.

Teal shook her head and felt every hairpin holding her chignon gouge into her scalp. Amy wasn't the only person feeling annoyed. Teal took a deep breath.

"That was uncalled for. You can dig harder here when you get back from Michigan—"

"By Friday I hope," Amy said.

"I'm thinking of staying over for the weekend," Teal mentioned.

"Whatever for when we could be out of there by as early as Thursday?" Amy asked.

"I like the lake." Teal couldn't explain how Michigan had been her rival for her mother's attention every summer growing up, and had won. She thought it might be time to see why. Maybe distance would clear her mind of the dead faces of that sad Reesy Mars and Emma Browne and Laura Smart. Maybe Malley would have found his murderer by the time she returned. She didn't want to think about other people's guilt or innocence when there was nothing she could do to help.

"Teal?" Barbara lowered her voice as she spoke into the pay telephone. She scanned the FNEB lobby. "It's Barbara Singer."

"Oh Barbara, how are you?" Teal asked.

"Poorly. Roger's got himself in trouble. He is, isn't he?"

Barbara scratched her manicured nails against the metal box. She didn't like the long pause. Anxiety worked her jaw.

"I'm not sure I know what you mean," Teal said, sounding cautious.

"Yes you do," Barbara snapped at the receiver. "The police. They think Roger beat Emma to death and poisoned that disgusting Laura. Roger would kill me, but I need to know what you've heard. Has your secretary's husband said anything yet?"

"Detective Malley?" Teal asked. "About Roger?"

"Yes." Barbara made hurry-up motions with her free hand and swallowed the fear in her throat. That sex-pot Laura Smart would get her husband into a mess.

"No," Teal said. "Barbara, you're letting your imagination make things worse. Detective Malley will be thorough. He won't go after the wrong guy."

"But they don't want Roger to leave the state," Barbara said.

"Think of it as for his protection," Teal suggested.

Barbara hated the low, professional voice, the voice Teal reserved for work. Barbara should know. Teal had been out to the old house often enough over the years when she'd relaxed and let go.

"But the thing is, Teal, I don't," Barbara said and slammed down the phone.

Teal wanted to let it ring. She didn't want to go another round with Barbara Singer. She hardly had time to talk to anyone before she left for her four o'clock engagement. She let Kathy pick up the phone.

Kathy buzzed twice on the intercom, the signal for an important call.

Barbara would say that, Teal thought. She swallowed her groan as she said "Hello."

But Barbara Singer's wasn't the voice saying, "Detective Malley has advised me to hire a lawyer."

TWENTY-THREE

Teal pressed her thumbs into her temples and tried a deep, controlled sigh, but everyone in the evening commuter traffic remained stalled, her taxi included. It made her want to jump out, watching the pedestrians make progress. She should have taken the T to this afternoon's meeting and would have if Roger hadn't called.

One week ago she had arrived at an evening Children's Charity Fund meeting on time, in her own car, before anyone had died. One week ago, the most surprising item in Teal's day had been her lunch with Julia Clarke.

The cab inched to the right, the driver avoiding eye contact with the motorists he cut off. He knew those BMW and Saab owners had a good deal more to lose than BosCheck #105. The cab caught the green at Beacon and Arlington and hung a right down Berkeley and west onto Storrow Drive.

Teal's back stuck to the hot, plastic seat and she heard the vinyl hiss as she shifted. Someone at BosCheck had taken every precaution and removed the cranks for the back windows. The sheet of Plexiglas separating her from the driver prevented the air conditioning from offering her relief.

As if anything could after Roger's call.

"Detective Malley has advised me to hire a lawyer," Roger had said, worry squeezing his voice an octave higher. "I fought with Emma Monday night. I never expected to run into her in the office—"

"The office?" Teal had repeated.

"Yes, and since she was there, I tried to apologize. She started screaming 'why?' and laughing, like I'd done her a big favor. I lost it and started yelling, and maybe I took her arm." Despair had colored Roger's voice. "Laura saw us."

"But she's dead—"

"That's the problem. The cops think I killed them both. But they have nothing to go on."

Teal had let silence hold the line, her fingers wrapped tight and her eyes closed. Malley wouldn't have suggested a lawyer unless he had something he hadn't had a day ago. Dan wasn't the innocent young officer of two years ago. He didn't work as someone's junior now, and when he ran a case, he ran it right.

"You'll help me, won't you Teal?" Roger had finally asked.

Her moment of hesitation had shocked her.

"Of course," she'd replied, too quickly.

That halting conversation ended, but her discomfort had not. Teal had never worked in opposition to Dan Malley. And what had made Roger think that helping would be feasible? The assignment out in Michigan meant the investigation would take its course without her intervening. Roger was on his own.

The cab pulled up at the CCF office, cutting off a bicyclist with a squeal. Teal checked her watch, amazed to see she had arrived on time. She could think about children now and leave telling Roger she couldn't help him for later.

Roger did not realize the importance of the outside foil and paper wrapper the police had sorted from the trash.

Kathy did. She had overheard Dan's subordinate tell Dan about the search of the Clayborne Whittier rubbish.

Each night Martha emptied the forty-eighth floor baskets right into the garage dumpster for collection twice a week, every Thursday and Saturday mornings. Last Friday, after Teal had discovered Laura's body, the police had taken custody of the trash that had been dumped Thursday night. Their lab identified Roger's thumb and Laura's thumb and index fingerprints together on the foil and paper gum wrappers. The prints weren't difficult to match. All Clayborne Whittier personnel had been fingerprinted after Emma Browne's murder. The cyanide analysis was as easy.

Kathy wanted Laura's murderer to meet her or his just reward, but she did not want it to be Roger.

Kathy turned to divert herself from worrying about what more Dan might have found. Like most mirrors in a restroom, it did not go to the floor but cut her off at the waist. She rose on her toes, squinted, and exhaled. Her stomach flattened. Disappointment made her want to check the size of each breast in a cupped palm, but a strict upbringing had left her uncomfortable with that kind of touching. Dan had eased her over more than a few inhibitions to get her into this state.

She squinted, still disappointed. There wasn't enough

change. Certainly not as much as her new status—current wife and future mother—deserved, future being counted in months, less than nine and more than seven. Her uterus held a January child, a Capricorn. Her tenacious little goat would leave the womb and start the climb. Kathy smiled. Dan had been delighted.

She wasn't as confident in Teal. She'd heard stories about single female executives in their thirties turning sharp and angry with staff who became pregnant. Kathy had tried to talk through these fears with Laura. She almost never talked about her boss to anyone at Clayborne Whittier, but Dan had not understood and Kathy thought Laura, being a woman, would.

But Laura hadn't, not really.

"What do you care if Teal isn't happy?" Laura had asked. "What's your baby got to do with her?"

"Nothing," Kathy admitted. "It's just. . . . She's a friend, and she doesn't have anyone. I hope my situation doesn't make her jealous—"

"How can you think someone you work for is a friend? And what about me?" Laura had responded and effectively turned the subject to herself. "Who do I have? Who that's available, I mean? Anyway, you don't look knocked up. Don't worry about her yet. My advice is screw everyone else. They'd screw you fast enough."

Kathy smoothed a hand over the suggestion of roundness below her tummy. She didn't want to think about Laura right now, but she did laugh, remembering how Laura's indifference had been transformed by the next day when she couldn't show enough interest in Kathy's condition, asking for details on how it felt, how being pregnant made her behave, if there'd been any hidden physical changes. Kathy had tired of the subject herself, and after a joke about pickles, Laura had finally let the subject drop.

Kathy turned away from the mirror. Teal would come around if she did take it the wrong way.

Who didn't love a baby?

Julia Clarke handed the heavy, sweet-smelling infant with reluctance to the agency social worker.

"We are always pleased to see the reason for CCF's work," the board president said. "Thank you for sharing this baby with us."

The HIV-infected child opened her eyes and yawned before she reached out a chubby fist with a smile. The social worker patted the blanket into place and carried the baby from the room.

Julia felt a void as large as a crater in her heart.

"Next item of business, scrapbook materials from all of you for the past year. The office staff has made a start, clipping out what they find in the paper, but we need to give them more support—"

"I'm sorry," Teal interrupted, "but you've lost me on this."

The president gave a brisk nod. "We try to keep the CCF development staff current on our individual noteworthy activities to give them ideas for agency PR. You may remember that when Julia proposed you for the board, we immediately got items in the *Globe* and *Herald* announcing that E. Teal Stewart, new partner at Clayborne Whittier, had joined us—"

"Shameless promotion," someone piped up at the end of the table.

"And it works," another voice chimed in. "Remember the mileage we got out of Julia's handshake with former President Carter?"

Happy agreement buzzed around the room. Julia stiffened her smile.

Teal spoke again. "What are you talking about?"

"You didn't have Don hang it in his office?" The CCF board president turned to Julia. "I'd never be so modest."

"Look," interjected a new voice.

Julia hadn't noticed anyone leave or return, but the woman bearing the file must have left because here she was pulling the old magazine page out to hand it around.

Julia's fingers itched to rip the stupid paper into a million tiny parts.

Teal was watching Julia, who appeared distressed as the clipping made the rounds. It wasn't that Julia didn't continue to smile, but her smile wavered as the light in her eye, so evident when she had held the baby, went dark.

Teal was still staring at Julia when the woman on her right nudged her arm.

"Would you like to see?" she asked.

"Sure," she answered and glanced down.

A younger, gracious, and glowing Julia Clarke looked back, her hand extended to shake the hand of the former president. Teal squinted at the caption.

Commencement speaker former President Jimmy Carter and Alumni Representative-Elect to the Board of Trustees of Hillegonds College, Mrs. Donald M. Clarke, exchange greetings on the podium at Oostown's new civic center.

Teal shifted to hand the clipping over when her eye stopped her hand.

"May I?" Teal said to the baffled woman on her left and brought the picture back to scrutinize it at a tilt to catch a better light.

"Julia," Teal said before she could stop her mouth, "isn't this Emma Browne?"

Teal pointed at the profile on the other side of Jimmy Carter. When Teal straightened, she realized her mistake. Julia was turning away from the table, her face a mask.

"Is that the woman who tried to leap-frog your turn as Alumni Representative?" an older voice asked from the other side of the table. The voice addressed Teal. "Julia told us all about it. Shocking, girls these days. Everything in its good time is what I was taught, but it certainly isn't true—"

"Well, Julia is in the picture with Carter," the CCF president said in a voice designed to smooth troubled waters. "So, please heed this reminder to pass your good news on to the CCF office."

Teal didn't listen to the next topic. She thought about Julia on stage with Emma Browne at her alma mater, which meant they were both alumnae of Hillegonds College.

Julia didn't offer to drive Teal home but waved her regrets as she fled. Teal didn't mind. She had business in the CCF offices before she headed for the T.

She got off at Arlington and walked the seven blocks to Brimmer Street through a near perfect evening. Sea gulls clustered in the Public Garden, a sign of turbulence over the ocean. The wind smelled like a sea breeze. Teal wondered if it would rain in the morning and end the glorious, sunny streak.

Home, Teal stared out her kitchen window and enjoyed the black river. She flipped on the lights after a minute and tossed up a salad heavy with lettuce, brown rice, and adzuki beans with a raisin-pecan roll and goat cheese. The glass of Calera pinot noir looked lovely in the evening light and tasted better. She considered food a pleasure and ate from a lacquered tray.

The copy of Julia's handshake with Carter lay on the counter. The CCF copy machine had done a better job than Teal had expected. Carter looked like Carter, Julia looked like Julia, Emma looked like Emma, even if blotched and a bit streaky. The photographer's credit could be read along with "Oostown, MI" along one side.

Teal caught her breath. Hillegonds College in Oostown, Michigan. Oostown on the west side of the state where a population of Dutch immigrants had first settled in the 1700s. She thought back to her first conversations with Julia, who, doing her duty at a firm function, had asked Teal about her advanced degree.

"My MBA is from Stanford," Teal had said.

"Oh, how lucky for you. I wish I'd gone on for an MS in social work out west. My degree's in English from a college in Oostown, Michigan. Hillegonds, on the lake. It is a beautiful place, but then so is California."

Julia had explained more, about her Chicago grandmother and her Dutch ancestry and the family tie to Michigan and Hillegonds College. These places took on a new meaning for Teal now. She was headed to Oostown on Clayborne Whittier business the day after tomorrow. Teal wondered if the MicroAnswer assignment might take on an unexpected usefulness.

She didn't know what it meant that Julia and Emma had graduated from the same college. Certainly they would have attended in different decades, but, from the buzz at the CCF meeting tonight, they'd crossed paths as alumnae. Perhaps swords better described their encounter from the anger Teal had seen in Julia's eyes when the picture had come around. Given the animosity Julia had displayed, it was less of a wonder that Don had not supported Emma.

One mystery solved, another found, Teal thought.

Roger's "help me" pinged about in Teal's head with her new doubts about Julia. She spread a patch of cheese on the bread and bit down. Divine, and better chased by the wine.

She decided to ask a few questions at Hillegonds College, not for Roger or for Julia, but to satisfy herself.

TUESDAY

TWENTY-FOUR

"Neither of us needs to talk to Midori," Hunt said. "She handled Beej for herself."

"Oh," Teal said.

She wove a stray tendril of hair back up into her chignon. It would drop back to her neck with the first turn of her head. The inside of her skull thumped with a scratchy ache. The day had been too long, with reviewing the BiMedics' quarterly report and worrying about MicroAnswer tomorrow.

"Are you even interested?" Hunt grumbled from his end of the line.

"Of course," she said, but she lied.

"No you're not," he said. "You're hardly paying attention."

"Yes I am," she defended. She tried to remember what they had been talking about. "So, what did Midori do?"

"Told Beej she was flattered by his kind attentions and said he was just like an American *ani* to her."

"An *ani?*"

"Japanese for elder brother. Took the starch right out of our Beej. He's picking on a woman his own age now."

"Who?" she asked in an effort to keep her end of the bargain.

"The consultant we're using to design the megaplex security system. Best in the U.S. and she thinks BG's a hoot."

"She must be desperate."

"And you?"

She caught the subtle shift in his voice, moving between reluctance and a new desire to probe. She rubbed her right temple with a thumb and closed her eyes for a moment. *Am I desperate?*

Don Clarke had acted decidedly odd this morning in the hall. Roger had stopped in her office four times during the day to check on her progress. "Like what progress?" she'd snapped on the last go-round, causing Roger to slink out. Amy had not been herself during either of their exchanges, but Teal couldn't put her finger on what was off. Only Frank had remained true to form.

He had stood in her office doorway not a half hour ago, to say he wanted to talk. She hadn't paid much attention, with Michigan on her mind and ruining her day. She managed to get rid of him by promising to stop in and listen later, after she'd finished with seeing Ted.

Teal saw she still held the phone.

"Hunt?" she ventured.

"I haven't hung up," he said.

"Maybe you should have," she whispered.

"Maybe not," he offered. "Maybe I'm desperate myself."

That's right, Teal realized. Hunt had been joking about

his partner. Teal fixed her eyes on the mess on her desk. Her clock read six past seven.

"I have to fly out to Michigan tomorrow and I'm staying through the weekend to take a break, so what do you say to dinner at my place?" she said.

"Tonight?"

"Tonight. I'll pick up something at Savenors, maybe grill up a tuna steak—"

"And your salad?"

"Okay," Teal agreed. "We can make it simple and easy."

"I've missed you, Teal," Hunt said. The pause was not awkward. She felt the same way. "Is eight thirty too late?" he concluded.

"It'll get me out of here." She knew he couldn't see her spin her hand to indicate her office, but it was one thing she knew he understood.

"Me, too. It'll get me out of here," he said.

She didn't tell him to bring Argyle, knowing he would. Seeing Hunt was hard and easy, the familiar and the familiar. She could never sort which, the hard or easy, should win out.

Martha pushed through the door behind the rattle of the cleaning cart.

"I'll be out of my office in a minute," Teal said.

She wondered if she sounded as defensive to Martha as she did to herself. Martha shook with laughter.

"Girl, you get on your way. Po-lice-man gave me the okay, and I'm going to turn this floor upside down. Anyway, time you got back together with that boy—"

"Martha! How do you—"

"How you think I know? I been waiting outside your

door and you don't have no teeny-baby voice, I can tell you, girl." Martha glared as if to dare Teal to say more.

"I'm not accusing you—"

"Damned right you not accusing me, because if you are, I have the same words for you as I had for that snoop Miz Firestone."

"Amy? Snooping in here?"

Martha snorted. "Bet she would if you had something she was after. I caught her hanging outside—"

"Ready to spare a minute, Teal?" Ted extended his head into the office.

Teal turned from Martha's umbrage in the middle of the room to Ted at the door.

"Give me a second, Ted, and I'll be in."

He bobbed a sharp nod and was gone.

"Martha, I sounded all wrong."

Martha gave a curt nod.

"Amy is a snoop?" Teal asked.

Martha eyed Teal up and down.

"Sure looked like it Thursday night, but it's not my place to say. Not my place. I accept your apology, honey. Now you get through with him." Martha lifted her chin at the door. "You don't want that nice man of yours to be ringing the door at an empty house."

Martha knew Hunt from all the nights he'd waited for Teal in her office in years past. He had liked Martha and always acted charming as he'd listened to her complaints about the failings in the FNEB building design. On her part, Martha had never let Teal forget she thought her dumb not to pursue a life with the attractive architect. All of Teal's degrees made Martha shrug, a career being no substitute for a live-in love. Martha'd been married since she was eighteen and had raised two boys and one girl with her Wilbur.

Martha refused to divulge a word more on Amy. Teal packed her briefcase, changed to her sneakers, then walked down the hall to Ted's open door.

"I'm here," she said.

"Won't take a minute." He motioned her in.

He was what her mother would have described as a "fine-looking man."

"An uncomfortable minute, I'm afraid." He motioned to a chair and waited until she sat. "It's about MicroAnswer and Amy."

Ted was giving voice to what Teal had been avoiding.

"I thought I should say something before I send you off with her for the next two days, but this is a difficult subject."

"I understand," Teal said.

"Amy came to me accusing Roger of overlooking some funny activity with sales at MicroAnswer."

Teal nodded, and Ted went on.

Frank hated waiting. He paced his office, up and down, reaming one ear and then the other with a baby finger, using the opposite thumb to scrape the wax from under the nail and roll it into a ball. He didn't much like Teal Stewart. No, he didn't like her at all, but she was friends with that cop.

The police had turned Laura's office upside down, Frank had heard the rumor from his secretary. They must have found the memo by now and realized Frank was the partner to be kicked out. They must have, but Frank hated speculating when he could have confirmation from a better source.

Teal Stewart.

He picked at his tie, wriggled the knot tighter. He hoped he hadn't blown it. He could imagine Teal's surprise when he offered to trade support for her little protégé if that was the way to find out. He wasn't a fool. Footsteps sounded from the hall, and an eager Frank spun around.

Amy Firestone smoothed the impatience from her face. Frank Sweeny could be as obstinate and stupid as a mule. *Could be? Was,* Amy reminded herself, and getting him into a state would not help her cause.

"What do you know about Roger being transitioned out?" Frank asked.

Amy felt his eyes bore into her face. Roger was not who she'd come to talk about, so she shook her head.

"I haven't heard that rumor."

"It's all over the office!" Frank's voice scratched up and down. "Roger is out."

"I'm not surprised," Amy said half to herself. She contemplated the floor, wondering if she should go on.

"No? Why not?" Frank pounced.

She turned her head back to Frank. She did not raise her voice. "There could be something wrong at MicroAnswer."

"Is that why Ted came out from California? Because of something Roger did?" Frank appeared excited. He went on talking to himself. "Then the change could have been right!"

Amy did not know what he was going on about but didn't mind when he hurried her out of his office without saying a thing about Funsters. If he wasn't going to blame her, she didn't see any reason to explain.

"I can't believe Amy would go around Roger," Teal said, but she heard her own doubt and anger. This was what she'd advised Amy not to do.

Ted inclined his head. "It wasn't comfortable for me or anyone else. I've talked with Don and agreed we need to extend testing—"

"Should Amy and I take a look in Michigan?" Teal asked.

"Yes, but I'd be happier if Amy was not aware of any special interest on your part."

"But she raised the issue," Teal said.

"A nervous senior manager, Teal. I've seen it before when someone's up for admission. I'm not as convinced as Amy that Roger's done a bad job—"

"Or been involved in a deliberate fraud?" Teal asked.

"I didn't say fraud," Ted responded. "You said fraud. We don't know enough yet, which is my point. Amy could be wrong. All I'm asking is that you make a special investigation and report directly to me."

"All right," Teal said.

He stood. "I'm counting on your discretion."

Teal had considered saying no. She couldn't, of course. Not with Ted rumored to run Boston when Don moved up. She wondered if Hunt would understand. She'd have made fun of acquiescence herself if she didn't harbor her own doubts. That's what made judging so difficult—from the inside things looked different. She was a partner now.

"I don't believe Roger could—"

Ted stopped her from continuing. "If anything is wrong, I am sure MicroAnswer's Massachusetts management will be the problem. But really, I expect Amy is off base on this."

Teal nodded. "I hope so."

"If we can get this straightened out, I want to support your Amy for partnership." Ted held the door.

The thrill of being on the inside tickled Teal's spine. Ted was suggesting she could help make Amy a partner. She understood this was an unusual invitation. The power to make partners came with seniority, and Teal did not have seniority.

This had to do with Emma Browne. Clayborne Whittier would be knocking itself out to admit women until its reputation as a bad employer for half the workforce calmed down. Teal was right to sense Amy was up for admission at a good time. It wouldn't hurt her to be credited for some of Amy's success.

There was the flip side, of course. It would hurt to back the wrong horse.

Teal ran into Julia Clarke on her way out.

"The second time this week!" Julia smiled. "I'm going to make my husband take me to dinner. He's been working such unreasonable hours."

"Things should get better now," Teal said, her tongue unguarded.

She was thinking about Julia sitting outside Laura's house. Laura's death would free up a good deal of Don's time. Julia's smile wavered.

"Yes, once these terrible investigations are done," Julia said, smoothing her sleek Charles Sumner dress with a restless hand. "I never liked Laura Smart.

Julia's voice sounded direct and hard. She wasn't lying.

"Or Emma Browne?" Teal suggested.

Julia's eyes flicked up, then down.

"I hadn't realized you and Emma were graduates of the same college."

"Hillegonds," Julia said. "Separated by years, of course."

"And you were on the board?" Teal asked.

"You career women confuse me," Julia said, head shaking.

The statement made Teal pause, but Julia went on.

"What did she want?" Julia tightened her lips to a ghastly smile. "Emma had a profession, all that importance, but she loved causing problems, didn't she? I can't say I regret having her out of my life."

"And Laura?" Teal asked. She could see the agitation in Julia's eyes.

Julia stopped smiling. "She was fucking my husband."

"Fucking" sounded wrong from Julia Clarke. Teal did not try to say "How do you know?" or "Oh, I'm so sorry."

"Don't look so upset," Julia said, her voice back to normal. "The wife is always the last to know. I'm not blaming you, dear—"

"Blaming Teal for what?" Don crossed the reception hall to place an arm around his wife. In the most quiet of motions, she shook him off.

"Nothing, darling," she said. "Just a bunch of silly CCF raffle talk. Teal's co-chair!"

"I know that," Don said and thumped Teal's back. "Off to Michigan, are you?"

Teal nodded.

Don turned to his wife. "She'll be out in that town where you went to college."

Teal noticed his solicitous tone and how his arm went back around Julia's shoulders.

"Business?" Julia asked.

"For two days," Teal said. "Then I think I'll fly up to Traverse City—"

"Planning on a visit to the Upper Peninsula?" Don asked.

"Maybe," Teal said. She'd been thinking more about Interlochen.

"Then try to stay at Annchris House in Gordon Park—"

"It's awfully far," Julia objected, her voice tense.

"Yes, yes it is," Don agreed.

Don and Julia walked the hall to his office. Teal turned to jab the elevator button when she remembered Frank.

"Sorry it took me so long," Teal said.

"You didn't get my message?" Frank asked.

"I've been out of my office."

"Well, I have the information I wanted."

"Great," Teal said. She could see the clock on the credenza behind his desk. Eight ten. "You're working late."

"You bet," Frank agreed. "It pays some days."

Teal couldn't imagine what he meant, but tried to look pleasant.

Back at the elevator, she stopped thinking about Emma and Laura and Julia and Frank and the rest of Clayborne Whittier. She thought about Hunt instead.

TWENTY-FIVE

Hunt was thinking about Teal as he cleared his desk. A part of him wanted to kick himself. The call to Teal about Midori had been a flimsy excuse. What did he expect? The old affair to come alive? Teal to offer him a break from the loneliness of his empty office and emptier loft?

Argyle whined.

"Okay. I know. I've got you, pal," Hunt said as he knelt to scratch the fine, alert head. "But it's not the same."

Argyle's eyes shone, the hazel irises rimmed with a line of coal.

"Don't believe me? Try it for yourself." Hunt put his hands at his hips and looked at the deerhound. "Hunt!"

Argyle swished his tail and raised his head, alert.

"Teal!" Hunt said.

Argyle sprang erect, his long, tapered muzzle poking the architect toward the door. The dog let out a low whine from deep within his chest. When Hunt didn't move, Argyle barked, once, urgent and loud.

Man and dog regarded each other.

"Point taken," Hunt said.

Argyle loped half the length of the drafting room, turned, and tried a soft moan. His curved nails clicked a clean percussion on the hardwood floor as he danced between Hunt and the door, alert and impatient.

Hunt punched off the light angled over his board. He promised himself he would not talk about the megaplex project tonight. Teal thought the investment of public money in a commercial enterprise wrong. "Republican welfare," she'd said when Huntington BG Associates had won the commission.

He had to smile. People always got the two of them wrong, assuming he was the liberal architect and she the conservative, being a CPA. Who they were had never been divided like that, not from the start.

They had met at a party given by friends of friends of friends of his at MIT, just another way to pass a Saturday evening. Teal had stood beside a bucket full of iced beer talking to the host, an acquaintance from her childhood. He remembered watching her come through the living room a little later to search for the hostess.

In those days, her hair had hung to her waist and when she leaned forward it draped like a great, heavy curtain over her shoulder to hide her face, a face that had stopped him cold in the middle of his sentence. He never had finished his story but walked to meet her in the middle of the floor. He learned she'd just arrived in Boston from California.

He hadn't been able to take his eyes off her that night. He'd been jealous when she'd kissed the host good-bye, even though it had been him, not her casual date, who had accompanied her out of the graduate-student dorm.

She was someone Hunt realized he never would get over.

Her hair still showed the effect of the Pacific sun in streaks of honey gold, but she wasn't leaving parties with him anymore, not like that.

Argyle accepted the leash at the outside door, beneficiary of Teal's patient and consistent training. She never had confused love with license. As a result, living with Argyle was a joy.

Living with Teal had not been as easy, Hunt reminded himself as man and dog turned down Newbury Street.

But the memory of their meeting still made his heart race. He had thought her beautiful then. He thought her beautiful now. Beautiful and smart and difficult. She might say it a different way, leaving "difficult" attached to his role in their relationship.

They still pretended it had been a no-fault break, but each attributed to the other an uncomfortable measure of blame. Evenings like this, he was uncertain how to view their end.

He wasn't sure what he would change and understood that there was nothing he could. She had gone her way. He had gone his. They had stayed friends, intimate even, until the freeze last summer. He realized he had not been gracious about her uncertain, new-partner behavior.

The Newbury Street sidewalks were crowded in the late heat of the day. The line for ice cream at Emack & Bolio's bulged out the door. Argyle, who favored chocolate flake in a plain waffle cone, did not hesitate but kept going straight. Teal's house at the flat of Beacon Hill was still ten minutes of fast walking away.

Hunt turned on Dartmouth when he couldn't take the crowd a moment longer. Five pedestrians, two dogs, and a vagrant curled on a bench were the only traffic on the Commonwealth Avenue mall. He and Argyle made good time. At eight-thirty one, he lifted his finger to hit her buzzer.

And again at eight-thirty five.

At eight forty-seven, he looked up from where he sat on the steps to see her wave. She arrived, out of breath and glazed with sweat.

"Sorry. I ran into one person after another trying to leave the office—"

"And you couldn't tell them you had to go." Hunt did not raise his voice.

Argyle didn't understand how to be angry. He circled Teal and rubbed his head up against the hand clenched at her side. His persistence made her palm open to give him a reassuring stroke.

"No," she said, "I couldn't."

They glared.

"This isn't how I wanted things to turn out tonight," Teal said. She raised the bag in her hand. "Tuna steak, greens for salad—"

"And I can see the batard," Hunt conceded. It was his favorite bread from the store.

"I would have been on time if Savenor's hadn't had a line—"

"And you'd been willing to tell Clayborne Whittier to flip off," Hunt said.

"But you don't understand. I'm not," Teal said.

Even Argyle did not try to bridge the silence.

Hunt stood and took the bag.

"So, what's up at the great firm? Any new bodies dropping tonight?" He worked to keep the anger out of his voice.

"None that I know of," Teal said.

The words hit him low and cold.

"Do you want to eat or go home?" Neither her inflection nor her gesture indicated her choice.

"Eat," he said and cleared his throat. "So, looking forward to Michigan?"

He was trying.

"I'm not sure," Teal said. She spun around from unlocking the door. "Roger's in trouble, Hunt."

Hunt remembered when Roger had made partner, the pompous bluster. Teal had been something of an ass herself. *One sorry rite of passage,* Hunt thought, his arm tired from holding the bag and keeping Argyle from taking all the steps inside at a single bound.

"You're thinking he doesn't deserve my concern," Teal said.

He tried a noncommittal shrug.

"Dan Malley's telling Roger to hire a lawyer," she said.

"And what do you think?"

"I think maybe he should if that's Dan's advice."

Dinner was delicious, and Argyle licked his plate of stewed ground round. He lay at Teal's feet, gnawing away on Ronnie Savenor's bonus of a bone for the dog.

Hunt had been attentive as they ate, asking questions about progress on the murders, and she'd admitted she didn't know what Dan had found. They weren't working together on this one.

"What's up with Huntington BG Associates?" she said to change the subject. She watched him shrug. "The megaplex, right?"

Hunt nodded.

She could feel the irritation, the blood pressure pounding up, the flush to her cheeks, and over nothing—a disagreement on how government should invest tax money. *Not in a stupid sports complex,* Teal thought, and hated that Hunt had any part in bringing the plan to fruition. Hunt was watching her with his best black Irish grin. She wanted to kick him.

"You're laughing at me," she said.

"Better than what you're thinking," he suggested.

"So, you have the security all figured out?" she said. She could be civil, interested in his business.

"There are a bunch of sometimes conflicting issues, according to our consultant—security for employees, security for convention activities, security for fans, security for the teams. You wouldn't believe the technical changes from the days of laminated picture IDs and metal keys . . ."

Teal had stopped listening.

Security. Like Jean sitting in the FNEB lobby and running plastic cards past the scanner after six. She remembered the reaction at Clayborne Whittier when the new system had been installed.

"Big Brother is watching" signs had blossomed in all the johns. The slogan had reflected more than a paranoid fear. It was true that Clayborne Whittier now received routine reports of every employee's comings and goings after 6:00 in the evening and before 8:00 in the morning. The reports went to the partner in charge. Kathy had kept Teal informed since Kathy knew from Laura what happened to the reports.

This is where the paranoids were wrong.

Don Clarke wasn't a bit interested in the role of time

cop. He dropped the unopened envelope on Laura's desk each week to be filed. Cheating on hours still resulted in staff being fired, but the building security reports had not become the means by which one was caught. Dishonesty continued to come to light at Clayborne Whittier the old-fashioned way—when a manager reviewed the reports of time charges accumulated by a client and asked tough questions about unusual or excessive staff hours.

But the high-tech computer record of night office comings and goings existed, should anyone look. *Like the police,* Teal thought.

She glanced at her watch. Jean would be on his shift in the lobby. She wondered what he knew about the security system.

There was only one way to find out.

Frank straightened up his desk, feeling fine. Better than ever since the rumor about Roger had come out. He could tell Margaret it wasn't a mistake. He picked at a small car-buncle on his face. Amy Firestone had him a little worried, seeing his relief, but he could handle her. He'd handled worse.

He packed up his briefcase with selected memos from his bottom drawer and a file with more detail. He considered putting in a call to the senior manager who had worked with him on the internal review in California but decided his lit-tle bit of gossip could be delayed until tomorrow. He wanted to get home. Margaret would be pleased, proud and pleased.

Amy Firestone had astonished him. She was no novice at the Clayborne Whittier game. It wasn't much different from the military—stay in the chain, let the commander take the first bow. He had never considered her in his corner. He smiled. Her accusations about Roger deliberately overlooking the false shipments could get Frank off the transitioned-out hook. Or get her fired. It had surprised Frank, her saying so much.

Once in a while it was nice being surprised.

"You're crazy," Hunt said.

Argyle was tangling Hunt's legs with the leash as the three of them hurried down Beacon Street.

"And you're angry," Teal said.

She had changed before they'd sped out of the house, but still she felt sweaty under her Cirque du Soleil T-shirt, the sharp sweat of anxiety.

Hunt spun to face her at a stop and momentum slammed her into his body.

They recoiled one from the other.

"You're right, I'm angry. I'm furious—"

"Because what? Because I'm loyal? Because I'm worried about a friend—"

"Roger's been a turkey," he said. "He doesn't deserve your concern."

Her mouth dropped open. "How would you feel if I said that about Beej? It's the same. Roger's my partner—" Her own labored breathing stopped her.

"It's not the same," Hunt said. "What's Clayborne Whittier? An intimate partnership of eight hundred souls? And how many staff? Huntington BG Associates is just BG and me."

"And staff like Midori. Anyway, Roger only started a

year before me. We are close, like you and BG. Roger may be annoying, but he isn't guilty, Hunt. He couldn't have killed Emma Browne or Laura Smart, I don't care who thinks he did." Her voice cracked, then rose. "You don't have to come with me."

Argyle whined. He hated their fights, the raised voices. The day Teal's temper led her to hurl Hunt's glass of wine against the wall had set a younger Argyle to miserable howling. She never threw a thing after that day, but they still fought and were setting up to rip into an argument now.

"I'll help."

"What?" Teal snapped.

"I'll help. Look at the security with you," Hunt said. He took the leash from her hand. "Heel, Argyle."

The deerhound nuzzled Teal with an aquiline nose, and the three resumed at a walk.

"I just want you prepared to be wrong," he said.

"Well, I'm not," she responded, but she didn't pull ahead.

She wasn't prepared for Roger to be a murderer, but she couldn't come up with the better alternative, yet.

They waved at Frank across the lobby. He was headed for the garage, where another security light would read his card and record his exit time.

Teal asked her questions of Jean, only to be disappointed. He could not access the security data from his desk, only scan the employee key card and read the most recent activity on the screen. If the card wasn't valid or had been stolen, a warning message came up while the silent alarm was dialed to the police.

"That's all I know about this," Jean said. "I am sorry."

Hunt pulled Teal aside before her frustration erupted.

"I have an idea," he said.

"Make it good," she snapped.

"It is."

WEDNESDAY

TWENTY-SIX

Hunt, famed and controversial architect of the First New England Bank building, had hurried Teal up to her office, asked her to wait in the hall, and made one phone call. Teal had pretended she didn't mind, and hadn't once he'd produced his results—a fax of the FNEB security log from the Monday night Emma had been murdered and the same from the Thursday Laura had died.

The pages lay heavy on Teal's lap in the morning.

She waited until the plane taxied off the runway. Amy was seated a good seven rows behind. The distance between the partner and senior manager followed Teal's rule for business travel.

"Never," she had instructed Kathy on Kathy's first day at work, "seat me beside a colleague on a plane. Make any excuse."

Kathy had failed only once, when Teal had flown to a New York meeting with Don Clarke. Laura Smart had made those arrangements.

Teal looked down at the stack of data. Hunt's renowned consultant on the megaplex had been responsible for the design and installation of FNEB's security. The woman had used her hacker's skill and privileged knowledge to call up the information. Twenty-five pages of gibberish lay in Teal's lap.

Teal held a third report in her hand. These pages paired the pass code assigned each individual at Clayborne Whittier to a name. She squinted at the small print until she found herself: 9230320, E. Teal Stewart.

She bent to her briefcase and withdrew a yellow marker. The section 923s denoted Clayborne Whittier, so she scanned for 0320 on Monday. What had she done that day? Finally she found: 9230320 6:20 P.M. OUT.

She could have sworn she had left later, but how could she sort one memory of a long day from another? "9230320" did not return. She could see this was going to be tedious. A person entering the building after 8:00 A.M. and leaving for good by 6:00 P.M. through either the garage or front lobby would not appear on the report.

Emma Browne had died after hours. So had Laura Smart.

An average workday being what it was in public accounting, that both the women had died after dark eliminated just about no one. Teal groaned. The gentleman beside her clutched his *Forbes* tight up to his nose.

"Don't mind me," she said turning. "A project."

She rattled her papers. He shrank farther away. *So much for meeting someone engaging and congenial on a plane,* Teal thought.

The captain announced the trip to Detroit would benefit from a tail wind. Teal flipped open her service tray, turned on the overhead light and set to work.

Amy wondered what was going on. Teal always refused to sit next to people from work, but she acted different today. Actually, their relations had been strained for a week. She wanted to press a hand against the place on her chest where her heart pounded her ribs in and out but worried she would look strange.

How could Teal know? Teal couldn't know.

The only witness to Amy's confrontation with Emma had been Laura.

Now a funny taste invaded Amy's mouth, the taste of the vomit she had puked when Teal had told her she had found Emma dead.

SUE. How Emma had laughed and slapped at Amy's arm. Amy had been so pleased to see Emma in Boston. So proud of SUE.

Amy had drafted the first issue of the subversive newsletter herself to answer the Clayborne Whittier management committee statement issued to "all professional staff" with its platitudes about women and opportunity and Emma Browne's "misguided" lawsuit. The statement had made Amy gag. She had never cared about Emma Browne, not personally. She cared about the righteousness of Emma's fight. She cared about equality.

And that's what she'd written, copied, and distributed in the Boston office under the byline "Anonymous." Then the avalanche had started—women in Clayborne Whittier offices across the country calling Boston for copies.

Amy raised her eyes to the small rectangle of window. She saw not her own but Emma's face. She heard the echo of Emma's derisive howls bouncing off the women's room tile.

She could smell the exotic perfume as Laura had stepped out of a stall.

Amy shook her head, but the history of that night remained engraved in her brain.

Laura had been everything Amy despised—a woman who used her sexuality to get ahead, a woman who refused to work for other women and fawned over men, a woman who laughed at Amy's clothes and her vision of a gender-neutral world.

That woman had overheard.

The cause of the argument with Emma made the situation more ludicrous, had Amy been in a position to see the humor. Frank Sweeny.

Amy did not want to be flying to Michigan with the Boston police looking into her actions the night Emma had died.

The tedious job was going to take forever. Teal wrestled to sort out the facts of Monday. Emma must have entered Clayborne Whittier during normal hours because she had not been signed in as a guest by anyone else. Everyone knew now that Emma had never departed.

Jean maintained that the security routine required each building tenant to use a card to go in and out after hours and each guest to be authorized and to sign the log. Don Clarke had come in early and departed late. Laura Smart had paid a night visit to the office.

Teal scanned her list of employees. Roger Singer. Frank Sweeny. Amy Firestone. Ted Grey. Kathy Malley. The names of people to look for went on and on.

Her own record of activity that night challenged Martha's constant advice to "get a life, girl!" It looked like she had not worked particularly late, for once, having left long before Emma had died. She stopped to rub spots from her eyes. A crackle and whine preceded the announcement from the plane's intercom.

"Please place your tray tables and seats in the upright and locked position to prepare for our final descent into Detroit."

Teal didn't mind. She was tired of chasing a murderer on paper. She was generally tired today. Maybe she should drop Martha a note. "Have a life. How's yours?"

Argyle's whine, not an alarm, had brought her awake that morning. Hunt had carried her near flat overnight bag out to the cab. Some things felt like they had before. Better even.

The landing gear released with a grind and Teal's ears began to pop.

Amy caught up with her at the gate. The next plane would take them to Grand Rapids. They'd be in Oostown before too long.

Frank loved his Cadillac. He loved the calfskin interior, soft as a baby's butt. He loved driving around with a sound system better than most people could afford for their homes. Most of all, he loved that no one else in his family came close to owning such an automobile.

He never hesitated to lend it to his brother, his older and only brother, the child his parents had banked on for their old age, and Billy had made the Boston College grade in academics and at hoops. Frank had squeaked into the community junior college and had transferred to a local four-year institution for a major in accounting when he had the grades. It had taken him five years for his BS.

Today Billy made under forty thousand teaching math and coaching junior high basketball. Frank made over two hundred thousand in a bad year and didn't have to deal with teenagers.

He never said a word to his parents, never said you should have believed in me, just paid the deposit and the annual assessment on the senior community they'd chosen. He'd never made Billy feel like the failure, except to offer to pay when Billy tutored the kids.

Still, it bothered Frank that his brother didn't seem to notice, didn't go out of his way to guarantee that Frank's children made the grade or to fall all over Frank with thanks for loaning the car. Billy hadn't said a word last night, just left the Caddy with the keys in plain sight. Any fool could have stolen it from the drive. Billy refused to learn how to operate the control to open the garage. A math teacher and he couldn't be bothered!

Frank turned the key. Billy at least had left a full tank, as he did every time, as though Frank couldn't just be gracious and make the loan without expecting payment.

Frank realized he was plucking at his bald spot, caught in his jumble of thoughts. Margaret was waving from inside the front door, the morning sun catching her face and the shine of her hair. She made the baby wave. Frank waved back and put the auto into reverse. He didn't have to brake but curved to the street, where he flipped into drive.

Margaret blew him a kiss.

His parents had expected him to move south—Hingham or Cohasset or maybe Marshfield—but Margaret had refused.

"I'm not living on the Irish Riviera," she'd said.

Frank wished she would. His best friend lived down there, but Margaret had insisted on Concord because that's where Louisa May Alcott had once had a house. Margaret owned a first edition of *Little Women.* So the Sweenys had bought a big reproduction colonial not far from the center of town.

The good news was that it gave Frank an easy commute to work. He made it a policy to wait until the worst of the morning traffic died down. Where Route 2 widened at the intersection with 128, Frank eased the Cadillac into the fast lane. He liked fast cars and slow women, that's the joke he told Margaret.

The car climbed the hill at the Arlington and Belmont line. Winter sleet or snow could make the steep incline slick and dangerous with ice. Today the hill gave only enjoyment, with a stunning view of Boston from the top. He didn't know why, but seeing the buildings shimmer made him think of *Planet of the Apes,* where the city rose in the distance from the barren landscape.

The car came over the top and Frank eased off the gas to touch the brake. His tap sunk the petal to the floor—no resistance, no response. The car sped down the long, steep slope, Boston dropping from view like it had never been in front of him.

He did not notice with his blood pounding. He pumped and pumped his foot up and down, but the car did not slow. It did not stop. The wheels spun faster.

Frank saw himself in the car as if from above or beside,

saw fear goggle his eyes, saw that the coast to eternal life was not clear, saw how garish the makeup had made Emma Browne, saw Laura Smart laugh in his face. What had they done to deserve their fate?

He prayed like he had never prayed before, offering to make a confession and a new start. His car flew past the other traffic as he fought to steer. When the Cadillac missed a Wagoner by inches, Frank crossed himself to thank God.

He didn't see the pickup truck.

TWENTY-SEVEN

"You aren't going to believe this," Kathy said.

Teal readjusted the telephone between her shoulder and ear as she twisted to watch Amy one tele-space over. Airport noise gave unexpected privacy to the open booth.

"Really, you aren't," Kathy repeated.

She stopped looking at Amy and obliged.

"What?" she asked.

"Frank Sweeny nearly killed himself this morning!"

Teal jerked alert. "He what?"

"I guess his car brakes let go. Can you imagine, no brakes on Route 2 at the hill—"

"You're joking," Teal said.

She remembered following the paper trail on Frank. He had been out and in and out that Monday night. She had starred his security code, someone to point out to Malley, who Kathy admitted had the same report. Teal wasn't sure she had the patience to work on the dense data anymore. So many Clayborne Whittier staff and partners had been in and out. The cops could do the job.

"He's all right. Shaken, but all right. Some guy in a

pickup realized Frank was in trouble and forced him to take the exit that turns. You know the one. Anyway, the guy saved Frank's life. He was just in here looking for you."

"You told him I'm in Michigan?" Teal said.

"Yep. And speaking of cars, your mechanic called."

"And?"

"And the 190SL will be ready at the beginning of the week."

"And?" Teal prompted.

"He wouldn't tell me. Except he said to remind you of your love for your car and the garage still only accepts cash, so bring a full wallet. Oh yes, and it's running 'like a top.' "

"An expensive top."

"You said it, I didn't," Kathy agreed.

Teal ran a fingernail along the small perforations in the sound divider to her right. It didn't give the satisfaction of connecting dots. No happy bunny or cozy country cottage emerged from chaos.

"I know, I could drive a Honda. Should I call Frank, did he say?"

She could hear Kathy's hand lift from the mouthpiece, where she must have put it to mask her laughter. Kathy disapproved of Teal's attachment to the ancient Mercedes.

"Frank will try you in Michigan later. I gave him the number. Did I do okay?"

"Perfectly." Teal paused, but knew she had to ask. "Kathy, what's Dan saying about Roger?"

Kathy did not replace her hand over the phone to block the line, but the distance between Boston and Grand Rapids grew longer. Somewhere in the terminal, a child screamed for her father. The intercom announced last boarding for a flight. Amy, finished with her call, motioned to Teal with impatience.

Teal knew her question placed Kathy in a difficult position. Secretary and partner never had faced an issue this way. But here it was, Teal putting Mrs. Detective Malley on the spot.

"I have to ask, Kath," Teal said.

The silence lingered.

"Dan's a cop." Kathy sighed. "You know Don Clarke specially put in the request for Dan to be assigned this case."

"Yes," Teal said.

"I don't know what to say."

Teal heard the sigh across the line.

"My fault. I can't expect you to talk behind Dan's back," Teal said.

"You hoped," Kathy said.

"Yes."

Teal understood it must be difficult, the tug between old friend and new husband.

"He doesn't tell me anything anyway," Kathy said in a too perky voice. "Oh, but I found this out myself. Roger isn't the one about to be fired."

"It's Frank."

"You knew! How?" Kathy sounded disappointed.

"Your husband let it slip, but it makes more sense," Teal said, not wanting to fuel a marital fire.

"Laura lied," Kathy said. "I guess I'm not surprised. But Laura could be like that, making trouble for someone, making them think twice."

"But why pick Roger?" Teal asked.

"Why not? When he's thinking about a divorce—"

"He's what?"

"When Laura told me, I thought you must know—"

"Roger and Barbara?" Teal heard the hurt in her voice. How would Laura know? Roger didn't talk to Laura.

"Maybe I'm wrong. And maybe Roger wasn't even Laura's target," Kathy said.

Teal could imagine Kathy's tolerant shrug and her pale, clear face concentrating in thought.

"That's what Dan and I have to find out, right? And notice the *and*," Teal tried to joke. "I'm all for helping your spouse—"

"You just hope the murderer isn't your buddy," Kathy said.

"Right."

"I'm on the same side, Teal," Kathy said.

"So, do I have any other messages?" she asked in her best brisk, professional voice.

"The Fidelity guy who follows BiMedics? He called and would you call him back, please. Something about the revenue recognition policy," Kathy said.

Teal raised her eyes to where Amy stood and mouthed "BiMedics, revenue recognition," through mute lips. Amy cocked her thumb and forefinger like a gun.

Amy had predicted the question.

"Some analyst will be all over you with the release of these numbers," she had said when Clayborne Whittier had finished the quarterly review at BiMedics.

Teal had hoped Amy wouldn't be right. Hot-shot technology companies like BiMedics received too much hype, went public at high, distorted stock prices, then garnered quarterly calls from anxious analysts.

The fact that BiMedics had adopted a conservative revenue recognition policy actually made it worse on occasion. Similar companies with more aggressive accounting were reporting better short-term sales than BiMedics. Every few months, Teal fielded the questions and explained the positive effect of the company's accounting on the long-term outlook to the brokerage house analysts and *The Wall Street Journal.* BiMedics had been the subject of more than one favorable "Heard on the Street" column after these talks. She wished analysts were smart enough not to need the quarterly repeat.

"What's his number, Kathy?" Teal said, resigned.

She held up a finger to Amy and made the call.

"Everything okay?" Amy asked when Teal stepped away from the telephone.

Teal nodded. "Fidelity is satisfied. Ready for the drive to Oostown?"

Teal closed her eyes and tried not to get too excited by her new thought. What if Amy was right about the MicroAnswer sales? It could be that someone at Clayborne Whittier other than Roger knew that everything at MicroAnswer was not right, someone like the partner in charge of the corporate account, someone like Ted.

Ted Grey, wonder boy. Pre-med in college, he'd decided to work a few years before going on to become a doctor. But he'd never left his first job and had taken a special masters in accounting designed for talented young people who wanted a program of study with employment. He'd passed the CPA exam in one sitting and became the firm's youngest senior manager, then youngest admission to the partnership, and had headed the firm's participation in the decade's most spectacular IPO, MicroAnswer. Now he was the rumored candidate for a partner in charge assignment to the Boston office.

Teal sat straighter.

"Did you happen to tell Emma about your trouble with the MicroAnswer sales number? What you thought about Roger?" she asked Amy.

She couldn't read Amy's face because the manager had her eyes on the road.

"Yes," Amy said, after a moment of hesitation.

"And what did Emma say?"

Amy swung her head to Teal. Honking erupted from the car in the lane to their right. Amy faced the road and wrenched the wheel straight.

"Anything? Did she say anything?" Teal asked.

Amy shrugged. "No."

But Emma might have said a lot to Ted. And Emma was dead.

"Did you tell Laura?" Teal asked.

"No!" Amy stabbed her chin at Teal in annoyance.

Teal watched the edge of the city blur in expanded fields of green and clustered trees, here and there interrupted by a billboard. She thought about Emma.

"There was what Roger said," Amy said. "Last Wednesday? I told you I tried to talk to him, and he acted like my worry about sales was some big joke in front of Ted and Laura."

"And Laura heard you?" Teal asked, wondering if she would have welcomed Emma Browne as a partner.

"I said so earlier, didn't I," Amy snapped. "She wasn't deaf."

Teal noticed Amy's knuckles go white.

Laura Smart had been an operator. Had she been capable of blackmailing Ted? The idea didn't strike Teal as far-fetched. And, like Emma Browne, Laura Smart was dead.

Kathy had said Frank had been almost killed this morning. Frank, the partner who had headed the internal review out in Ted Grey's California office where MicroAnswer was the biggest client. Frank's team had to have taken a close look at that audit.

"Did you ever ask Frank if he noticed something funny with our work on MicroAnswer in California?" Teal asked.

Amy's "no" rattled the rental car interior.

"I'm surprised," Teal said, her voice quiet, "considering MicroAnswer's Massachusetts subsidiary has you worried. I'd have talked to Fra—"

"But I'm not you!" Amy set her mouth in a line.

"I can ask him myself," Teal said.

Amy had her surprised, not pressing Frank. What was wrong with this picture? Amy had to have wondered about Ted. He had much more to gain than Roger. Teal glanced at the senior manager.

"Is everything all right?" she asked.

"Fine." Amy did not invite further discussion.

Don Clarke stood from his chair.

"Frank." He motioned to the couch.

Don hated the couch no matter what the firm's human resources department said about their creating "islands of equality with a hierarchical neutral comfort zone" in the office. It had taken Laura to make him enjoy the fool thing.

He sighed to mask a moan. Laura had been many things, trouble first among them, and he hated himself for missing their stolen pleasures on the couch. A sharp tongue's lick. No. He could not let himself think of this. Her death offered an escape from disaster. That's how he needed to think of it.

Frank cleared his throat. He had said it was a personal problem he wanted to discuss, which was why Don sat them on the couch. Don hated personal problems.

"I don't like to be the one to tell you." Frank shifted the phlegm in his throat. "But your wife knows."

Don watched Frank run a hand over the velvet plush and felt the chill. His hand had traveled the same distance up Laura's leg on this spot. His fingers had found the elastic bands of her nylon panties about where Frank sat. His body began to react, and he shifted with embarrassed discomfort.

Personal, Frank had said. He never identified for whom. Don had assumed wrong.

"I saw Julia the other night," Frank said.

Don watched Frank trail his fingertips where Laura's head would have arched to receive a kiss.

"It was the night Laura died," Frank said as if his statement needed to be clarified.

Don turned a stiff neck to look outside. Julia's behavior—did she know he had called their lawyer? He wished he could take out his handkerchief and wipe his face, but it wouldn't do with Frank so close.

Frank pulled at his shirt collar and swallowed.

"I need your help deciding," Frank choked out. Nothing more came but a rattle of throat noise.

"Deciding what," Don snapped.

Frank's face remained guileless as he replied. "If I should mention that Julia was up here to the police. I feel uncomfortable, knowing how Julia must feel about Laura. And with Laura being murdered . . ."

Don dug a nail into his palm. "So you were in the office."

He waited to see if Frank got it.

"I love Clayborne Whittier. Margaret loves being a partner's wife—" Frank's voice deteriorated to a whine. "Is it true about Roger? The rumor?"

"Rumor?" Don repeated. The partner in charge was the last to hear rumors.

Frank worked his mouth open, distinctly nervous. "Laura told me Roger was going to be fired—"

"We voted on you," Don interrupted, his voice harsh.

This was not how he had intended to make the announcement, but Frank's attempt at coercion was infuriating. Frank was almost talking to himself. "The memo in Laura's office about Roger? I thought, after all, that the trouble with MicroAnswer had made the management committee change its mind."

Don had no idea what Frank was going on about.

"I don't want to find another job. I saw Julia—"

"You said that," Don said to cut Frank off and get him out of his office.

Julia stared down the hall, then swiveled her head to follow Frank's retreating back.

"That wasn't like Frank," she said. "You don't imagine Margaret is going to have another baby?"

Her husband remained rooted to the carpet.

"No! Really?" Julia said, astounded. The thought of Margaret pregnant broke Julia's heart.

"No," Don barked.

Julia jumped. "Are we grumpy today?" she asked.

"Busy."

Julia pulled her arms to her side and stepped back. "I just thought since I was so close by—"

"I don't have a lot of time," Don said.

Julia watched his hurried motion. She could feel the migraine starting. This was going to be harder than she'd hoped.

"I just thought I should know, with the police asking and all. What were you doing the night your friend Laura died?"

Teal expected Ted to call at the end of the day.

"Anything new to report?" he asked.

"I'll be finished with my look at the shipping and billing activity tomorrow," Teal replied.

"Oh." He sounded disappointed.

"And you still prefer I not discuss my assignment with Amy? It doesn't feel right," Teal said.

"I'm grateful she's been so astute, but I think we don't want to encourage more speculation at this point."

"She's discrete," Teal said in Amy's defense. "I expected she would have talked with Frank about what he found out in California, but she didn't."

The moment the words left her mouth, she wished she could snatch them back. Internal reviews like the one Frank had led in Palo Alto were to evaluate the competence of

Clayborne Whittier partners and staff and were not a reaudit of a company's books. The results were highly confidential within the firm. She'd as good as told Ted she suspected he could be crooked.

He didn't take offense but chuckled at his end.

"No harm to check. I've had Roger at the Massachusetts numbers again. I'll get my manager out in California to check over our sales testing, and why don't you talk directly with Frank?"

Teal didn't have to say she planned to because Ted made it easy. He transferred the call.

THURSDAY

TWENTY-EIGHT

Teal closed the binder of sales reports. She leaned back in the old, wooden desk chair and shut her eyes. The MicroAnswer review in Michigan was done. Sales reports, shipping logs, bills of lading, even the answers to her questions of company customers—all the data tied together to support the propriety of each recorded transaction.

Her study of the FNEB security logs, after she'd woken up tense with insomnia and turned to them as a last resort, had yielded no more revealing results.

Teal set her fingertips to her forehead, but she could not rub away the lines of fatigue marking her brow.

The number of Clayborne Whittier staff and partners and guests entering and exiting the FNEB building on the night when Emma had died had exhausted Teal's patience. But one thing was clear—Ted Grey made no appearance in the report.

Teal hated to let go of such a tidy suspect, but unlike MicroAnswer's sales, the data on Ted Grey weren't there. Nothing going on with his big client, and he hadn't been around when Emma had died. She opened her eyes and sighed.

"Bad timing?"

She swiveled her chair, which gave a reluctant yowl, and tried to smile.

"You're working too hard," Amy said.

"Unlike you, right?"

They laughed together, the sound pleasant and pure.

"I called the airline. I can get on the earlier flight if I skip lunch," Amy said.

"Hot date tonight?" Teal asked.

Nervous giggles distorted Amy's mouth.

"Who?" Teal pressed, intrigued.

"No one, really. It's . . . nothing like that," Amy fumbled.

Amy looked awkward standing in her navy wool suit and white shirt with a paisley bow. Teal felt a flash of compassion.

"Look," Teal said. "It's only fair you know the results of my review—"

"There's a problem with sales?" Amy interrupted, her head tilted to the side.

"No." Teal lifted her hands, palms open and empty. "MicroAnswer isn't doing anything funny here in Michigan or anywhere else."

"Oh," Amy said without disappointment or surprise.

"It's the issue you raised. Remember? You were so angry about Roger's reaction that you went to Ted?"

"Guess I was wrong," Amy said.

Teal hoped she was in control of her face. "Guess you were wrong? Well, you were. But not before your suspicion made me stick my neck out and wonder about Ted. The corporate partner on the account has a lot more to gain than the partner on subsidiary work. Imagine the damage to Ted's career if MicroAnswer's roaring success had been based on sham sales he had helped to generate."

Amy fingered the loop of her bow. She didn't meet Teal's eyes.

"I went so far that I talked to Frank about the review in California. Then I discussed your testing with Roger. The company came up with the proper documents."

"Yes," Amy mumbled.

"Yes? What does 'yes' mean?"

"That I made it up."

"You what?" Teal didn't understand what Amy was saying. Amy had to be joking. But Amy's face held no humor.

"I made it up about MicroAnswer—no, please don't interrupt. This is hard enough. If only I had known Emma was willing to get me in trouble—get anyone in trouble—for her own ends, I wouldn't have done it. When I heard about her lawsuit, I just cared about the gender-bias issue, then I realized it had happened to a real woman. The only way to make men get it was to put one of them in her position. Make him feel like a pariah. Roger was easy for me to use because of Ted being in Boston."

Teal held up a hand. "May I ask a question?"

Amy shrugged.

"You're telling me the MicroAnswer accounting for sales is correct."

"Always has been," Amy said.

"But you decided to make up a problem and lay the

blame on Roger." Teal inspected the ceiling. She couldn't bring herself to acknowledge this was her Amy.

"Sort of," Amy mumbled.

"Why didn't you let it go after Emma's murder? Say your extended testing proved things were fine and forget it." She was examining Amy's face now.

"I don't know." Amy squirmed. "I was worried because I'd had this huge fight with Emma the night she was murdered and Laura had seen us and I was scared, so I let it go on to keep the attention on Roger. I made a mistake," Amy whispered.

"Yes," Teal agreed. "A hell of a mistake."

"I took the small trunk with the workpapers I wanted from Roger's office the night Laura died—"

"You took a trunk?"

"Not the big one, the little one," Amy clarified as if Teal had been concerned about the size and weight. "Anyway, I took it down on the freight elevator so no one would see me. I planned to make a few changes to the documentation to help make my accusations look right."

Amy started chewing on her lips.

"You haven't helped the cause," Teal said.

Amy had been on the security report. Teal hadn't thought twice about what the senior manager might have been up to that night. She had assumed Amy had been keeping her usual hours. She'd never thought it might be to sabotage an audit. Or a reputation.

"It's a mess, isn't it?" Amy's mouth twisted.

"Did you alter the workpaper files?" Teal asked.

"No. I worried about it all night and went back about five A.M. so Roger would never know I'd had them. His office was a mess, everything from the big trunk dumped on the floor, and it was gone. I couldn't figure out what was going on but didn't want him to blame me, so I got another trunk from supplies and cleaned up."

"It could have been his mess."

Amy shook her head. "Uh-uh. I saw him leave."

No wonder Roger had not missed his trunk. No wonder the police thought his denial a cover-up. Teal saw shame on Amy's face. Her next words would offer no great comfort.

"You're off my list of suspects and on my—"

"Shit list, right?"

"Yes."

Partner and senior manager sat in unhappy silence.

"What are you going to do about me?" Amy asked.

Teal had not decided. She glanced at her watch. "I know if we don't get moving, you'll miss your plane."

"I can't let Boston off the hook. You can make an exchange, but no escaping the cut," the head of the firm barked across the fiber optic miles from New York as clear as if he spoke in Don's office. "What is this really about?"

"Morale," Don said. "The rumors, the articles about Clayborne Whittier cleaning shop, I think it may not be the time with what's happened in this office—"

"Jesus, Don! I regret those murders, but we chewed this damned decision around for months, called in McKinsey to consult and wet our pants at the alternative. Do you want to lower your compensation to keep a partner like Sweeny?"

The question hung between them.

Why had Frank seen Julia? Don repeated to himself. Laura was still creating problems.

"I think maybe Roger Singer should be the one to go," Don tried out.

"And how's that going to look? Like we kick a man the minute he's down? That's good for morale?" the firm's managing partner sounded annoyed. "You said you don't think the guy is guilty."

Don's palm slid on the receiver as he allowed something between a yes and a no.

"Singer stays. Sweeny goes." The click from New York brought the conversation to a close.

Ted Grey picked up the telephone and dialed.

"I'm sorry, sir, Ms. Stewart just left," the MicroAnswer receptionist in Oostown said.

"And she'll be back when?" Ted asked.

"I believe the review is complete."

"Then Ms. Stewart is heading home?" Ted suggested.

"I wouldn't know. Let me pass you on to the chief financial officer."

That conversation was reassuring as it came to a close.

"Your team did a nice job," the CFO said.

"I'll discuss the review with Teal and give you a call tomorrow," Ted said.

"I think Teal has plans to stay here in Michigan for the weekend."

"Right. I'd forgotten," Ted said. "Well, I'll be back in California, but the three of us can conference call on Monday."

Dan Malley didn't like interrupting a partner on the line, so he waited for Ted's temporary assistant to tell him when Mr. Grey was off. He preferred that the assistant warn Grey of his arrival.

Dan couldn't say he'd enjoyed any of his partner interviews. None of them understood that he could be smart and accept a pay check his size. Police service marked Dan a loser in their eyes, and Dan knew it. A few individuals had been helpful, if brusque. Others, like Roger Singer, had just acted nervous.

Fright didn't mean a thing to Dan. Police upset honest people more than criminals. Criminals could lie without blinking.

Frank Sweeny had been interesting. Emma Browne's name had brought Sweeny's skin up in welts and Laura Smart had added something akin to hives. Frank didn't have a good alibi for either night, and when Dan mentioned the two memos, the man came close to being undone.

Don Clarke had been a different sort. Clarke had crushed Dan's fingers in his grip. But Clarke's explanation of his whereabouts was not convincing, and Dan suspected something important had been left out.

"Sir? Detective?" Grey's temporary assistant tugged Dan's arm. "He's off."

Grey didn't try to mask his surprise, but nothing unusual came out of his mouth.

"You're not from this office, are you?" Dan asked, when the standard list of questions had diminished.

"California, for now," Ted said.

"My wife tells me you are the leading candidate to take over this office when Don Clarke goes to New York."

"Your wife?" Ted asked.

"Kathy Malley—"

Ted nodded. "Right, Teal Stewart's girl."

Dan decided he wouldn't mention "girl" to Kathy.

"What do you think of the operation in Boston?" Dan asked.

"Top notch, officer. What do you expect me to say?"

They laughed in a companionable acknowledgment of all internal politics.

"What did you think of Emma Browne?" Dan asked.

Both men accepted this as standard police practice, the repeat of an earlier question when the interviewee had relaxed.

"A big mistake," Ted Grey said.

"Her murder?"

Ted shrugged. "Perhaps. But I meant how most of the committee evaluated her performance—"

"How you documented the discussion?" Dan pressed.

He knew what Kathy had said. Ever since the mess with Emma Browne, Clayborne Whittier had become very careful with what was written in personnel files. Now all real performance appraisals happened word-of-mouth.

Ted waved his hand to dismiss the comment.

"No. You are right, of course, we are more careful, but the mistake was fighting against her qualifications to be a partner. Emma wasn't a nice person to have around, but she was effective. I thought she deserved to be welcomed as one of us."

"And that's what you said? At the time?" Dan asked.

"Yes."

Dan had to give the man credit. Roger Singer remained the best suspect, Dan concluded. Some important folks at Clayborne Whittier blamed him for the Emma Browne case, the problems he'd brought to the great firm. Laura Smart's malicious rumor didn't help his future. The physical evidence linked to Singer, and he had been in the office both nights.

Singer seemed to be the man, if Dan ignored Kathy's doubts.

"Anything else, Detective?" Ted said.

"No," Dan said.

Teal loved walking a campus again. Hillegonds College formed a cohesive whole, the gothic chapel anchoring one end of a central grove of pines and paths, the elegant new library arching to the sky at the other. Preparations for graduation ceremonies were everywhere evident as seniors lolled on the spongy, grass slopes, their final exams over. One cluster of students directed Teal to the Office of Alumni Relations.

"Julia Clarke?" the young woman at the desk repeated and checked her book. "Julia Wade Clarke, class of 1960."

"And a past alumni representative on your Board of Trustees," Teal added.

The young woman scanned the Alumni Directory. "No, I don't think so."

"But I'm sure I saw a newspaper picture with Julia Clarke and former President Carter here at Hillegonds. She was identified as alumni representative to the Board—"

An older woman stopped her filing and spoke. "I'm afraid it was a mistake. The vote was so close that Ms. Browne insisted on a recount. Julia Wade Clarke came up two short. Of course, it is a tragedy about Ms. Browne."

The woman's compressed lips told another story. The

younger woman, unfamiliar with either Julia or Emma, showed no emotion.

"I told Mrs. Clarke she as good as had grounds for a lawsuit," the older woman let out.

"A lawsuit?" Teal repeated.

"Ms. Browne said terrible things when she made us do that recount. I thought Mrs. Clarke should take legal action, defend her good name, but she refused to stoop to the level of—"

"Emma Browne?"

"You said it. That girl caused problems from the start. Take her senior paper and the fuss it stirred up." The silver-haired woman took a noisy, aggravated breath. "Well, it's all history now and Ms. Browne no better off for the trouble she caused. I said then Mrs. Clarke was too loyal to the college for her own good. But—" the woman shook her head with vigor. "What can you do?"

The library was easy to locate. Teal enjoyed the hush and quiet, the sour smell of paper and ink. Emma's senior thesis was available from the closed stacks. The natural light which washed the page made Emma's words no less dark. She had written of what was now categorized as date rape. Teal could imagine how, at the time Emma had tackled the subject, Hillegonds College had not enjoyed the notoriety Emma's scholarship brought. The thesis, according to the reference desk, had been featured in an article in *Time*, leaving a false impression back then that Hillegonds College had the problem.

To discuss the meaning and ramifications of nonconsensual sex for the victim, Emma had organized her exposition around one story, an alleged rape in Michigan's Upper Peninsula, in a town called Gordon Park.

The name resonated. Gordon Park. Teal rifled through her folder of personal notes on places to visit. Gordon Park! "Annchris House, Gordon Park" was the bed and breakfast Don Clarke had recommended. Teal thought back to the woman in the alumni office.

> That girl caused problems from the start. Take her senior paper and the fuss it stirred up. But—what can you do?

Murder, Teal thought. *You could do murder.*

TWENTY-NINE

"Shouldn't you be hanging up?" Hunt asked.

"I still have time to kill before the flight to Traverse City boards," Teal said. Her life seemed to be spent on telephones, an earring in one hand, receiver in the other. "I could switch and come home."

"Why? You said you need a break." Hunt sounded annoyed.

She knew she was contradicting herself. Couldn't she admit she didn't want to be seeing another new place alone?

"But I have stuff for Malley," she said.

"Then call him."

Argyle's whine rustled the line.

"Does he recognize my voice," Teal asked, eager.

"Malley? How do I know?" Hunt said.

"What's eating at you today?" Teal snapped. "Lose a bid? BG up to his old tricks?"

Not even static broke up the long pause.

"Yes," Hunt said.

"So which? Bid? BG?"

"The latter," Hunt said.

"Still can't control his libido?"

"You got it."

"And he's standing beside you right now?" Teal offered.

"Um-hum."

"Partners—they can make your life awful. Anyway, I'll change the subject so you can talk. I'm thinking it could be Julia," Teal said.

"You're thinking who could be Julia?"

"Julia Clarke—the killer. You remember Emma Browne? Laura Smart?" Teal's voice lifted with impatience.

"Right. So what happened to the Ted Grey theory you went on and on about?" Hunt asked.

"Nada. He wasn't even in the office the night Emma got it, and MicroAnswer doesn't have a revenue recognition problem."

"I think you'd be better off talking to Malley than me right now," Hunt said.

He probably meant it to be helpful, Teal decided, trying not to read rejection into his suggestion.

"Maybe I'd be better off coming home," she offered again.

She turned her lips in over her teeth and stared straight at the departures board. *"Boston Gate 4"* showed opposite the status, which flashed "boarding." She could make the distance in a sprint.

"If you think you can't communicate with Malley by phone," Hunt said, his voice hesitant, "I should tell you I'm not available this weekend. Plans—"

"No need to say more." Teal pronounced each word short and hard with a terminal punctuation. "I might try the bed and breakfast Don Clarke suggested."

She made this sentence breezy and light, then explained Emma's senior thesis on the story of a date rape in Gordon Park. Julia had been uncomfortable when Don had opened his mouth to recommend Annchris House.

"Do you think I should I give the place a try?" she asked at the end.

"What about Interlochen? Wasn't that the plan? To see where your mother studied and performed?" Hunt said.

She wanted to snarl "what about it?" but she didn't. Hunt meant why wasn't she going to visit the place her mother, a retired concert pianist, had spent most of Teal's childhood summers far away from husband and children teaching other people's offspring, giving them attention. Teal had never been to Interlochen in all those years, not once. And she didn't feel like taking on her rival from the past today.

"So, where is it you're going to go?" Hunt asked in a let's-be-friends voice.

Teal considered hanging up.

"I'm not sure. I think I'll just play it by ear."

She didn't consider her remark much of a joke until she heard his laughter over the telephone. Interlochen—play it by ear. Her teeth clamped down.

"Well, have a good time, Sherlock," Hunt said. "I've got to run."

This time she did slam down the phone.

Malley, if possible, made her feel worse.

"Cleaning woman says she saw s-s-someone hanging outside the women's room door the night of Browne's murder," Dan said.

"What does that mean?" Teal asked. "Who? When?"

"She got a late start, something about the T breaking down—"

"Did it?" Teal interrupted.

She knew she must feel contentious. Martha didn't lie, and the Metropolitan Boston Transit Authority system did experience breakdowns now and again like everything in life.

"Water main burst and flooded a switching station. Orange Line lost four hours of service. Ms. Washington got to your floor late." Dan's voice never swerved.

Teal sighed. "So, who'd she see?"

Martha would not have been on the printout that Teal had received. Martha was employed by a service company, not Clayborne Whittier. Teal realized she had missed a whole population of individuals with access to the offices in her research.

"So, who'd she see?" Teal repeated. She hadn't been listening.

"A man in a green trench coat. No, let me get this r-r-right. An 'ugly' green trench coat—"

"Roger's." Teal could not deny the description. "Ugliest thing Martha and I have ever seen. Barbara made him buy it in London at Harrods, and it must have set him back a fortune. She loved the color. He can't find it for you?"

"No."

"Dan, I just don't think it's Roger," Teal said.

"That's what friends are for, but I'm a cop. His trench coat is missing. He had a motive."

"So, everyone knows he leaves it at work. Did Martha use his name?" Teal asked. She amended her question. "Who does Martha say she saw?"

Teal heard Dan crack a knuckle.

"She didn't pay attention. She was rushing to get home and had done the bathroom."

"Well, when did Roger leave the office compared to Martha?" Teal asked. She'd given up on the tedious security reports and couldn't have made this comparison in any case, but tedium was a part of Malley's job.

"No way to know precisely. The time setting has been off since the new year turned over."

Teal thought she heard Malley chuckle.

"What do you mean?" she asked.

"I mean I know you m-m-managed to get a bootlegged copy, but the data are wrong. You people never use the damned things, so no one noticed."

"Great!" Teal groaned, annoyed at her wasted hours. "You guys going to make it right?"

"The security company is trying," Malley said.

"Did you ask Martha if it could have been a woman in the green coat?"

Roger wasn't tall even if he wasn't short.

"I d-d-don't know," Malley said.

"You didn't ask."

"No."

Teal wanted to push an idea forward. "I just learned that Julia Clarke had reason to loathe Emma Browne."

She told Dan about her discovery of Julia's thwarted election to the Board of Hillegonds College as well as her reason to despise Laura Smart. She left out her speculation on events at Gordon Park.

The boarding call for Traverse City caught Teal's ear.

"Look, Dan, I've got to go. I may have more for you by the end of tomorrow—"

"Teal, stay clear of this. You work with these folks—"

"I don't have time. Sorry," Teal said and placed the receiver on the cradle.

Then she ran across the busy corridor as the door to the walkway was being closed.

"Just in time," the steward said.

"Sometimes that's how it goes," Teal apologized.

He grinned and waved her through.

"You enjoy your visit up north."

She certainly hoped to.

The rental cars in the Traverse City airport were parked right outside the airport door.

Teal took a practice turn around the asphalt lot before she let herself head off. A near fatal mistake in a rental had taught her to be cautious. She experienced many joys in owning the 190SL, but her driving habits applied to an automatic always suffered, and she felt awkward without her stick shift.

She enjoyed the long evening at the western edge of the eastern time zone once she was in the boring routine of pointing the car and holding steady on the gas, her left foot tucked safely up and away from misusing the brake as a clutch. At this hour, Boston would look like night. Michigan's Lower Peninsula rose and fell in a landscape of gentle hills thick with cherry orchards. Farmhouses and barns marked the countryside, while the towns seemed to have as many churches as homes.

Teal considered the list of pleasures she would miss by

heading straight north: The Sleeping Bear Dunes National Park where the sand cliffs rose like mounds of sugar from Lake Michigan's turquoise shores. A sunset from the Coast Guard station at Crystal Lake. The tart tang of a slice of Cherry Hut cherry pie in Beulah. Teal should know, she'd heard her mother's excited descriptions of these delights at the end of every summer.

Teal didn't want to judge her decision. She didn't want to think what it might be about. Mixed memories of childhood could be addressed at another time. She had Roger to worry about, and another mother's fate to decide.

For the moment, Teal concentrated on following the signs to take the car onto the graceful incline of the Mackinac Bridge. Lake Michigan lay below on her left, and Lake Huron and Mackinaw Island to the right. The Upper Peninsula welcomed her on the other side, with a different terrain from that she'd left behind.

This land reminded her of Maine's northern Aroostook County. The year she and Hunt had tried camping together, they had gone to remote, inland Maine. That landscape was no flatter than what Teal saw before her, the houses, few as they were, no farther apart. The spareness of both places appealed to a faint longing for perfect solitude.

Almost every car she passed was a pickup outfitted with a serious hunter's gun rack. The mom and pop convenience stores all carried large-letter signs for bait and tackle and offered volume discounts on dressing game. Calculations off her road map told her she'd be in Gordon Park in less than two hours.

———————

By the time she arrived, evening had darkened to a black canvas and the stars had become sharp pricks of light. Annchris House was off the main road to the right. A black cat beat the owner to the door.

"You've met Jelly Bean, I see. I hope you're not allergic. Two more are wandering about." Patricia Mock extended a hand. "Call me Trisha and don't worry if a cat gets out."

The house, a large Victorian, contrasted with the simpler summer bungalows in town. Moonlight showed trees and shrubs and flowers in the yard. An old-fashioned seat-swing swayed on the gazebo to one side.

"Your room is up to the left. We have a full house," Trisha said.

Few women made Teal feel small, but Trisha Mock was sufficiently tall and broad to give her a taste. The woman displayed the no-nonsense attitude of an able innkeeper, but she opened the door to a warmer relationship.

"Sherry is in the library. Settle in, then come join us. I'm afraid your only convenient dinner choice is down the road at the old Gordon Park Inn, and if you want to eat there I'd better call. The square dancers have the restaurant booked, but the Inn takes people for me last minute. And the food's good."

"I hadn't realized Gordon Park had an inn," Teal said.

"Well, not so as it rents out rooms anymore, just the dining and big dancefloor are in operation. Years ago we were quite a resort."

"Did you grow up in Gordon Park?" Teal asked.

Trisha's laugh made Teal smile.

"Yes and no. I worked at the Inn every summer it was open. The sixties and seventies weren't very prosperous for us up here, and it closed. Annchris House was built by the resort's first owner. Named it after his daughters, Anna and Christina. I bought it from the bankruptcy court—"

"And invested a fortune," Teal said. The house glowed with signs of care and was filled with restored antiques.

Trisha chuckled. "Which I have, my dear. I made too much money in the lower part of the state and I'm happy to bring it home. Now—"

Trisha ticked off the few rules of the house, then let Teal go.

The room pleased Teal, being everything she did not buy for her home—frilled, Victorian, and dense with dark furniture. The bathroom pleased her even more, with its enormous ball and claw foot enamel tub and separate water spouts for the hot and cold. It was deep enough to guarantee she'd be warm to her neck. She turned the handles full on to fill the tub for a soak after she unpacked.

She had planned to read the in-box of mail she'd taken from her office, but the comfortable bath made her lazy. She took up the stack after she dressed, planning to skim the few office memos and a *CW/Alumni*, the glossy firm publication targeted to those who had left, with a sherry in the sitting room.

Downstairs a fire burned against the late spring chill, cooling the earth this far north. Cheese, labeled as from the Mennonite farm up the road, lay out with crackers on a plate. An etched glass decanter stood beside matching, fragile crystal glasses. Teal poured a scant half inch of aperitif and settled into the sofa.

She started at the top of her pile with an alert from the Securities and Exchange Commission specialists in the Clayborne Whittier practice. The memo called attention to the recent scrutiny by the SEC of revenue recognition accounting standards, particularly in the biotech and software industries. *Nothing I don't know,* she thought, and flipped forward.

The second piece of paper announced the office outing. The day would start with golf and end too late. Teal decided she could come up with plausible regrets. She tossed the paper into the fireplace and watched the flame.

Voices moved closer from down the hall, then her solitary occupation of the parlor ended as four square dancing partners do-si-doed into the room. Teal was happy to lay down the *CW/Alumni* unread.

Trisha joined the group for introductions.

"Boston!" everyone exclaimed as though Teal had traveled from Mars. "We don't get many people from out your way around these parts!"

"But you should," Teal said. "This is beautiful."

"Wait till you see Pictured Rocks National Lakeshore and you won't want to go home," one woman said.

"Oh, I don't know. Lake Superior scares me to death," another voice said. "Lake of shipwrecks."

"You be sure to stop in Lefebvre's in Grand Marais and pick up smoked whitefish. With bread and beer from the general store, you've got a picnic," a lanky young man advised.

Teal couldn't get a word in edgewise, the happy advice came so quickly. She couldn't protest the square dancers' invitation to join them for dinner at the inn.

Trisha Mock was staring down at the *CW/Alumni* as the group stood to go.

"See anyone you recognize?" Teal joked.

Trisha looked up.

"The Clarkes?" Teal suggested.

Trisha shook her head. "Clarkes? No. Not a name I know."

Teal couldn't delay the group spiriting her out of Annchris House. On the short walk to the Inn, she tried to remember who was on the front page of the *CW/Alumni*. The pictures were from last month's partner and manager dinner dance. Julia and Don Clarke, Roger and Barbara Singer, Amy Firestone, and Frank and Margaret Sweeny were among the crowd captured by the camera.

Or maybe Trisha had been reading the headline two-thirds of the way below.

Firm Responds to Emma Browne.

THURSDAY TO
FRIDAY

THIRTY

The four square dancers and Teal joined a crowd of people streaming through the huge double doors of the old Gordon Park Inn. The Annchris House guests had driven up from Chicago, Teal learned. The less affluent square dance enthusiasts from the south lodged at modest strip motels down the road, but most of the group lived in the Upper Peninsula. All shared high spirits and a dance jargon which left Teal in the dark.

She managed to hold up her end of the conversation through dinner with the folks from Chicago. After the coffee had been cleared and everyone mingled in the foyer waiting for the ballroom to open, Teal found keeping up with the subject matter another story.

"Enjoy contra dancing?" a fellow in a plaid shirt asked in the crush. "Contra dancing," he repeated, louder. "Comes from your parts."

He stared at her from under a furrowed brow, brown eyes fired with passion.

Teal didn't know what to do with her expression. Contras, to her memory, had to do with dirty money and double dealing and former President Bush professing he hadn't been in the loop.

Plaid shirt's wife tapped Teal's arm. "It's an early form of line dancing out of New England. Contra means opposite you, like your partner."

Teal was saved when the ballroom doors opened. Her dinner friends from Chicago encouraged her to stay, but she shook her head as they funneled by. When the foyer emptied, Teal scanned the hundreds of pictures from past seasons which covered the walls. Hunters and fishers beaming beside big and small catch, every face lit with pride. Women portaging wooden canoes down steep slopes, sober with determination. Mist off a waterfall spraying the camera lens to a fog. "Tahquamenon Falls" captioned that shot. Teenaged workers giggling in rows in front of the Inn summer after summer.

She caught on to the chronological order and started with the oldest snaps of the original Inn, a building of rough timber and logs. A series of flame shots and ruins ended with a picture of the firemen in a row of soot-blackened faces and bodies listing with exhaustion. The year was 1924.

She studied the last completed wall of pictures as she eased on her coat. These dated from the 1950s through the early 1970s when Gordon Park Inn had closed, not to reopen until three years ago as a dining and dancing only facility. She viewed families eating lunch on blankets spread over lush grass and tennis players swinging wooden rackets at blurry balls on the red clay courts. In one series, small children perched on ponies led by teenaged boys.

Each year was marked by a large group shot of Inn staff from manager to bellhop. The changing fashion in coiffure was evident on this wall. Boys went from near bald crewcuts to hair curling over starched collars. Girls went from pert pageboys and flips to the straight and mournful style of 1960s folk singers.

Here and there Teal stopped at a face or posture which seemed too familiar.

"Feel like you know them?"

Teal whipped around to face the manager as he walked over.

"Yes," she said and turned back to squint. "I'm almost sure I do—"

The manager took her arm and guided her back to the first wall.

"Starts here, then repeats in families, both the guests and staff. See this young man?" The manager pointed to a boastful fisher. He walked Teal to the next wall over. "His son."

The son dangled his day's catch.

"Happened over decades. Parents came as guests, kids came as summer employees. Now it's the next generation bankrolling our return. Place gets into your blood."

Teal looked around the room, its walls and ceiling of age-darkened fir, its floor bright from scrubbing and rubbing. Outside was all the desolation and beauty of a once inhabited place now empty. She could see, as she had at remote lakeshore camps in Maine, how Gordon Park could captivate.

"Where did the guests come from?" Teal asked.

"Same place as now. Big money folks from Chicago, the smaller money from less far south."

"And their kids provided all the help?"

The manager laughed. "No. I hear half the time summer

kids were given jobs to keep the parents happy. The real work's always been done by locals."

"Which you are?" Teal asked.

"Which I am, and proud of it. I started here as a pony boy. Now I run the Inn. You staying at Annchris House?"

"Yes," Teal said.

"Patricia Mock, now she's a hybrid. Mother lived over to Beaver, not twenty miles from here. Father came from a city down south. They met at the Inn. Patricia was never quite a local and never quite a summer kid. She's one of us working hard to save the town from extinction."

"I hope you succeed," Teal said.

She stopped for a moment in front of a group photograph of staff. A girl's laughing, adolescent face held Teal's interest. Surprise registered as Teal identified the tall woman in her early twenties who stood beside the teenager as a young Trisha Mock. She made her way through the dark to Annchris House, satisfied with this explanation for her fascination with the photo.

That's not how she felt when she jerked from a deep sleep in the middle of the night. She squeezed closed her eyes to recompose the picture in her mind. Girls in front, boys behind. The laughing girl in the middle flanked to the right by Trisha. And to the left by Julia Clarke. Julia Wade Clarke, her grandmother from Chicago. Teal sat up, sure she remembered right, but she could check her memory. Trisha had pointed to a collection of scrapbooks on the history of Gordon Park in the parlor. There was a good chance some of the contents duplicated the display at the Inn.

Teal wrapped herself in her trench coat, the traveler's

best bathrobe, and slipped on two pairs of athletic socks to warm her feet and mute their fall.

She didn't make a sound.

The parlor didn't have a door to close, so Teal moved the lamp off the round Victorian table covered with a shawl and set it behind the dark cloth. Switched on, the light came like a pale and eerie fog through the fabric, not enough to disturb anyone not in the room but adequate to find the stack of albums.

She flipped through the first, Gordon Park's founding. The second documented the effect of the First World War. The third showed generations of Mocks. The fourth confirmed Teal's first suspicion about Julia Clarke. Trisha could have been an archivist in her neat presentation. Where the Inn had mounted mostly unlabeled photos, Trisha's careful hand had penciled in every name, every date.

Teal recalled Trisha's first response.

"Clarkes? No. Not a name I know." That's what Trisha had said.

Teal doubted she'd get the same answer on Julia Wade in the morning.

"Julia Wade? Of course." Trisha smiled and stroked the tabby purring in her lap.

Longing quickened Teal's heart. She missed the comforts of a warm, furry body. She missed Argyle. The cat pressed its head to Trisha's palm. Argyle preferred to set his nose under a forearm and flip his head to initiate a rub. Once the scratching started, the deerhound would sink closer and closer to the ground until Teal found herself bent down, a chair arm cutting into her side. But Argyle was not here now.

"So you knew Julia?" Teal asked.

"Some. Not much. She came to Gordon Park with her grandmother one year for a few weeks in the summer. The next she came to work at the Inn. I think the job was arranged by her grandmother. It lasted under a month. Julia was older than I by a few years and done with college that spring. She seemed a sweet person," Trisha said. Her hand stopped the patient stroking. "Except for the once."

"The once?" Teal queried.

Trisha shifted her imposing body until the cat became annoyed at the disruption and jumped to the floor. Early morning's angled sunlight flooded the dining room. The cat found a bright, warm spot and set to a course of self grooming.

"At the time I thought it funny, kind of good for her. I don't imagine it seemed like that to the other girl. Julia had a little thing with the cook's son. An unlikely pair." Trisha chuckled, but shook her head.

"And?" Teal offered a prompt.

"And the cook's son's girlfriend became rather unhappy. They were both from around here. Julia coming from the south and with the hint of her grandmother's Chicago money, well, I think the cook's son thought he might give it a run. At first Julia didn't realize he satisfied himself otherwise on the side."

"Sex?"

"My yes, with his girlfriend, who put her long-term plan into action. Pregnancy and marriage and I can say she got her way." Trisha shrugged. "Divorced now for over nineteen years for all the good it did her—"

"But Julia," Teal interrupted.

"Julia caught them in the back barn and took the poor girl by the throat. Almost killed her. Came away with a handful of bleached hair and the girl's skin and blood under her nails. Julia sure surprised the rest of us, having been all milquetoast and honey. Grandmother spirited her back home that day, and that was the end of my knowing Julia Wade." Trisha stood.

"Was there ever talk of a rape?" Teal asked.

"And Julia? Not that I heard." Trisha's hands looked for a cat and ended smoothing and resmoothing a fold of trouser.

"But there have been rapes in Gordon Park?" Teal prodded.

"Yes," Trisha confirmed. "Nothing we talk about. You off to visit the Pictured Rocks?"

Another reminder of Maine. No loose talk to strangers.

"Take your time and enjoy," Trisha said and ended the audience.

Teal tried. She slowed the car to absorb the majesty of the thick birch forest and gasped in delight when a startled deer bounded across the red dirt road. She pulled in the marked lot for an easy view of Lake Superior before she started to hike the trail she had chosen. The eroded cliffs reminded her of birthday cake cut straight and clean with a knife. One peninsula of striated rock rose like the rough turrets of a fantasy castle.

A quickening wind disturbed the smooth water, and

clouds covered the still early sun. She shifted and saw a different shore of weathered rock. From a distance, the tall outcropping looked like a slab or a tombstone. The cold tug of the wind made her shiver, or maybe it was that this vacation could not bring an escape from memories of Theresa Mars, Emma Browne, and Laura Smart. They would not leave.

It was time to go home.

She drove back to the gas station she'd passed not a half mile outside the entrance to the park. The Gas—Convenience—Bait—Traps store had a pay phone inside. Directory assistance gave her the numbers. She booked a seat on a mid-day flight, Traverse City to Detroit, Detroit to Boston.

The next number she punched in, knowing it by heart.

BG answered.

"Is Hunt around?" Teal asked.

"El nope."

"Want to disclose a little more?" Teal didn't have time for BG's shenanigans.

A sigh rattled the line. "He's at the State House showing off the model for the megaplex to the guv and his buddies. Aren't you supposed to be away?"

"I am away."

"Oh. Where?"

"Michigan," Teal said. "But tell Hunt I'm coming home. I expect I can make it in time for a Clayborne Whittier dinner for Ted Grey tonight. Hunt said something about being busy for the weekend, but I was hoping he could come."

"Sure you don't want to ask the better man—"

"Beej!"

"He'll be free. Promise," BG said. "Ciao, bella baby."

"Ciao, yourself," Teal managed.

She decided she must make one more stop before packing.

The Inn was empty and quiet, the front door shut and bolted. Teal walked around to the back and buzzed at "Deliveries" as instructed. A fifteen-year-old kid answered and said the manager was not in for the morning. The kid shrugged when she used the excuse she'd left something in the coat room. He let her enter and turned back to the kitchen. Teal watched him reposition his earphones and heard the waspish buzz leaking from the personal stereo. He'd be oblivious to anything she did short of set the place on fire.

Her intention was far more modest, but perhaps no less alarming, at least to one person.

She walked the walls of pictures and studied each one, group by group, year by year. Here was a boy cleaning game. Here the girl laughing in the middle. Teal guessed the relative ages, ticking off years with her fingers. The children and young adults ranged from maybe eleven to twenty-four. Teal watched Patricia Mock literally grow up on the wall, over ten years, from average to tall, slim to imposing as she matured. She'd been an arresting girl. So had some of the others.

Teal identified a snap of Julia's grandmother, a distinguished and gracious lady. Julia could have become that woman in a different era. Teal moved on until she found another familiar face, the one she wanted to discuss with Trisha Mock.

———

The square dancers were finally up and out, and Trisha also gone, "Back by 4:00 P.M." tacked to the front door. Teal would not make it to Boston if she waited. She filled her one bag and dropped it in the hall while she searched for the *CW/Alumni* she'd left in the parlor. She wasn't surprised to find it was gone.

THIRTY-ONE

Barbara Singer stormed out of the walk-in closet.

"What do you mean you don't feel like going?" The muscles at her temples contracted and narrowed her eyes.

"Barbara, please . . ." Roger sighed.

She hated that sound.

"What do you think?" she yelled. "You think I really feel like going? That I ever feel like going to your stupid partner and manager dances, your damned national meetings, your Clayborne Coffees? Do you think I'll enjoy being on display as the perfect little *fired* partner's wife tonight? But I'm not going to let your . . . your stupid partnership push me, or you, around!"

The swell of fury left her gasping.

"But you've always complained about Clayborne Whittier. You should be happy I'm about to be fired," Roger said.

She wanted to slap him, wipe the secretive expression off his face.

"Stop looking at me like that. You are going to be the perfect little partner tonight and I'm going to be the perfect little wife because I'm not going to let those bastards get me down—"

"It's not those bastards actually, Barbara. It's the police," Roger said.

"Because those bastards, your partners, would just as soon you be charged with murder as find out the truth. They just want the whole thing over with. Well, I don't feel like making it easy."

The telephone made them both swing around.

"Hello?" Roger answered.

Barbara made who-is-it motions.

"Teal," Roger mouthed.

"Nothing. Barbara asking who," he said aloud.

Barbara hated the silence as Roger listened. She edged closer and watched him shake his head. She wanted to grab the receiver. Roger half-turned away as he nodded to the wall.

"Yes, okay. Amy was asked to Ted's dinner tonight, but I don't know if she'll be there—yes, Barbara is telling me yes." Roger paused. "Who else besides Barbara and me? Don and Julia of course, Amy and—"

Roger put his hand over the mouthpiece.

"Are Frank and Margaret invited?" he asked Barbara.

"What's this about?" she hissed.

Roger shrugged. "Teal, asking who's coming to the good-bye dinner."

Barbara plucked the telephone from her husband.

"Hi, Teal, it's me," she said. "Frank didn't work with Ted on anything so, no, I don't think he was invited."

Barbara listened for a moment, then spoke. "Right,

Frank's time in California? If you think he should go . . . I can try, but with babysitting—"

She shrugged and nodded. "Kathy Malley? If she wants to spend her Friday night looking after all those Sweenys, fine." Another nod. "See you then, okay. Bye."

Barbara turned to Roger.

"I think Teal was calling from a plane," Barbara said.

Roger lifted his shoulders.

"Anyway," she said between tight teeth, "Teal is going to make the dinner tonight and wants Frank and Margaret to be invited. Can you ever imagine why?"

Margaret Sweeny put down the telephone.

"I guess it isn't hard to read our life," she said.

"Meaning?"

Frank turned from his youngest son to his wife.

"That was Barbara Singer. There's a good-bye dinner or something for Ted Grey tonight and we were supposed to have been invited. Some glitch with the hospitality committee list and we didn't get our notice."

Frank's eyes brightened. "We are?"

Margaret knew he thought it some kind of positive sign, reassurance everything at the great firm would come out all right. He didn't seem offended by the late contact or the oversight. She wasn't feeling optimistic herself, but she wasn't going to disappoint her husband now, not with him so pleased.

"Yes, and babysitting's provided. Teal's secretary, Kathy—"

"Malley," Frank said. His face contracted into a frown.

"What's wrong, dear?" Margaret asked, arms stretched out to take the youngest off Frank's hands.

"Kathy Malley's married to that damned detective."

"So what?"

"So I don't like the idea of her hanging around our house."

Margaret laughed. "You have something to hide?"

"You agreed to what?" Dan tried to keep his voice down. It still came out too sharp and loud.

"Do a favor," Kathy said. "You don't have to yell, I can hear you fine on this phone line."

"M-m-my mother—"

"Understands. I only needed to say the word baby."

"You l-l-lied," Dan said.

"I did not. I just neglected to go into details about whose baby. She thinks I'm having morning sickness at night. Honestly, Dan, we eat dinner at her house every Friday. She'll survive."

"So, I'm supposed to hang around the Locke-Ober bar while Teal is upstairs at some fancy private party?" Dan asked.

He shoved the Browne file across his desk, then leaned forward to fish it back.

"You know what this is about?"

He listened as he flipped the folder open and fanned a few pages into a semi-circle of fractured lines—*Trauma blow to the/First responded/According to Teal Stewart.* He hadn't made any more progress on Laura Smart. The case against Roger Singer relied on what? Roger's prints on his marble tombstone. The empty gum package in his trash, one wrapper dusted with cyanide. Emma's threat to his career. Laura's spreading the rumor Roger was about to be fired. His missing coat.

Nothing good enough for Dan to want to take to court. He tuned back into the conversation with Kathy.

"If Teal's got something," he said, "I guess I don't have a choice."

Amy had decided not to go home. Why bother? Locke-Ober's was two blocks up and three over from the FNEB building and she had no intention of changing. Amy did not understand the concept of cocktail clothes, which, in any event, applied only to wives.

Teal had said she'd stop at the office before going on to the restaurant.

Amy had not minded Teal's prying on the telephone. Some things were easier to disclose long distance, like how Emma had infuriated her. She could still hear Emma's derision ring in her ears. Amy had been proud of her plan for ruining Roger, and Emma had just howled.

Amy told it all to Teal.

"I wanted to kill her," Amy said. "I could have, except for Laura. She came out of a stall, and I left."

"Lucky for you," Teal said.

"I went back to find Emma, thinking I should apologize, but she was arguing with Roger in the hall in front of the women's room," Amy had explained to Teal. "So where did Emma get off being judge and jury on my stupid plan to embarrass Roger?"

"Perhaps it is judging yourself that has you worried,"

Teal had said. "Isn't that why you wanted to return to Boston?"

Amy had nodded, unseen at her end. "The morning I surprised you at BiMedics—when I stopped because of Roger's car in the lot?—I was sure he'd come to confront me, tell me he'd figured out what I was doing to make him look bad. I felt a wave of nausea at myself. It didn't go away in Michigan."

Amy had graduated near the top of her Lake Forest class. She'd won the medal on the CPA examination for highest score in the state. She'd been rated "technically outstanding" every year at Clayborne Whittier. But she had been stupid about Emma and cruel with Roger. Anxiety squeezed her chest. She had something else to tell Teal.

"I heard Roger and Laura in his office the night Laura died. Laura kept saying, 'You don't want my help with the divorce? Well, tough—too late,' like she was funny. He said he was in enough trouble already. Because of Emma, I guess, and me. MicroAnswer. But I still took the stuff, after he left."

"After he left?" Teal had asked.

"Yeah, remember I told you I saw him leave his office. I think I did see him way down the hall later, maybe, in his trench coat. I worried he might go back to his office, but I figured I could just make some excuse in the morning."

"I think I have a way you could really apologize to Roger," Teal had said. "I could use your help tonight."

Amy wondered if she'd been smart to agree. But it was too late to worry about being smart.

"Are you sorry?" Julia asked.

She stopped fiddling with her hair and turned to Don.

He wasn't a handsome man anymore, not like when they'd first met. Time had dragged his varsity athlete's body out of shape despite the new hours at the gym. Age had thinned the once thick hair. She wondered if she still loved him.

Disappointed as she might be, there was nothing she willingly would give up. Not him, certainly. Not after the years of investment or the great pleasures and small comforts. She'd made that clear in what she'd done. A chill crawled up the back of her neck.

"Am I sorry? About what?" Don asked.

Julia tried to stop the tremor in her voice. "For yourself, losing Ted, Clayborne Whittier's comer," she said.

"Oh Ted. He's a good man. He'll be good for Boston." Don flipped the newspaper onto the coffee table. "You about ready?"

"If you like this dress." Julia spun in a slow circle, letting the fine fabric swirl around her legs.

"You look lovely, my dear. Really, lovely." His eyes locked with hers. "I'll just drop off my briefcase and brush up."

He had looked, had seen the dress she'd chosen to set off her still slim figure, had cared. His eyes had told her that and much more. Hope mixed with fear.

"We never talk," she said.

She watched Don's back stiffen as he hesitated on the stairs.

"I have to confess." Julia twisted her engagement ring in a circle around her finger. The diamond twinkled and extinguished as she pressed it round and round.

Don turned then, his head awkward over his left shoulder. "No. I don't want to hear. Not tonight," he said.

"But—"

"It's my fault. I've been a terrible fool, and all I can say is I am sorry," he said and took the steps away from her two at a time.

Ted caught a glimpse of Amy in the hall and waved, but she didn't notice. He didn't try harder, figuring he'd see her at the dinner.

He wondered what ax Amy had to grind, causing all the furor on MicroAnswer, arguing with Roger, then coming to him and over what? Nothing. A re-review of the books and discussion with management and the issue was settled without finding a problem. She hadn't done herself any favors.

His worry had been genuine. The lead partners on high-profile accounts took high-profile falls, and even if they weren't involved, the taint of the questions remained. He rubbed the weariness from his face. At least these unhappy thoughts would not apply to him. He had other issues to think about, like when Don Clarke would get the official call to move to New York.

Ted grinned. He'd like running Boston. It was a good office.

"You don't have the time to stop at Clayborne Whittier," Hunt said.

"That's why I'm taking the Blue Line," Teal insisted.

"Can't you let it go for tonight?" Hunt asked. "Forget the office for once and be grateful you found yourself a date?"

Teal grinned into the telephone. "I am. I am. And it isn't like it's such awful duty—dinner in a private dining room at Locke-Ober's—"

"With a group of Clayborne Whittier CPAs."

"How many times have I put up with you and BG and some dreadful client of your firm?" Teal asked. "But I'm asking you to come for another reason."

"Make it good," Hunt said.

"I finally reached Patricia Mock. She understands why I took the photo. I'll send it back to her and she's agreed to fax me the other. The more important one."

"From Michigan?"

"Yes, and it should be arriving in my office about now. Anyway, I may need you. I know who killed—" Teal caught a glimpse of the bus and raised her carry-on luggage as if Hunt could see. "Look, I see the shuttle for the T. Just meet me in half an hour—"

"Or so."

Teal thought she heard a groan as she jammed down the phone.

Public transportation from Logan Airport into the city beat any cab ride on a Friday night.

Martha stood watching as Teal ran by to her office.

"Girl, you living here," Martha called after her. "You about need a bed in there for the long nights."

Teal skidded to a stop.

"What did you say?" she called back to Martha.

"You about need a bed if you going to keep on staying the night—"

"Thanks Martha!" Teal shouted, delighted.

She didn't have time to look at the fax she grabbed off Kathy's machine, but she didn't expect to be surprised.

THIRTY-TWO

Teal stopped short. Someone jostled her elbow and the smiling face in her hand went out of focus. This was not who she had expected.

"Teal!"

Hunt's voice caught her.

"Come on," he said, taking her arm in an uncompromising grip and propelling her to walk. "We'll be late."

Locke-Ober's was tucked down a lane off a through street. Wait staff outfitted in black with crisp white aprons hurried among the upstairs diners. Hunt and Teal climbed one more floor to find the private space. The other guests from Clayborne Whittier had arrived and were seated in a room dark with wood paneling and heavy with a sense of history. Commercial history.

"Didn't think you'd make it," Don Clarke said to Teal before he extended a hand to Hunt.

Greetings went round the table. Only Ted Grey needed a special introduction, Hunt having met the others.

Ted sat to the right of Don, Teal to the left. Husbands and wives had been split apart, a mark of Julia's adherence to the old art of etiquette. The conversation moved from work to charity through the appetizer and salad courses. Oysters Rockerfeller and mixed greens had been preordered.

Julia promoted the CCF car raffle in terms designed to move every member of the group to write a check and joked that Teal must maintain an accounting of the pledges.

The entrees came with the usual litany of Clayborne Whittier war stories, many featuring Ted. It had to be boring for Hunt and the spouses. The brandy snifters set down at each place for desert stimulated the first toasts to Ted's hard work and his continued good fortune in California.

"Or Boston," Don suggested.

"When you join the management committee and he comes here as partner in charge?" Barbara Singer spoke for the group.

"There's no guarantee on either," Don demurred. "But, to Ted's continued success!"

Teal watched the smiles, some tense and some filled with hope, as glasses touched and clinked. One among them had committed murder. The brandy warmed her constricted throat.

"Some of you asked why I returned early," Teal said.

"To celebrate?" Julia suggested with a sharp, fixed smile.

"To discover the truth," Teal said.

One hand shook a scatter of drops on the cloth. Someone swallowed a choke.

"Truth of what?" Barbara asked.

"Truth of who killed Emma Browne and Laura Smart."

"Now Teal!" Don pushed back his chair and stood. "I don't think this is the time—"

"Or place?" Barbara Singer glared. "No, you'd rather let my husband take the blame and have the problem off your conscience when he's charged!"

"This has nothing to do with me, I don't know about the rest of you," Amy said and set her napkin down.

Teal's heartbeat accelerated. The play had begun. She had called Amy from the plane, after the conversation with Patricia Mock and before reaching Roger, and together they had worked out the first act. But Teal had not confided how her script would end. Had not known, exactly. Still didn't.

"This has nothing to do with me," Amy repeated.

"Actually," Teal responded to her cue, "that's not true. My understanding of Emma's death started with you."

Every mouth tightened. Teal gazed past Roger, her eyes on Amy.

"You were Emma's big defender. The whole situation with Emma had you furious—at Clayborne Whittier's sexist behavior, at Roger for—"

"Telling her to dress more like a woman. How revolting!" Amy threw in.

"That passion made you decide there had to be something more you could do. Even more than SUE. Something to vindicate the crusading woman you had read about but never met. If you could make one partner understand what it meant to have his professional reputation challenged—"

"MicroAnswer," Roger said, bemused. He rotated his attention from Teal to the senior manager. "Your worry about sales was a set-up! You wanted me on the defensive—"

"It worked to reinforce your own rumor," Teal said.

"Rumor?" Julia repeated.

"That Roger was going to be fired?" Barbara's voice hit each word with a sound like a pebble dropped on a tile.

Margaret Sweeny raised her eyes to Frank and shifted them as fast.

Teal's attention did not leave Amy. Her senior manager made a good show at spontaneous anger. Time for her contribution.

"Amy, when you met Emma Browne and told her what you were doing, Emma laughed at you—"

"She said she could take care of herself. Made it clear she didn't need my help."

Real hurt glazed Amy's eyes.

"That's why you were upset when I told you Emma was dead. I mistook guilt for sorrow," Teal said.

"What did Amy have to be guilty about?" Ted asked.

"Amy had a ripping fight over Roger with Emma the night of Emma's murder."

"She made a joke of my plan to embarrass Roger, then laughed that I was being blamed for sending Frank to Funsters! And I couldn't believe someone in her position could think it funny," Amy complained.

"But what really upset you was feeling responsible for Emma's death," Teal said, ignoring the too early introduction of Frank.

"I shouldn't have left her . . ." Amy's voice dropped so low people craned their necks.

"She was alive when you left the women's room," Teal said.

"Yes," Amy whispered. "Alive."

"Just like Laura Smart the night she died—"

"Laura caught me in Roger's office looking through the

325

MicroAnswer trunk. I'd heard her in with Roger before, arguing about his divorce—"

"Divorce?" Barbara shrilled. "What divorce?"

"Laura said Roger had lied—"

"That's crazy," Roger said. "You just admitted making up the mess with MicroAnswer. What's this? Another way to get me in trouble?"

Teal shushed him with a hand but spoke to Amy. "But the conversation with Laura had you enough on edge—"

"To kill?" Margaret Sweeny interjected. Her eyes couldn't have opened wider.

Teal shook her head in denial. "To call me on an impulse, wanting advice and the chance to confess. But not about murder. Emma and Laura were killed by someone else."

"And you have an idea who," Ted suggested.

"Yes."

Frank hated the flush he felt mottle his neck. It was just his bad luck to be seated next to Amy, all those eager faces turned his way. He dabbed his napkin to his lips and wished he could disappear behind the cloth like a magician's rabbit.

"You fought with Emma over the Funsters joke," Teal reminded Amy.

Frank wanted to die.

Amy turned to face him. "It wasn't me, Frank. That's what I wanted to say to you the other night, but you were only interested in Roger's being fired. Honest."

Everyone waited for him to speak, their attention too fixed, eyes too attentive.

His Adam's apple strangled his voice.

"No," he squeaked. "It wasn't you."

"Then who?" Margaret asked.

Margaret, his wife and friend, was making everything worse.

"Who?"

She'd turned to Teal.

"Emma Browne," Teal said.

Frank fingered his collar. Pulling harder and harder until he heard the button pop. He could see Emma's garish face leering up at him.

"Emma planned to use you in her lawsuit," Amy rushed in. "As proof an incompetent male at Clayborne Whittier had no trouble getting to the partnership."

"A variation on your little game with Roger," Barbara said, her voice taut.

"Emma brought in whole agencies of the California and Federal governments, when Frank had to chase Funsters. She thought it was so amusing and didn't mind if people thought I'd done it. Emma didn't care whose future she ruined. At least I wasn't getting anyone else in trouble."

"But Roger," Barbara hissed.

"And someone did care," Teal said. "Emma was murdered."

Frank could close his eyes and see Emma's cow face flare with malice as she told him to watch out for Amy Firestone. He'd believed her until Laura Smart had set him straight.

"Sending me to . . . to that bar wasn't a joke. The bitch did it on purpose. She deserved murder."

"And Laura Smart?" Roger asked Frank. "What did she deserve?"

"It's not true," Frank said. "It's not me. I didn't kill

Emma Browne or Laura Smart. Laura started the rumor about you, that you were the one to be transitioned out."

Roger watched Frank's finger lift and point at him.

"What's this? Another accusation?" Ted snorted his disbelief.

"I think Frank is trying to suggest Roger remains our best suspect," Teal said.

"All the physical evidence," Frank put in.

"All suggesting I did it. I'd be that stupid?" Roger countered.

But he had been. He knew he had been. Asking Laura to spread the false rumor in an attempt to learn what his wife really valued before he went further on a divorce. Which did Barbara love, he had wondered, him or the partnership position and money? Laura had been game to stir things up. She had let slip that Roger would be fired. The trouble was, Laura had refused to stop when the calamity with Emma happened.

And now he knew that Amy had overheard the fight. His situation was not good.

"You couldn't believe it was Roger who would be fired," Teal said to Frank.

Roger made himself listen.

Teal leaned forward. "You thought Laura was up to some trick—"

"That's not true!" Spittle flew out of Frank's mouth.

"You went through Laura's office the night she died," Teal said. "You found out you had been right from the start. You were the one management voted out."

Roger gyrated his head back and forth like everyone else.

"You know this from reading the stars?" he asked Teal.

328

Roger couldn't say he liked Frank, but the guy didn't deserve this any more than he did himself.

"No. It will be in Detective Malley's report. Laura's office is covered with Frank's fingerprints."

"Okay, I broke into the personnel files. There was a memo about me. But there was one with Roger's name on it under her blotter."

"And you believed it?" Amy asked with incredulity.

"With Roger screwing up on MicroAnswer, sure, it could have been true, the change. But I wasn't the only person interested in Laura's office," Frank's voice broke into pleading. He pointed across the table.

Every pair of eyes followed Frank's finger.

"She was a perfect bitch" came out with a smile.

Now everyone stared at Julia Clarke.

She saw Don's hand rise to stop, heard the words come from his mouth. "This isn't the time or place."

Julia could feel the inappropriate smile curling on her face. She watched discomfort color the circle of faces.

"Julia was there," Frank said to no one in particular. "While I stood in the ante-room between Laura and Don's offices—"

"I wanted to talk to my husband. I couldn't find him, so I went looking for her to confirm the worst," Julia's voice stumbled.

"Please, don't say more," Don pleaded.

Julia turned to her husband. "Then I went back to your office. This time the light was on and I heard—"

"Julia, please!" Don said.

"I'm not that crude. I didn't have to look through the

keyhole. I understood what she was doing with you. I went back to her office and left her a message."

"That's enough." Don's words slurred in his hurry. "I tried to protect you. I destroyed the letter you left on Laura's desk."

"After I called to tell you she was dead," Teal mused. "I called you before I called the police, out of respect. You used the time to destroy evidence."

The migraine hammered into Julia's forehead.

"I contacted our lawyer," Don said from the other end of the table. "I wanted to save you from this."

"And then there's Emma Browne," Teal interjected.

Julia met Teal's eyes.

"Yes. I never liked her."

"I know. The CCF picture of you with Jimmy Carter in Michigan? Curiosity about you and Emma made me stop in at Hillegonds College."

"She insisted on that recount. She enjoyed my humiliation when she put me off the board. Last week she enjoyed my humiliation again when she called for Don and told me the truth about my husband and Laura Smart. It wasn't news to any of you." Julia's mirthless chuckle echoed in the wooden room. "Yes, I hated Emma Browne."

Julia watched each face at the table. Don's was red with guilt, Teal's smooth with calm. Frank picked at his chin, as though relieved the attention had shifted from him. Amy balanced on her chair, young and energized by the tension. Roger sat still with shock. Margaret's eyes shone with compassion. Barbara glared. Ted looked uncomfortable at the exposure of raw emotion. Hunt leaned forward, alert. Julia could imagine her own fixed smirk.

Ted spoke first in an appeal to Teal.

"You make it sound like everyone wanted Emma and Laura dead," Ted said.

"Yes," Teal agreed. "Even you."

"Me?"

"I kept thinking about the question of MicroAnswer sales. Had the company shipped bricks?" Teal said.

"But Amy just admitted that she made up the problem."

"Who benefits when a company like MicroAnswer goes public?" Teal said. "Management who owns stock, true, but also the partner at the accounting firm, like you. MicroAnswer made your career, shot you to the top. How many times have I heard that you were the youngest partner at Clayborne Whittier, youngest up to run a major office."

Ted let his jaw drop. Teal had an interesting way of adding up two and two. And he wasn't hearing four.

He shook his head. "Teal, this has gone the limit. I listened when Amy came to me. I took her concerns to Don. And now she agrees it was a fraud. Her fraud."

Amy nodded.

"I sent you to Michigan with specific instructions to audit sales. You found—"

"Nothing. You're right," Teal said. "But it would have been neat, you making sure MicroAnswer didn't disappoint Wall Street. I knew Emma would have guessed it was you who stood to gain, not Roger. And Laura overhearing Amy and you and Roger and catching on."

"And what? Blackmailing me?" Ted snorted. "But why are we dragging this out when nothing was wrong at MicroAnswer? How do we even know those women died because of anything at Clayborne Whittier?"

"Nothing was wrong," Teal agreed. "But it took me a while to see. And you're right, Emma and Laura weren't killed over anything at work."

"How do you know?" Margaret asked.

"Because I learned something in Michigan."

Teal laid an envelope on the table and drew out the photograph she'd taken from Annchris House that morning when Trisha had gone.

Ted saw young people in front of a lodge.

Julia hissed, "Oh my God!"

THIRTY-THREE

A shy Julia Wade beamed out at the camera from where she stood beside the other staff at Gordon Park.

"This is enough for now," Don said.

He came around the table to put a protective hand on his wife's shoulder.

"You think she murdered Emma Browne and Laura Smart," Teal said.

"I'm tired of this." Frank began to push back out of his chair.

Margaret held up a restraining hand. "No, I'd like to hear."

Heads nodded, apprehensive and curious, for Teal to continue.

"People do such strange things and call it love," Teal said. "Julia going to visit Laura Smart at her house—"

"It *was* your car!" Julia hid her face in her hands, then raised it to stare back. "I wanted to make her leave Don alone, make her see what she was doing to us, but I couldn't. Not and barge in at that hour. I finally drove round back to see if she was up, but I left when I heard voices."

Julia was crying now, the sound soft and thin.

"The thing is," Don said, his hand delivering awkward pats, "I knew I'd made a mistake the moment it started. It's no excuse, Julia."

Teal scrutinized the faces around the room.

"There was something to cast suspicion on all of you. Julia's lies after she missed our CCF meeting—"

"Don and that . . . that girl had me so angry," Julia said.

"Grieving," Margaret corrected.

"Yes," Teal agreed. "The first thing I realized was every one of you was in and out of the office on the nights Emma and Laura died. Or almost every one of you."

Teal addressed Julia first.

"Julia, you talked your way past the guard Thursday night. Jean remembered when I asked him. Then there was Martha, who told Detective Malley she'd seen Roger outside the women's room where Emma was murdered—no, don't protest," Teal said to Barbara. "I am going to use every clue to the truth."

Teal caught Roger's eye. Did she look as weary? Hunt was out of his seat and ready by the door. She couldn't afford to lose anyone's attention.

"The jealous wife, the faithless husband," Ted said. "Where can you go with all this?"

Frank laughed.

"That's disgusting." Amy said to Frank, then turned to Teal. "Don't forget the incompetent partner about to be fired."

"I won't," Teal agreed. "I didn't."

The titter stopped in Frank's throat.

Barbara had a hand to her chest. "You're going to say it was Roger, aren't you. Amy saw him, and then Martha."

Teal smoothed the photo on the table. "I found the truth in the most unlikely place. Gordon Park."

Julia pressed Don's hand off and set her shoulders. "I didn't want her to go, Don. I told you!"

Hunt slipped from the room unobserved by all but Teal.

"Patricia Mock didn't remember a Julia Clarke, but I think she remembered Julia Wade when she saw you in the *CW/Alumni*. After all, Julia, you were the first college girl to come up to Gordon Park Inn and try to kill a local girl—"

"I found them together in the barn. He'd said he loved me!" Julia lifted her chin. "I hated that place."

"But you told me such wonderful stories—"

"Because I didn't want you to find out." Julia shifted her attention from Don back to Teal. "Patricia Mock." Julia's voice wavered.

"Yes, she identified you in the photograph. And someone else." Teal pulled a thick sheaf of papers out of her envelope. "Patricia recognized the name 'Emma Browne.' This is Emma's senior thesis at Hillegonds College. She wrote about date rape before we used those words, and profiled a case in Gordon Park—"

Don grabbed at Teal's stack of papers. "What are you trying to say?"

"Emma was sixteen when she read a paragraph about it in the Chicago papers. The coverage wasn't much, didn't mention names, but did identify the Michigan town. She remembered when she had to come up with a topic four years later. She booked at Annchris House and went up to Gordon Park. She met the victim through Trisha Mock."

335

Teal remembered the relief she had felt when she'd recognized the picture of Emma Browne in Trisha Mock's scrapbook. She had not identified Emma the first time but had realized who was pictured when she returned to the parlor this morning. Seeing Emma explained why she'd recognized another face on the wall at the Inn.

She considered what Trisha Mock had told her about Emma's visit in her call to Trisha from the airplane.

"The story was about this girl." Teal slid the photograph Trisha had faxed from the bottom of the paper pile. Everyone craned to see the smiling face.

"So who is she?" Julia asked, the puzzlement lightening her voice.

Frank bent closer and snapped straight. "That beggar at the FNEB door—"

"Theresa Mars," Teal said, her hand holding the page down, "grew up near Gordon Park and worked at the Inn. I saw her in a few group pictures, but it took seeing Emma's face to tie her portrait to the story. Emma wrote about Theresa Mars's rape at age fourteen. Raped by a guest at the Gordon Inn."

"Who?" Don asked.

"This boy," Teal said and moved her hand to the left. The other side of the photo was exposed. The smiling face had been the unknown bonus of hard proof when Trisha had offered to fax "her picture of Reesy, not one I leave in the scrapbook" to help Teal.

Ted grinned. "Is this a joke?"

"No," she said. "You were the young man whose parents bought off the girl's family in Gordon Park. The girl never named you to the police, she was too upset. Then your family stepped forward and ended the threat of prosecution. They let you get away with behavior that should have been punished. The girl became unbalanced and tormented. Twenty-three years ago, and she never recovered, did she?"

"I wouldn't know since I have no idea of what this is about," Ted said.

Teal tapped her finger to the image of the adolescent girl clowning on the pony the boy led around.

"Think again," Teal suggested.

Ted looked down.

"That's the young Reesy Mars, the woman I found, her head bashed in with a brick—"

"Like Emma Browne," Amy Firestone blurted out. She darted her eyes between the living Ted and the photo. "It is him."

"A nineteen-year-old Ted Grey and a fourteen-year-old Theresa Mars. Jail bait, and he walked away," Teal said.

"What does a picture prove?" Ted scoffed. "I knew the girl? I'm not denying it, am I?"

"You must have panicked when you saw them together, Reesy and Emma," Teal said. She addressed the table. "Emma was one person who stopped to give money to Reesy Mars. Ted already knew all about Emma's senior paper, he'd read the coverage himself, years ago in *Time*. He could tell from the article that Reesy and her family had kept their word of the settlement, not daring to tell who—"

"So all the years he worked with her in California, he never worried that Emma would tie him to the rape," Margaret said, piecing the puzzle out loud.

"But Reesy could, and she might have said something to Emma when they recognized each other," Teal agreed. "Ted already had one problem with Reesy asking him for money."

"I'm not listening to this." Ted lurched out of his chair.

"You should. What dumb bad luck that Reesy should have ended up in Boston. She must have been as surprised by you. Surprised, but not confused about what to do. The security guard saw her approach, and you pull out a big bill. That was your mistake."

"Am I the only one at this table who feels for the homeless? So a guard saw me give her something," Ted protested.

"Unfortunately, Reesy had grown street smart. She considered you a resource and demanded more, but you had no intention of running the Boston office with Theresa Mars around your neck. She was your one mistake in a lifetime of perfect performances, and you decided to put the threat to an end."

"And this fantasy proves I killed her and Emma Browne? I wasn't even in the building the night Emma was murdered," Ted scoffed. "I'm no suspect. Ask your friend Malley."

Unsettled faces looked from Ted to Teal.

"I didn't understand myself, until tonight when Martha couldn't resist kidding me. She said I as good as lived at Clayborne Whittier, and I thought, what if I did?"

The group didn't offer an explanation.

"If I lived at Clayborne Whittier, I wouldn't come or go after hours. Security wouldn't have any record of my movements. Like they didn't have any on you, Ted, because I think you slept on your office couch after beating Emma to death. Roger's trench coat kept you out of the worst of the mess, and you disposed of that the next morning, after the

338

building opened. You didn't mind that he could be a suspect—"

"This is ridiculous," Ted said.

"I saw you," Amy whispered.

"How can you live with yourself?" Teal asked, her voice quiet and tired.

"Oh, so now it's holier than thou, and you've got me charged and convicted. Well, I can tell you this. No one has ever questioned my actions before because I've done everything anyone ever expected of me. I'm the most successful partner Clayborne Whittier has ever seen. I'm going to run your office, and you're going to wish you had never cooked this up to smear me." Ted started for the door.

"Sit down, Ted. I'd like her explanation about Laura," Don said.

Ted lowered himself to the edge of a chair.

Teal didn't blink as she spoke to Don. "Laura liked the idea of becoming a partner's wife. Ted strung her along—"

"Ted?" Julia whipped her head back and forth between Ted and her husband, then fixed on Don. "She didn't love you."

"Or Ted," Teal said. "She loved opportunity. She decided Ted offered a better future than your husband. You may not believe it, but Don would never leave you, and Laura knew it."

Ted laughed. "Laura took it on herself to be a full service welcoming committee. You heard me with Laura in Somerville, Julia. Sorry, old man."

Teal smoothed the fold of the napkin still on her lap. The setting was so civilized, the food so delicious, the material rewards of being associated with the partnership numerous. No wonder Laura had wanted to join the party.

"Laura knew you had supported Emma against most of your partners. To a woman like Laura, there could be only one explanation. Sexual attraction. She was in a state of frenzy anticipating Emma's arrival."

Frank was making a sound like a giggle.

"It's not funny, Frank. Like Amy, Laura knew nothing of Emma. Laura came up with a plan. She decided to be pregnant before Ted met with Emma," Teal said.

"You can't believe this," Ted snapped.

"Met with Emma?" Don blasted at Ted.

"I broke the firm rule," Ted shrugged. "I wanted to help with the suit. Get her story Monday so we could use it."

"You wanted to kill her," Teal said. "And you did."

Frank made a gagging sound. "She was grotesque. I . . . I was crazy to pay Amy back for Funsters and thought I could catch her Tuesday morning. You know how she comes in so early." He surveyed the table.

"Five A.M.," Amy confirmed. "But I went to MicroAnswer first Tuesday."

"I even looked in the women's room," Frank said. "It was horrid."

Julia looked confused. "But I don't understand about Laura. How could you know about her condition?"

"Don't forget my sources," Teal said. "Kathy caught on first to Laura's questions about pregnancy, Laura's missed days at work. Laura's condition had Ted worried about a paternity suit."

Julia clutched Don's arm. "It couldn't have been—"

"The autopsy showed she wasn't pregnant with anyone's

child," Teal said. "But Ted didn't know. Laura was becoming a threat, like Reesy, like Emma Browne. He overheard Roger agree to leave his car for me, an unexpected opportunity. Roger even provided him with a trunk. Amy had taken the small trunk from Roger's office, packed it with files—"

Amy dropped her eyes away from Roger. "I didn't do anything but return them in the morning."

"Ted dumped the contents of the bigger trunk out in Roger's office and wheeled it into Don's—"

"I heard!" Frank yelped. "I heard someone go into Don's office. I thought it was Don."

Julia turned to her husband. "You weren't the man with Laura."

"No," he said.

"Martha complained to me that Roger had left his office a mess. That's not like him. One reason he was never my suspect," Teal said.

"And I cleaned up in the morning," Amy said.

"That's why the police didn't believe me." Roger sounded dazed. "I never knew what they were talking about."

Ted chuckled, a mean sound in his throat. "Convenient for me, your leaving the car keys right next to a pack of gum. I added poor Laura's last empty wrapper, and tossed it all into your trash."

"Ted did what Amy had done and took the freight elevator straight to the garage to dump the trunk with Laura's body into Roger's car, but he didn't check out then. He returned to Clayborne Whittier to drop off Roger's keys and leave past the lobby security like any ordinary night."

"But why dress Emma in Laura's clothes?" Amy wrinkled her face at Teal and avoided Ted. "Why Laura?"

"I think the clothes served two purposes. Tie in to Roger's injudicious comments to Emma and warn Laura off her mission to become Mrs. Edwin D. Grey," Teal said.

"No way," Ted said. "No way. She promised to force me to marry her or lose in court. She thought I could go on with the great firm as before. She didn't understand my relationship with her would mean the end. I've given Clayborne Whittier everything—my talent, my time, my loyalty—"

"An unquestioned loyalty," Amy muttered, "and look at what it's got you."

Roger stared across to Ted. "You thought you could get away with—"

"Murder?" Teal said. "It's not that easy."

AFTERWORD

Hunt walked her home through the cooling night. Clouds covered the moon.

"Think it will rain tomorrow?" Teal asked.

"Maybe."

The Common lights turned them both a ghoulish gray. Hunt had explained again and again that the strong illumination made the park safer.

What was safety, Teal wondered. Roger had spent a lifetime playing it safe, except this once.

"Poor Roger," she said.

"Poor Roger?"

"Asking Laura to start that rumor about him being the one to get the boot. It wasn't a mortgage loan he was off to sign the morning Frank went to Funsters, but a check for a retainer on a divorce attorney. He never talked with Barbara, never asked her how she felt, or why they were losing touch."

"Men," Hunt said.

"You're an incomprehensible species." Teal leaned into Hunt's shoulder. "Roger thought he could force Barbara to show her true feelings, and if she didn't really want him, he'd go for a divorce. Malley found preliminary papers in Roger's car under the Clayborne Whittier trunk, where Roger had hidden them the night before I took the car, before Ted had covered Roger's guilty secret with something much worse in the trunk."

Laura's clever game had left her dead. She didn't doubt that Laura had planned to use her as a pawn in the midnight call, had probably intended to hint she was going to have a partner's baby, preparing to throw the danger of exposure at Ted. Funny Laura had picked her. No, not so funny.

"Kathy and Dan are going to have a child," Teal said. She smiled.

"Think you'll lose your secretary?" Hunt asked.

Teal narrowed her eyes. "Kathy worried about that reaction, too. She worried about something more—that I'd be jealous."

"And are you?"

"I don't think so. I have a few family issues to work out before I worry about children. Kathy and Dan have asked me to be the godmother," Teal said, her voice lifting. She and Kathy had talked about more than tonight in the conversation from the airplane.

"Argyle will be jealous."

They laughed, a companionable sound.

"Jealousy," Teal said. "Not a pleasant sight. You know, Julia handled it pretty well. She wasn't going to let Laura Smart destroy her marriage and was willing to play hard ball, very hard ball. Tell Laura just what opposition she faced. That's what she wrote in the note Don destroyed."

"And Don thought his wife killed Emma and Laura?"

"Don thought it was Julia, and Julia worried it was Don. You know where she was that night after she and I had lunch? When she skipped the CCF meeting?"

Hunt shook his head.

"Driving around like I do when I'm upset. I never thought of Julia as comforted by the highway."

"What are you going to do about your senior manager? About Amy?" Hunt asked.

"She took the decision out of my hands," Teal said. "Her letter of resignation is on Don's desk."

Amy had made it easy and spared Teal that tug of conflicting allegiance. Amy's behavior had been unacceptable for Clayborne Whittier, even if Teal felt a sympathy for the passion and anger of her convictions.

"Who was after Frank?" Hunt asked as they crossed into the Public Garden. "Ted?"

"No," Teal said. "Sadder than that. His brother. I guess Frank had rubbed it in for too long. Kathy told me the poor bastard committed himself at McLean Hospital this morning."

"Frank really drove someone crazy," Hunt said, bemused.

The gas streetlights cast a softer glow on Brimmer Street. The clouds had coalesced into a ground mist and the damp wrapped under Teal's dress, around her shoulders, in her hair.

"Want to come up?" she asked when they came to her steps.

Hunt shook his head. Teal didn't want to let go.

"Think Argyle will need another walk tomorrow morning?"

"I'm sorry, Teal, I said I wasn't free this weekend. But why don't you take Argyle?" Hunt offered.

Teal snapped her words from between tense lips. "Is she allergic?"

Hunt grinned.

"Doesn't like dogs?" Teal persisted.

Hunt shrugged. "Nope, Dad's fine with Argyle, it's just Argyle upsets the fish."

"You're going fishing with your father." Teal let out a long held breath. "Give him my love."

"He misses you, too," Hunt said.

The kiss they exchanged spoke of confusion and forgiveness. Teal drew back to hold Hunt an arm's length away.

"Go on," she said. "You have to be up by dawn and you know how your dad gets when you're late."

Like you, Hunt was kind enough not to say.

Teal thought of this evening, at the end of Ted's farewell dinner as Don, Frank, and Roger had walked out with Julia, Margaret, and Barbara at their sides, each with private struggles. She wondered if she knew any better what partnership was all about, at Clayborne Whittier or in love. She looked at Hunt.

Amy had a point. You didn't get quality with unquestioned loyalty.